CRAZY LIKE A FOX

Books by Melinda Metz

Crazy Like a Fox

Fox Crossing

Talk to the Paw

The Secret Life of Mac

Mac on a Hot Tin Roof

CRAZY LIKE A FOX

MELINDA METZ

KENSINGTON
PUBLISHING CORP.

www.kensingtonbooks.com

In memory of Jen Jones, connected to so many
with cords of warm and glowing light.

PROLOGUE

The Fox sat alone on her hill. She had not had a mate or kits in many years. Her life had been long, longer than any of her kind. Now she felt more kin to the trees, the stars, and the water of the lake. At times it felt as if she and they were one.

But she was still connected to those that roamed the earth. Cords of pulsing light bound her to each of them, from the soaring hawk to the trembling rabbit it hunted; from the bats navigating the darkness to the woodchuck foraging at sunrise, from the otter sliding on its belly on the grass to the snake sunning on a rock.

Though she found the nearby humans harder to understand, she was bound to them as well. It had been so since that day, so long ago, when The Woman had shown her mercy and returned her to life.

CHAPTER 1

"You obviously don't want me to come, so fine. I'm not coming."

Gavin watched as Rebecca yanked her duffle out of the trunk, wincing as he heard the ping of metal hitting metal. The big buckle on her bag had hit his bumper, leaving a small scratch in the Copenhagen Blue paint of his Porsche 944. No big. He could polish it out. Probably wouldn't take more than toothpaste.

Rebecca laughed, pulling Gavin out of his thoughts. "For a second, it actually seemed as if you were bothered that I'm not going with you. But you're more bothered by that." She pointed at the scratch. "And you can hardly even see it." She grabbed the handle of the suitcase that matched the duffle, giving a grunt as she tried to heave it free from the trunk. Gavin took it away from her and lowered it safely to the ground. One of its wheels could have done some serious damage.

"So, that's it. You're just going to help me get my stuff out of your car, and bye-bye?"

What did she want from him? She'd already decided. Or else

she was being dramatic. Rebecca was one of those women who thrived on drama. Look at her, eyes sparkling, cheeks flushed. Kinda unfair that she was extra hot when he wanted to be around her the least. "I never said I didn't want you to come."

"Of course, you didn't. That's not you. You never actually say anything. You just find little ways to push me away." Rebecca slammed the trunk so hard the car jounced. "You're Mr. Passive Aggressive."

"Where does that come from?" It wasn't the first time she'd thrown the accusation at him. It was one of her go-tos whenever they had a fight. And every time it sounded like made-up psychobabble crap.

Rebecca laughed again. Sometimes he hated the sound of her laugh. "Where? So many places. Like when my friend Sofia was in town. My oldest friend. I could tell you didn't want to meet her, not that you said so. Of course, like always, you pretended everything was fine, then you showed up late and said you'd already eaten. You didn't even order an appetizer, just sat there pouting."

That was unfair on a multitude of levels. "That was more than two months ago, Rebecca." It was like she kept a database of every wrong move he'd made. Everything she *considered* a wrong move. Most of them weren't anything. Including this one. "And, like I explained at the time, my study group ran late, because Dom showed up without the notes. I couldn't leave until we'd gone over all the material, or I wouldn't have passed the final."

He half expected her to jump on him for still being in school at twenty-seven, one of her usual fight moves. Even though, what did it matter? So he'd taken a few semesters off, changed his major a couple times. He was almost finished now, just a few more credits left. Since she didn't start with the school stuff, he kept going. "And, like I told you, somebody got hungry, so we ordered pizza, which is why I was late and didn't feel like eating. But I got there. Who cares if I ate or not? And it's not like the two of you didn't have plenty to talk about before I got there." He'd already explained this to her easily twenty times, but it was like she didn't even hear him. "If you're being honest, I bet you were even glad to have some time without me around. I'm sure Sofia had stuff she wanted to say to you that she didn't want to talk about in front of a stranger."

"That's not the point. The point is—passive aggressive. Like now. You don't want me to come with you. But instead of saying so, you start doing all the things you know make me crazy, like playing your video game so late that I went to bed without you on Saturday, and then yesterday, I wanted to make us a nice dinner for our last night in the apartment, so I decided to make the marinara from scratch. And what do you do? You kept sneaking in red pepper flakes until it was so spicy, I knew if I ate it, we'd have to stop at every gas station between here and Maine. So I had to have Cheerios."

"You eat lots of spicy food. You—"

She held up one hand like she was directing traffic and wanted him to stop. So, he stopped. Even though that hand was as bad as interrupting, and she always got on his case for interrupting her.

"I can eat some spicy food, just not spicy food that also has tomatoes, which I know that you know. And you've been acting like a jerk for weeks in all kinds of ways, just so I'd get mad enough to tell you to go by yourself. Well, it worked. Go by yourself. I'm done. We're done."

"Because I put in a few too many red pepper flakes?" Unbelievable.

"No. That's not what I'm saying. I'm saying you've been pushing me away in all kinds of little ways, nothing too big, nothing you couldn't dismiss as me being crazy."

Gavin couldn't stop a sigh. "You *are* being crazy, Bec. Why wouldn't I want you to come? Are you PMSing or what?" He should have known that was the wrong thing to say. The expected explosion came fast and hard.

"See? And now you want to make it my fault. Because that's you. You never accept the blame for anything." She pulled out her phone. "If you had just been upfront and said you wanted to break up, I wouldn't be standing here calling an Uber to go to my sister's because I sublet our place, without your help, thank you very much, and I did it because . . . because I don't know. I should have seen this coming a mile away. You've been acting like a jerk for the past month. You've probably been freaking out because I kept giving you more chances instead of kicking you to the curb."

Her voice was getting that quaver, and he could tell she was moments away from crying, and he didn't even know why. Nothing she'd said was any big thing. One night when he went to bed after her. Or maybe a few nights, because he'd had that tournament. And a few too many pepper flakes? And the thing with her friend? It wasn't like he blew it off. He'd been a little late, yeah, and yeah, he hadn't ordered anything, which made no difference whatsoever. He had been there, what did it matter if he ate or not? And it was freaking months ago. But he couldn't say any of that, because now she was crying.

He pulled in a deep breath and gave it one more try. "Rebecca, we just moved in together a few months ago. Why would I have agreed to that if I didn't want to be with you?"

"You agreed to it. You *agreed* to it," she said again, her voice getting higher and more quavery. "Like you were doing me some kind of favor?"

"No. That's not what—Do you have to analyze every word? I just talk, you know. I just . . . talk. What I meant was, we just moved in together. Why would we have moved in together if I didn't want to be with you all the time?"

"I don't know. Maybe that's something you should do some

thinking about. Although, what does it matter now? We're over."

Should he try to change her mind? She sounded absolutely definite. "Well, okay, this is good-bye then." She didn't look up, even though he was sure she'd finished putting the address in.

He got in the car. When he glanced in the rearview mirror as he pulled away from the curb, Rebecca's head was still lowered toward her phone. Gavin got some Nick Cave going. Rebecca used to complain about the less-than-pure sound quality that came out of the Porsche's stereo when he used the FM transmitter and his phone, but it made Cave sound even better, especially the old stuff. Gavin tilted the sunroof and cranked the music as loud as it would go, until he could feel it in his bones. With every mile down the I-95, he felt the Rebecca-induced stress sliding out of his body. He gave all his focus to the music and the feel of the car, the tightness of the hydraulic power steering, the sound of the exhaust and the occasional rattle, the precision of the shifter.

About three and a half hours out of Newark, he got himself a Hot Mess sub, emphasis on the hot, at Cowabunga, a place he'd discovered road-trippin' it a few years before. Definitely not something Miss Rebecca would want to put in her delicate tum-tum. He took it down to the beach and kicked off his shoes so he could dig his toes in the sand while he ate. Warm sun. Good eats. Salt air. Life was good.

Back in the car he got some Limp Bizkit going, a move Rebecca would probably call passive-aggressive if she was with him. She always said it was angry music, and that he should have grown out of it. But, hell, his father hadn't been a teenager when he and Gavin were listening together. It brought up great memories of hanging out with his dad, and it was perfect driving music, although it did feel kinda out of place once he was off the highway on a dirt road with pines rising up on either side, like green walls.

He cut the music, and, a few seconds later, he spotted a sign up ahead that read "Welcome to Fox Crossing, Maine. Founded 1805," and smiled. This was what he needed. A real, old-school summer vacation. He deserved it. He'd busted his butt this semester and had worked almost full-time at his barista gig. And that was another thing Rebecca had disapproved of. His lack of a real job. But that's why he was in school, to get the marketing degree to get a real job. And, anyway, the tip money was prime. So yeah. He deserved some vacay. He'd be working, yeah, but mostly outside as an instructor getting hikers prepped for hiking the Appalachian Trail. Not exactly hard labor. It would—

Gavin slammed on the brakes hard enough for the Porsche to fishtail. "Please, you go first," he muttered as a fox trotted across the road in front of the car, taking her time, unfazed by the sound of him screeching to a stop to keep from mowing her down. Strange looking fox. The tip of the tail was black instead of white, and one sock was white instead of black.

Guess I should have taken that sign more literally, he thought as he watched the fox make her way under the Fox Crossing sign and disappear between a couple blueberry bushes. He did a quick check of both sides of the road to make sure there were no more critters headed his way, then put on the gas, eager to see the town again. He'd only spent a night there back when he had been hiking this end of the AT, so it would be mostly new. Gavin loved new. Maybe he'd meet someone. Have a nice, fun summer fling to go along with the summer vacation. Yeah, this summer in Fox Crossing was going to be exactly what he needed.

"A charm of foxes," Lillian Smith murmured, her gaze traveling around the cozy shop, taking in the fox kites flying near the ceiling, the string of cute little copper fox bells tied to the doorknob, fox socks waving from the clothesline stretched across the bay window, the fox pillows on the window seat beneath, the fox—

"I almost called the shop that." Lillian turned toward the voice and saw a petite woman, maybe in her seventies, with a pair of cloth fox ears perched on top of her head. "But I ended up going with Vixen's. I own the place, and I thought the name suited me as well as the store. Not in the ill-tempered sense. I'm as sweet as Honey, which is my name or at least what everyone calls me. My actual name is Ruth Allis, and I'm a vixen, in the sexually attractive sense." She winked at Lillian, and gave her skirt, a fifties-style poodle number, but with a fox where the poodle would usually be, a flirty swish-swish. "I've still got it."

"I can see that." But an endless number of coffee dates from a slew of dating apps had proven that she didn't have even a smidge. Her mother said all Lillian had to do was get herself out there, so she'd gotten herself out there. Over and over and over again. It wasn't that she didn't have the, well, the assets, but she didn't have the attitude. She couldn't flirt. At all. It made her feel squirmy and embarrassed, so squirmy and embarrassed that most of the time all she'd wanted was to put in enough time that she could leave. Usually, it seemed like the guy, whatever guy, had felt the same way.

Her stomach tensed as the negative thoughts threatened to take her over. She pictured them as little rat-like things with dozens and dozens of pointy yellow teeth. You know how to deal with them, she told herself. She imagined herself holding a glittery wand with a star on top. She flicked her wand at the rats—zing!—turning them into beautiful dappled gray horses that then galloped away.

Why did she still let those thoughts get to her? She didn't have to know how to flirt, not anymore. Not since Owen. Somehow, he'd had the patience to get through her squirmy and embarrassed, not to mention her awkward and shy, to see, well, what she thought of as the real her. And now, she was almost, pretty sure almost, about to be engaged to him. To be married to him. There had been a time when it had seemed there was no chance she'd be married before she was thirty, but then she had met Owen.

Honey chuckled. "I was just about to start telling you about how every single girl needs a little something foxy, but then I saw that smile come out. You've got the smile of a girl who's already lucky in love. Just nod if I'm right."

Lillian nodded once, then followed it up with five or six fast head bobs. "My boyfriend's doing a section hike. Last year he did Springer to Harpers Ferry. This year, Katahdin to Harpers. We're both teachers, me kindergarten, him sixth grade, and that's how we'll be spending this summer. I just dropped him off at Baxter State Park." Wow. She was talking a lot. And fast. She was just nervous. Excited. Nervous-excited. "He had me make a reservation at the Quarryman Inn the night he plans to arrive in Fox Crossing. I think, maybe, he might, maybe . . ." Lillian couldn't quite bring herself to say it. She might jinx it. That's where all the nervous-excited was coming from.

"Might pop the question?" Honey finished for her.

Lillian managed to keep it to one nod this time, her cheeks warming. "We're going to be able to spend the whole summer together. Well, in bits. Any time he gets to a town, I'll be there. And he hinted that maybe we'd kick off the summer by getting engaged. He showed me some rings in a window and asked which one I liked."

"It sounds like a done deal to me, then. A man doesn't show a woman engagement rings unless he's serious. But even though you don't need any fox luck on that front, you have to see the panties we carry." Honey winked. "I'm sure your man would like to see them—on you. There are some with little foxes all over, but my favorites are the ones with the fox face, just over the—Well, I'll let you see for yourself."

Lillian followed Honey deeper into the store, even though she liked her matching beige bra-and-panty sets. They worked with everything. Smooth lines, nothing to show through her clothes. Not that her clothes were see-through-able. She'd tried sexier lingerie a few times, but it gave her that same feeling trying to flirt did, just a squirmy sensation, and Owen seemed happy with her usual practical things.

"I have to know the story of your charm of foxes. There has to be a story, and I love stories," Lillian said as she looked at the undies display. Not for her, but she definitely wanted to buy something, a keepsake to remember the cute little town, especially if Owen ended up proposing to her here.

"Of course, there's a story, the story of how Fox Crossing came to be." Honey straightened her fox ears, then fluffed her blond curls. "It started with a fox, of course, and my husband's great-great-great-grandmother, Annabelle Hatherley. She'd recently been widowed, left with a little baby. The people of the settlement did what they could to help her, but they didn't have much to give. The community was one bad winter away from annihilation, and that winter was closing in. And even with all her sorrow, wondering how she and her child would survive, when she saw a fox with her leg caught in a trap, Annabelle saved it. My theory is that she couldn't stand the thought of even one more death, no matter how small. She took it home and some say—"

Honey leaned closer and lowered her voice. "Some say she nursed it with the same milk she used to feed her little boy, the milk from her own breast. The Fox survived, and so did the settlement. It wasn't too long after that that one of the settlers, Celyn Hanmer, discovered slate on Annabelle Hatherley's land, and that was the start of the Fox Crossing Mine Company. That company turned the settlement into a thriving town. Some say it never would have happened if Annabelle hadn't saved The Fox, and the mine and the town and my store were named after the vixen."

Honey adjusted the position of a ceramic fox on the shelf of a nearby curio cabinet. She was clearly waiting for Lillian to beg her to go on, and Lillian was happy to oblige. "I'm missing the connection. How did The Fox play a part in Celyn's finding the slate?" The way Honey said "The Fox," made it sound like it should be capitalized for extra importance, so that's how Lillian saw it in her mind, and she gave it the same emphasis when she said the words.

Honey made a second adjustment to the ceramic fox, then continued. "It so happened that a fox, The Fox, Annabelle Hatherley's fox, caused Celyn's horse to shy and dump Celyn on his butt. He had to go after the animal, and, when he did, he saw something sparkling in a cliffside. He knew it was mica. He'd done mining back in Wales before he immigrated, so he knew that where there's mica, there's usually slate. He had the knowhow, and Annabelle had the land. They teamed up on the mine. Some say that fox is still with us and that whoever sees it shares its luck. I'm one of them. I know—"

The shop door opened with a bang, setting the fox bells tinkling, and a little girl, brown hair pulled back with easily a dozen multicolored barrettes, maybe about eight years old, raced over to Honey and flung her arms around her waist. Honey took a step back to absorb the impact, then hugged the girl tight. "This is Evie," she told Lillian. "My great-niece," she added in a whisper.

The girl let Honey go. "She doesn't like the 'great' part. She thinks it makes her sound old. I'm staying here with Honey for the whole summer! Honey always comes to visit us, but, finally, I get to see Fox Crossing." She pulled a business card cut into the shape of a magnifying glass out of the bright blue purse she carried and handed it to Lillian. It read:

Evie Hendricks
P.I. (Private Investigator)
with the P.I. (Powerful Intelligence) to solve your
P.I. (Pressing Inquiries)
555-542-1743

"If you need my services, call the number. It's my sister Kristina's phone. My parents won't let me have one, even though I've explained that it's essential for my detective work and that if I got a special number that spelled out 'Call Evie P.I.,' I would earn more than enough money for a cell and the fees. I explained it would be a P.I., Priceless Investment, and they still said no. But Kristina will take a message if I'm not with her."

Lillian carefully slid the card into her wallet. "I'll only be here for about a week and a half, but you'll be the first person I call if I come across a mystery."

"Or it can just be if there's something you want me to find out for you. My mother says no secret is safe from me. For example, I know that you work at a preschool, that you have a boyfriend, and that although most visitors to this town are hikers, you are not."

"I was just telling Honey I'm a kindergarten teacher, so very, very close. But how did you know?"

"Your purse has a child's fingerprint on it in what I suspect is finger paint. She touched the small orange oval, which Lillian hadn't noticed. "Some might have thought that meant you had a young child, but I observed that you are wearing a silk blouse. My mom says she hasn't worn anything that isn't machine washable since my sister was born, so I deduced you work with little kids. Your tote says 'Miss Violet's Boardinghouse for Trail Widows,' and you aren't wearing a wedding ring, so I deduced you have a boyfriend, one who is out hiking. And if you were a hiker, you'd be with him; also, you wouldn't be nearly as clean or smell so nice."

The little girl had only looked at Lillian for about ten seconds before she'd made all those deductions. "Wow. I'm so impressed! Or should I say that I admire your"—Lillian paused for a moment, thinking—"Preternatural Insights?"

Evie grinned. "I don't actually know what that first word means, but it sounds good."

"Preternatural means extraordinary. A lot of times people use it to mean psychic."

"Thanks! I'm adding that to my list of *p* words. I'm not psychic, though, just observant. I know pretty much everything about everyone I meet," Evie bragged. "Like I knew there was some secret about my sister, Kristina. My parents knew something was wrong. I heard them talking about it. But they didn't know what. I investigated and found out she was being bullied by—"

Honey placed one hand over Evie's mouth. "She's bubbly. She gets that from me." She kissed the top of Evie's head. "Let's let Kristina talk about Kristina. I want to hear about you." She slid her hand away, and Evie immediately started talking again.

"Me? My Field Day team came in first in the Mummy Relay. I was the mummy. Everybody had to take toilet paper and—"

The fox bells on the door jingled, and a girl around fourteen, presumably Kristina, walked in, followed by a tall, white-haired man.

"Kristina! Get yourself over here!" Honey threw open her arms. The girl hugged her great-aunt as tightly as her little sister had. Lillian turned and picked up a fox paperweight from the curio and turned it over in her hands, trying to ease herself away from the family reunion.

Honey put her hand on Lillian's arm, pulling her into the group. "This is my gorgeous great-niece Kristina." She said "great-niece" in a whisper. "She gets the gorgeous from me."

Lillian didn't quite see how a great-aunt had passed down traits to her great-nieces, but Honey sounded certain that she deserved the credit. "And that's my gorgeous husband Charlie."

"He just had a birthday," Evie volunteered. "He's seventy-four years old and—"

"I'm much younger than he is," Honey cut in.

"She's actually—" Evie began.

"One more word, and it's the last you'll ever utter," Charlie warned. "I love you, but I will not be able to stop your Honey from plucking out your tongue." He wrapped his arm around Evie's shoulders. "Come on. We just got in an order of gummy fox candy, and they need a taste tester." He guided her through a curtain, fox print, of course, that must lead to the back room.

"I'm related to them. They have to think I'm gorgeous," Kristina muttered to Lillian, not quite meeting Lillian's gaze.

Lillian disagreed. Maybe Kristina wasn't *gorgeous* gorgeous, but she had lovely skin, her light brown hair was glossy, and her brown eyes were large and striking, flecked with gold. Lillian didn't try to tell Kristina that, knowing it would make her even more uncomfortable than she already seemed.

"We think you're gorgeous because you're gorgeous," Honey insisted.

"Honey was just telling me how Fox Crossing got its name." Lillian thought the girl could use a subject change.

Kristina smiled, a dimple appearing in one cheek. "I love that story. Start over, Honey."

Honey took off her fox ears and put them on Kristina's head. "You know it by heart. I tell it every time I come to visit. You tell . . ." She looked at Lillian. "We didn't get to names, at least not yours."

"Lillian Smith."

"You tell Lillian the rest. I was just saying how some of us believe The Fox is still with us."

Kristina shook her head. "No, you go. You tell it better."

"Somebody please tell me," Lillian begged. "The Fox would have to be more than two hundred years old! Or did you mean people see a ghost fox? Or feel The Fox's spirit?"

"Not the spirit, the actual fox!" Evie called. Her voice sounded like it had to make its way through a mouthful of those gummy foxes. A second later, she popped back through the curtain. She swallowed hard, then continued, "It's still living in the woods. Last year, my cousin Annie saw it, and if she hadn't, her boyfriend, well, he's her boyfriend now, would have died. He'd fallen into a river and gotten hypothermia, and The Fox got her to him just in time. She saved his life, but she wouldn't have if it weren't for The Fox. And the two of them never would have gotten together. Kristina is hoping she'll see it, now that we're finally getting to visit, because she—"

"How do people know it's the same fox?" Lillian asked. She didn't like to interrupt, and she hated the possibility of ruining the story with such a mundane question, but she had the feeling Evie had been about to say something that would mortify her sister.

"Evie, you still have a few more flavors to try," Charlie called, and Evie returned to the back room, throwing a wave over her shoulder.

"We know it's the same fox because Annabelle Hatherley wrote about it in her diary," Kristina explained. "She said it had one ear that was almost white, and that it had white on one leg where most foxes have black. And the tip of its tail is black, and ordinary foxes have white tips, not black."

"And everybody who has seen it has good luck. Everyone!" Evie yelled from the back, her words again sounding like they were pushing their way through gummy candy.

Lillian was enchanted. The story felt like a beautiful fairy tale, but with no poison apples or treacherous wolves. "That is the best story. Thank you for sharing. I think I want this." She plucked a necklace with a delicate silver chain from the jewelry holder on the curio. The small silver fox charm was beautifully detailed. "You can never have too much luck, right?"

"Right," Honey and Kristina answered in unison.

A few minutes later, Lillian was walking back toward Miss Violet's Boardinghouse, the fox charm resting lightly at the base of her throat. She pressed her fingers against it, and her heart gave a little flip. It was definitely going to happen. When Owen got to town, they'd have dinner at the inn, and he'd propose. She had the luck of The Fox on her side.

Not that she believed the story. Now back when she was Evie's age, she would have believed with her whole heart. She'd believed in wishing on the evening star, birthday candles, and dandelion fluff, and she'd had a collection of lucky pennies she'd found that she saved for use in wishing wells. Actually, she still made wishes, but she was a grown-up now and knew wishes didn't have any actual power. She'd loved hearing the tale, but she didn't actually believe it either.

Still, since she had a few days in Fox Crossing, maybe she'd take a few walks in the woods. She'd been wanting to get a closer look at the lake anyway. And if she happened to see a fox with unusual markings ... Well, it would be the product of some genetic mutation that had gotten passed on through the years, but it would be fun to get a glimpse of the town's local legend. Especially before Owen arrived in Fox Crossing.

Gavin grinned as he stepped into Wit's Beginning, his friend's pub. Banana stood on the bar, taking a bow. Gavin joined in the applause. When he had stopped to get gas a few towns back, he'd seen a tweet from Banana announcing that Banana had finally earned his damn mug.

Banana gave anyone who hiked the entire Appalachian Trail a special mug, and a mug full of their drink of choice every day for life. No one who wasn't a 2,000-miler was allowed one, and, until earlier today, that had included Banana. He'd hiked everything but the 100-Mile Wilderness, which started outside Fox Crossing, multiple times, but something had always stopped him from getting through that hundred-mile stretch, a couple times injuries, a couple times helping other people who got injured, a freak hailstorm once, and an assortment of other types of bad luck. That's how he and Gavin had met. Three years ago, Gavin and his then-girlfriend, Niri, had spotted Banana doing first aid on a hiker who'd fallen off an embankment and busted a leg. They'd stopped to help, and Gavin and Banana had been in touch on and off since then. It was Banana who'd hooked Gavin up with the summer gig teaching hikers what they needed to make it through the Wilderness—and the rest of the trail.

"Gavin! Welcome, my friend!" Banana scrambled off the bar and started toward him, pausing again and again for handshakes, back slaps, and hugs. "You made it," he said, when he reached Gavin, then gave him a hug, enveloping him with a cloud of just-off-the-trail stank. Brought back good memories. He looked good. He had to be sixty-something now, but his frame was still wiry, without the paunch a lot of guys his age sported.

"No, *you* made it. You made it through the Wilderness." As soon as the words were out of his mouth, the old Madonna song started playing in Gavin's brain, and he couldn't resist. He planted his hands on Banana's shoulders and started to sing in his best falsetto, which was pretty damn good, if he did say so himself. Heads immediately started to turn, and Gavin gestured for the crowd to join in. A few minutes later, he had everybody, except for a few clueless and/or inhibited, serenading Banana with "Like a Virgin." When Banana managed to stop laughing, he started singing too, then took another bow, getting even more applause.

"You're as crazy as ever," he told Gavin. "How'd you even know all the lyrics anyway? You weren't even born when Madonna put on the veil."

"I had a part-time gig hosting a karaoke night for a while. Heard it many, many times."

"Come on. Let me introduce you to Annie and Nick. They co-own the Boots Camp." Banana led the way through the crowd, getting stopped every few feet for more love. Banana was one of those guys who turned acquaintances into friends within minutes.

Gavin was sure there were a ton of locals in the place tonight, but he bet there were some who'd just met Banana and that they'd been applauding as hard as the people who'd known him for years. Gavin knew the power of the Banana. He'd made lots of buddies on the trail, but Banana was almost the only one he kept up with. He'd instabonded with the guy. Probably partly because they'd teamed up to get that hiker to the hospital, which involved swimming across a lake while towing him. But only partly. The rest was just Banana.

"Here's your new instructor," Banana announced as he came to a stop in front of a booth where a man and a woman, both around Gavin's age, clearly a couple, were sitting. The guy got to his feet and stuck out his hand. "I'm Nick. And this is Annie. Have a seat."

"Good to have you here." Annie reached across Nick so she could shake Gavin's hand too. "We only have a few courses going right now, but we're ramping up for the summer. Next Wednesday, we start the Boots Camp, the six-week intensive training course."

"Looking forward to it."

"Got your mug?" Banana asked.

"Would I walk into this place without my mug?" Gavin pulled it out of his backpack, and Banana took it from him.

"Spirited Banana?"

"Of course." The Spirited Banana was one of Banana's specialty microbrews.

Banana took a few steps toward the bar, then turned back. "Where's Psychick?" he asked, using the trail name of Gavin's old girlfriend. Well, former fiancée. Gavin didn't usually think of Niri that way, because she'd only been his fiancée for about two months. She'd also helped with the trail rescue. He hadn't told Banana they'd broken up? He could have sworn he had.

"Uh. We're not together anymore." Maybe he'd just leave it at that. He didn't need to get into how he'd started up a relationship with someone new—and then broken up with her too. With a couple more things, nothing serious, in between.

Banana sat down across from Gavin. "What happened?"

What had happened with Niri? He hadn't thought about it in a while. There wasn't one big thing that had led to his breakup. It wasn't like she'd cheated on him—or that he'd cheated on her—nothing like that. "I guess, I don't know, maybe we were on different timetables. I'd, let's say, taken a break from college, and was always working a couple jobs, which meant some nights and weekends. She'd just started working as a budget analyst and was all about the career." Gavin shrugged. Banana looked at him for a long moment, then stood back up. "I'll go get that drink."

Hopefully, when Banana got back, he'd wouldn't try to find out more about the breakup. Banana had a talent for getting people to spill their guts. Maybe it was a bartender thing. And Gavin preferred to keep his guts in place. "So, Banana said that you just started Boots last summer?" he asked. He definitely didn't want to do anymore talking about his relationship history with his new bosses.

"Yeah, Nick decided to try to put me out of business." Annie gave Nick's knee a squeeze.

"Actually, I wanted to team up with Hatherley's Outfitters,

which has been in Annie's family since before the town was even a town, but she refused."

"Because he decided to start a business practically overnight. It might have been two nights. And I had no desire to team up with someone who was so impulsive. I didn't think he'd even make it through the summer." Annie took a swig of her beer. "And then he starts making money. And just because he gave good customer service, while my Yelp reviews said I was, among other appellations, surly."

"Surly? Really?" Gavin wasn't getting any of that vibe from her, although she'd shot him an assessing glance when he'd been telling Banana about Niri. He'd probably sounded like a slacker, with the college break and low-ambition jobs. Not something a boss wanted in an employee. But, come on, none of that mattered when you were a hiking instructor. What mattered was time on the trail, and Gavin had that.

"If Annie thought you were ready to take on the Wilderness, she'd be sweet as sugar. If not, well, watch out." Nick smiled at Annie, and Gavin could see he was a goner, totally in love. "She has an incredibly big heart. She doesn't want anyone to get hurt. Sometimes that concern came out as—"

"Surly," Annie and Nick finished together.

"Which is why being an instructor at Boots is a much better fit for her than retail," Nick continued. "You'll need to put in some hours in the barn on the Boots grounds. We sell stuff there, and Annie and her family still have the Outfitters in town."

"Which is doing nicely, now that I'm no longer on the premises," Annie added.

Which didn't seem to bother her at all, Gavin thought. Good for her. Gotta play to your strengths. "I've been told that I'm charming." One of his strengths. "I've never done sales, not exactly, but I made a lot of tips serving up lattes, and I think that's because I gave good customer service. Not just making the drinks right. Remembering names, remembering all the little details they'd tell me about their lives. And I'm definitely familiar with pretty much all the hiking gear out there."

Nick pushed his horn-rimmed glasses—what Rebecca would have called geek chic—higher on his nose. "I'll get you on the schedule."

Gavin nodded, mind still on Rebecca. They'd had some good times together. He pulled out his cell, planning to shoot her a quick text, tell her how much she'd love it here. Maybe she'd decide to come out, and give him—them—another shot. Then he saw a barmaid with a laden tray weaving her way through the crowd, black hair, short skirt showing off long legs, smattering of freckles. He loved freckles, and wondered if she had them all over. Playing connect-the-dots on soft skin was one of his favorite activities. He put the phone away. He had been right when he'd pulled into town. It was time for a summer of fun with someone new. He caught the barmaid's eye and smiled, and got a smile back.

Old friend. Cool job. A smile from a cutie. What else did he need? Life was good.

"How'd you like your place? Does it have everything you need?" Annie asked.

Banana had set Gavin up with a summer sublet from a guy who was out on the trail. "Great. Great view of the lake. And more kitchen stuff than I know what to do with. Seriously, there was one thing, a metal cylinder with another cylinder on top that had a zigzaggy top. I have no idea what it does."

Nick laughed. "That would be a corn stripper, takes corn off the cob."

"Which seems kind of pointless when it's so easy to eat when it's on."

"I would have had no idea what it was either," Annie admitted. "Nick does all the cooking. Except breakfast. I pour a mean bowl of cereal. But most mornings we eat at Flappy

Jacks. If you're not into cooking, it's right on Main Street. Good food, good prices."

"I remember it. I hit it for one of those massive breakfasts before I started into the Wilderness. I'm sure I'll be a regular," Gavin answered as Banana sat back down and passed Gavin his beer.

"Looks like that fox luck is still with you. Congrats on earning the mug, man," a guy said to Banana as he passed by the booth.

Gavin had almost forgotten about the legend of the town fox, but Banana had been obsessed with seeing it. He'd gotten convinced a sighting was the only way he'd finally get through the Wilderness. "You really, honestly believe that some varmint has magical powers? Or is it just one of the tales you like to spin?" Banana had an endless supply of tall tales, one of the things that made him such entertaining company on the trail.

"Everything that passes my lips is the honest-to-heaven truth." Banana tried to look deeply offended as Nick, Annie, and Gavin laughed in his face.

"I can't vouch for the rest of what comes out of his mouth, but I will say The Fox saved my life," Nick answered.

"Actually, I saved his life," Annie said. "If I hadn't found him and dragged his frozen ass to the hospital, he'd have died of hypothermia."

"But she wouldn't have known she needed to find me, if she hadn't seen The Fox. She pulled out her phone to take a picture—and then she decided to check the tracker app to see how I was doing."

"Because I knew he wasn't ready for the Wilderness. For one thing, his calves, while very nice, did not have the circumference of those of someone who'd done the necessary conditioning."

"And because she saw The Fox and then checked the tracker when she had the phone out, she knew I was in trouble. She could tell I had been swept into the river, although it wasn't the actual me, it was my backpack with the tracker in it."

"So, you can take that as The Fox bringing him the luck he needed to survive. Or you can take that as me making sure he had a tracker before he left my store."

"I say a little of both," Banana told them, then turned to Nick. "And last year, I saw The Fox right before I got the call from my daughter asking if I'd take care of my granddaughter, Jordan, over the summer. Changed my life."

That was one of the things that Gavin and Banana had talked about when Gavin was avoiding talking about his relationship. He knew how much it meant that Banana had gotten close to both his granddaughter and his daughter after years with nothing but polite exchanges of Christmas and birthday gifts.

"I thought seeing it meant I'd finally get those last miles in, but what The Fox luck brought me was something much better."

"You know what? I think I saw The Fox on my way in."

Banana slammed his mug down on the table. "What?"

"It had weird markings. Your fox has weird markings, right?" The story Banana had told Gavin on the trail was coming back. "Mostly white ear, a white sock."

"Black tail tip." Banana ran his hand over his bald head. "You saw it?"

"Right as I was heading into town."

"Well, hold on to your butt, son, because, somehow, someway, your life is about to change."

CHAPTER 2

Lillian smiled as she heard Miss Violet reaching for one of the high notes in the Queen of the Night aria—and missing by quite a bit. She was giving it her all though, her voice charged with wrath and the desire for vengeance. Lillian realized she missed opera. She and another teacher and the teacher's husband used to have season tickets to the Asheville Light Opera, but she'd let her subscription slide around three years ago. She hadn't wanted to waste any Saturday nights, when she could be spending them with Owen.

Miss Violet hit, almost hit, another high note with gusto. The proprietress of the Boardinghouse for Trail Widows always sang when she made breakfast, which meant it was time to head downstairs. But first—Lillian pulled up the tracker app on her cell and checked on Owen. He was making good progress. He should make it into Fox Crossing about five and a half days from now, with time for a nap and a shower before their dinner reservation at the Quarryman Inn. She gave her fox pendant a tap for luck, the way she did every time she thought of their reunion dinner.

She started toward the door, then paused as she caught a glimpse of herself in the cheval mirror, a beautiful piece with a frame of cherry wood. A lock of her long, curly blond hair had escaped from her ponytail, and she tucked it back into place, then she pulled in a long, deep breath. She didn't have anything to feel anxious about, but tell her stomach that. It wasn't in knots, but it was tight. She'd been the only guest at the boardinghouse the first three nights, but last night, two other women—Ginger and Bailey—had checked in. Sometimes Lillian had a hard time talking to new people.

She took another step toward the door, then turned back to the mirror. Maybe she should change. The sky-blue T-shirt was one of her favorites, but it was slim cut. Was it too tight? She could never decide. Sometimes having big breasts was great, but sometimes . . . not so much. She got more than her share of embarrassing comments—some of them yelled from across the street. She wished Owen were there. He always told her if he thought she was wearing something that didn't make her look her best.

Should she change? She'd found sky-blue nail polish at the town mercantile that was an exact match to the shirt, and she'd used it to paint her toenails. On impulse, she'd bought a little package of tiny stick-on rhinestones and put them on her toenails too. They made her think of stars in a sunny summer sky, which wasn't possible, because stars and the sun weren't out at the same time, but which would be beautiful if it were possible. Owen only liked nail polish that was red or pink, but she'd have plenty of time to repaint her toes before he got to town, and it had amused her to paint them blue while she was hanging out in the room last night.

She wouldn't change, she decided. But then she thought of the two women downstairs. She'd been wearing a baggy shirt last night when she'd briefly chatted with them over tea and cookies in Miss Violet's parlor. Would they sneak looks at her chest? Because it wasn't only guys who looked. She was never sure if women were doing a comparison, and maybe wishing theirs were more like hers, or if they were thinking that she was somehow slutty.

Wand time, she told herself. She imagined zinging all the crazy, negative rat-thoughts, turning them into beautiful horses, and watching them gallop away. Other people had their own lives. Nobody was spending that much time thinking about her. Lillian was always reminding herself of that. But so many times when she'd been out with her mother, her mother would make these snide little comments about the women around them. That one had on too much makeup. No man wanted a woman with that much gunk smeared on. That one didn't wear any. Who thought they looked good with no makeup?

With a growl of frustration, Lillian grabbed a button-down from the dresser and pulled it on. Left unbuttoned it made her breasts less obvious. There. Now she was ready to go downstairs. It would be fine. No, it should be better than fine. Pleasant. It would be pleasant. Bailey and Ginger were both perfectly nice. Sitting at a table with them for breakfast should be fine. Pleasant.

So, get down there, she told herself. After one more deep breath and one last look in the mirror, she left the room and followed the sounds of Miss Violet's warblings to the kitchen. Ginger and Bailey were already seated at the big kitchen table.

Lillian did a quick mental review of what she'd learned about the two women the night before. Ginger's boyfriend, a college professor, had just started a SoBo hike, and would go as far as he could before he had to go back to school. Baileys husband was just hiking to Chairback Gap and back, so she'd only be in town a few more days.

Lillian's mother would say Bailey, with gray streaking her brown hair and an extra twenty pounds, was all but asking her husband to cheat on her. Lillian's mom had no patience for women who, in her opinion, had let themselves go once they got married. In her mother's opinion, a woman had to work as hard to keep a man as she did to get him in the first place. Not that keeping her hair colored and her weight the same as when she was a high school cheerleader had stopped Lillian's dad from cheating. Cheating, then leaving, back when Lillian was little. There were times Lillian was so tempted to remind her mom of that, but she never did. It would hurt her mom too much.

Ginger, on the other hand, would get full points from Mom, her hair falling in perfect waves, nails newly manicured, and a fresh, no-makeup look that Lillian knew from experience took a half an hour in front of the mirror to achieve.

"Morning," Lillian said, taking what, after only three days, had become her usual seat. She gave herself a mental reminder not to slouch. She had a tendency to hunch her shoulders, a bad habit Owen had helped her break. Miss Violet, still singing, headed for the table carrying a platter of scrambled eggs and home fries fresh from the skillet. She began to set them down, then froze, the platter a few inches from its destination. Her song petered out.

"Are you all right, Miss Violet?" Ginger exclaimed.

"Miss Violet!" Bailey cried.

Lillian gently tugged the platter away and set it down. "Miss Violet?" The woman's eyes were glassy. "This happens sometimes when she gets an idea," she explained to the other women. "She's a writer." Lillian gave Miss Violet's arm a light pat.

Miss Violet blinked once, twice, three times, then smiled. "I apologize, sweeties. I'm working on the end-of-summer play, and sometimes I get lost in my imagination. I thought I just had an idea that would work, but no." She gave a dramatic sigh. Everything about Miss Lillian was dramatic.

"What's the play about?" Bailey asked, spooning some eggs onto her plate.

"It's about—I'm not sure what it's about. Nothing feels right, so I keep starting again. It's vexing. Usually by now I'd have the whole thing done. I don't understand it. I never have writer's block."

"I'm sure it will come to you." Lillian gave Miss Violet's arm another pat.

"Of course, it will, my sweet." Miss Violet whirled around, setting her long lavender scarf flying, returned to the stove and pulled a baking sheet full of enormous cinnamon rolls out of the oven. She began to hum as she used a spatula to transfer the buns onto another serving platter. The humming turned to singing as she put the platter on the table, and the singing grew in pitch and enthusiasm as she wandered out of the room.

Lillian didn't know what her mother would make of Miss Violet. Probably she'd think it was pathetic of a woman who was pushing sixty—hard—to try to attract so much attention to herself, with those purple python-print wedge heels and the couldn't-be-natural red hair. By "trying to attract attention," Lillian's mother would mean trying to attract male attention, but Lillian got the sense that Miss Violet dressed to please herself and no one else, and that her style was part of what she'd heard Miss Violet describe as her "creative spirit."

"I think Miss V just got another new idea." Ginger picked up one of the rolls and dropped it on her plate, then waved her fingers. "Maybe wait a minute before you touch those."

"She reminds me of Jo March," Bailey commented.

Lillian smiled. Bailey and Ginger were both being so nice and normal. No side-eye. No hint of attitude. "Genius burns."

"Exactly." Bailey took a sip of pineapple juice. On her first day, Miss Violet had said every meal needed some flair, and Lillian thought the juice—served with little purple parasols—was this breakfast's.

"I don't get it." Ginger used one finger to test the temperature of the cinnamon roll.

"You know, *Little Women*," Bailey said. "That's what Jo's sisters would ask when she was frantically scribbling away on one of her stories or plays. 'Does genius burn, Jo?'"

Ginger shrugged. "I watched part of the movie, the one with what's her name from that movie where her father trained her to be an assassin since she was practically a baby."

"Saoirse Ronan," Bailey and Lillian said together.

"Sounds right. But I fell asleep. I'm horrible about falling asleep in movies. I fell asleep in all three parts of *Lord of the Rings*. Bryan was ready to dump me. He wrote his dissertation on some connection between Germanic heroes and the heroes in that movie—book. It had something to do with Beowulf. He's a Tolkiendil. I've learned not to say Tolkenite, unless I want to watch his head explode, which every once in a while, I admit I find amusing." Ginger laughed, then popped a piece of the roll into her mouth. "Still a little too hot, but worth the slight tongue damage," she said once she'd had a long swallow of her juice.

"I'm the opposite of you," Bailey told Ginger. "I live for movies. I like to sit right up front, so the screen fills my whole field of vision. The best part is, I know for those two hours—I go to the theater; I don't like watching at home—the phone won't ring and the text won't ping. If there's nothing I want to see, sometimes I'll go anyway, just for that. Sometimes, I'll treat myself to a triple feature, if I really need that down time."

She was talking like she didn't even have a husband. "Didn't that cut into Stan's conditioning time?" Lillian asked. A triple feature had to be six hours minimum, but probably more than that with time between shows and meal breaks. That meant pretty much a whole day off, and when you were prepping to hike even part of the Wilderness, you didn't take days off.

"Pfft." Bailey gave a dismissive hand wave. "I go by myself. Stan can't sit still for even one movie. He used to make me nuts wriggling around, then making trip after trip back to the lobby for a soda, then popcorn, then bathroom. And then he'd act like it was my fault that he got off his training regimen by eating junk. Our relationship got much better when we agreed to spend our Saturdays apart. He does his hiking thing. I do my movies, swim, hang with friends, and he hikes. Then Sunday is couple day. He gets in a short hike, but he makes sure he starts at dawn and is home and out of the shower in time to take me to brunch."

Lillian couldn't imagine going to the movies by herself, even if she were willing to give up the Owen time she got as they drove to and from whatever trail he'd chosen to tackle. She'd feel like everyone was looking at her, at the pathetic woman who obviously couldn't get someone to go to the movies with her.

"I hike with Bryan some, but only day hikes." Ginger pinched off another piece of her cinnamon roll and popped it into her mouth. "I spent one night in one of the shelters, and I'm never doing it again. A mouse ran right across my face, and one of the hikers was emitting baked-bean-and-beer farts all night long. Dis-gus-ting. What about you, Lillian?"

"I don't walk fast enough to do day hikes with Owen. Sometimes I'll do a little stroll on my own, then find a nice rock where I can sit and read in the sun. Or I go back to the car if the weather's icky," Lillian answered. "Speaking of Owen, I'm going to head out to the Boots Barn after breakfast to set up a food drop. You want to come, Bailey? Bryan will probably be needing fresh supplies before he gets through the Wilderness."

"He should have enough to make it from Katahdin to town. He prides himself on his ability to hike miles on one stick of jerky." Bailey shrugged. "I've stopped trying to understand it."

"Owen could definitely carry in everything he needed." Lillian somehow felt the need to defend him. "But I like to get him some little extras. A drop for Bryan could be a fun surprise, let him know you're thinking of him."

"He'd just get annoyed. I'd be messing up his man-against-wilderness thing, although it's not like he doesn't bring in multiple pouches of beef stroganoff. It's not exactly living off the land." Ginger shook her head, smiling fondly. "There are lots of things I don't get about him. And same goes for him about me. He is baffled by my desire to soak in the tub for two or three hours. He thinks of it as marinating in dirty water, although I've explained to him that I don't get all that dirty in a day of HR drama. On the important stuff, we're in sync, though. That's what matters. I'm going to go check out Junk & Disorderly. There's a local carpenter who makes beautiful things, and he sells them through the shop. Either of you want to come with? It's almost around the corner from here."

"Me." Bailey raised her hand like a schoolgirl.

"Mmmm." Lillian was tempted. She loved searching for treasure in junk stores. "Better not. I want to make sure I get the order in in time for it to be at White House Landing when Owen gets there."

"We should do dinner together," Ginger said.

Lillian had planned on making a quick dinner in Miss Violet's kitchen. Breakfast was the only meal served at the boardinghouse. That's what Lillian had done the last few nights, because she didn't want to sit in a restaurant by herself. But Ginger and Bailey were friendly. And the few times she'd gone out with Owen and his work friends, he had complained she didn't talk enough. This would give her some practice. "I'd like that."

Day four working at the Boots Barn, and Gavin had broken his sales record every day. Wasn't hard. The merchandise was high quality, and the prices were fair. Gavin stretched out in one of the hammocks displayed toward the back of the barn, along with some tents, and used one foot to get a gentle rocking motion going. Excellent breakfast in his belly. Some hammock time. Satisfaction of a job well done. Life was good.

"See, I told Nick you were industrious and hardworking," Banana called as he came through the big double doors.

Gavin grinned and kept swinging. "Inventory done. Shelf straightening done. New sign for sock sale done. Just waitin' until it's time to open up."

Banana walked over to the new display, where Gavin had strung a bunch of socks from fishing line over a sign that said "These'll Blow Your (Old) Socks Off!" Banana nodded his approval. "You been over to Flappy Jacks yet?"

"Yeah, including this morning. That omelet with the blueberries? I'm now addicted."

"Next time, sit in the last booth on the right."

"How come?"

"That would be telling."

"And you love to tell, so tell."

Banana grinned. "Actually, I can do better." He pulled his cell out of his pocket, tapped the screen a few times, then walked over and held it in front of Gavin.

"Wow." Gavin climbed out of the hammock and held out his hand for the phone so he could get a closer look. Banana handed it over, and Gavin stared down at the pic of the booth's tabletop—and the dozens of pictures of hikers under the glass. Including one of him and Niri, looking grungy as hell. Happy as hell too. "Blast from the past," he muttered.

"Three years ago."

"Feels like ten, and like a couple months ago at the same time." Gavin took a last look at Niri's smiling face. They'd burned hot for a while. Hot enough to get engaged. But . . . He gave a mental shrug and handed Banana back his phone.

Banana looked at the picture for a moment before he put the phone back in his pocket. "And, you said you split up because of timetables being out of sync? I didn't want to call bullshit on you in front of Nick and Annie that first night, but, I call bullshit. You two were good together. So, what really happened?"

Crap. "Honestly?"

"Otherwise, what's the point?"

"Honestly, I don't even know." Banana just stared at him. "I'm serious. I can't really remember. We just fizzled."

"I'm missing something. You were together when we talked about you two coming up here for the summer, and you're saying you can't remember why you split. It should still be raw."

Gavin had been hoping he wouldn't have to explain, but he wasn't going to lie to Banana's face. "The girl I was with when we talked, that wasn't Niri."

"You broke up with Psychick, got together with another woman, broke up with her, and you never said anything." Gavin thought Banana would start hitting him with questions, but he didn't say anything. "And you two were together how long?"

"Me and Niri?" Banana nodded. "A little more than a year. We didn't last that long after we finished the hike. It was one of those trail things. You know how things get really intense out there."

"Yeah." Banana drew the word out, sounding dubious. "But you two were engaged before you started the hike. Or do I have it wrong?"

"No. You're right." Gavin really didn't want to be having this conversation. The whole Niri thing, ancient history. No point in picking it apart. But Banana kept looking at him, not asking anything, but looking with that Banana stop-bullshitting-me face. "I gotta straighten up the maps before we open." Gavin turned and started for the display. The one he'd straightened as soon as he came in. He only made it about three steps, then he couldn't take being that guy, the guy who couldn't give a friend a straight answer.

He turned around. "Okay. You're right. Things were serious between Niri and me before we hit the trail. We were hiking the Wilderness partly to celebrate getting engaged. When we got back, we even started looking at houses. Her parents were going to help us with the down payment." His chest was feeling tight. This is why he didn't like looking back. And what was the point? It wasn't like it changed anything. "And . . . and I know I should have some big reason we split. You don't just break an engagement over nothing. But, I swear to you, there wasn't anything I can point to and say, yeah, that's what ended it. Maybe it's just because I was twenty-four. I had no business thinking of getting married."

Gavin tried to put himself back there, back to the day they broke it off. They'd been looking at houses. And . . ." Dang, it was fuzzy. It should be something that stuck in his memory. "I remember that I didn't like one of the houses we were looking at," he said slowly, trying to pull it up in his mind's eye. "She got pissed. Really pissed. Way out of proportion. And then I said something like, 'if we can't even agree on where to live, maybe we shouldn't be doing this.' Then she said maybe we shouldn't. And that was it. We just stared at each other. She started crying. . . ." Gavin shook his head. "She pulled off the ring. I took it. And that was it."

"You didn't talk about it again, after you'd both had a chance to cool off? Making a big purchase like a house, it can make anybody a little nuts."

"We didn't." Had she tried to call? Left him a message? He didn't think so. "And the more days that went by, the harder it felt, until it basically felt impossible. And that's it. That's the story of the end of Gavin and Niri."

"That's rough. If we were at the bar, I'd buy you a drink. So, you're owed a drink."

"I'll take it." Relief washed through Gavin. Banana wasn't going to try to suck more details out of him and analyze it all. Because Banana was a dude, for starters. "Although, it was probably a good thing. I'm not ready for marriage now, forget about three years ago. "

Banana rubbed the corner of one eye. "I was just reading that the brain isn't fully developed until age twenty-seven. So maybe now that you're firing on all cylinders that will change."

Gavin laughed. "Maybe. But I'm not looking for anything serious or long-term right now. I want some down time, no fights and craziness."

"Who wouldn't want a break from that? You know there are actually some relationships where fights and craziness aren't the norm."

"I was thinking we should get in more of a variety of Fox Crossing merch."

Banana held up both hands. "Okay, hint taken. No more relationship talk."

"I'm serious. Those socks with the LL Bean logo on them sell like crazy. All I have to do is point them out, tell them the mountain on the logo is Katahdin, and—sold. Hikers love this town. If we got in some—"

The door swung open, interrupting him. The woman standing there was like something from a fifties pin-up calendar, all curves, though she'd done a decent job disguising them under that shirt she wore on top of her tee. Had to be at least a couple sizes too big. "Are you open? Or am I too early?" she asked.

"We're open, and if we weren't, I'd open up just for you." He heard Banana give a snort, but ignored him. Yeah, what he'd said had been a little cheesy, but who cared? The important thing was he hadn't just stood there gawping at her.

"I'm interested in setting up a food drop at White House Landing. It needs to be there by Tuesday night."

"Sure. I can hook you up. You just need to choose the food." Gavin walked over to the wall with all the packets, protein bars, and other trail food and gestured for her to join him. "Is it for you . . ."

"Me? No. I'd never make it. I'm a walking through the park type."

He wasn't surprised. She looked soft. Not that that was a bad thing. But there was a look hikers got, men and women, and she didn't have it. Those cute little toes of hers, the nails painted sky blue with little sparkly bits stuck on, had clearly not spent time in a pair of hiking boots. For starters, all the nails were intact. No abrasions or bunions. No pieces of Leukotape covering blisters.

The toes on her left foot gave a little wiggle, and Gavin realized he'd been staring. At her feet. Like a freak. "So, you're looking for about five days' worth of supplies, I'm guessing. That right, Twinkle Toes?"

She gave a startled laugh. "You clearly haven't seen me dance."

"I betcha got some moves. But I was thinkin' more like twinkle, twinkle little star." He nodded toward her feet.

"If they were stars, they'd have to be on dark blue, right?"

"But stars in the sky on a summer day? I like it. And I think there's such a thing as too much reality."

"I completely agree." They locked eyes for a moment, and Gavin felt a rush of heat, then she blinked and turned away, reaching for a pack of tortillas. "Owen, my boyfriend, that's who the supplies are for, is getting sick of tortillas, but I know bread doesn't last well in a pack."

Boyfriend. Of course, boyfriend. A woman didn't walk around with the curves, and that curly blond hair—wasted, pulled back in a pony, but still—and those cute little toes, and not have a boyfriend. Oh, well. Couldn't win them all, so back to work. "You could go with bagels. Not as delicate as bread," Gavin suggested. "Or you could do crackers. I always tied some to my pack with a bandana."

"I think he'd like crackers. I'll send a bandana too."

"Maybe some pork rinds? They take a little more room, but

if he's sick of tortillas, he might like something with a little crunch. They're crammed with protein."

"I find them disgusting, but, good idea. I know he'll need more salmon packets and noodles and instant potatoes and nuts. He'll need more Greenbelly Meals. And seaweed. Because if he's eating pork rinds, he should also be eating something green, whether he likes it or not."

Gavin loaded her picks into a basket. "You know your stuff. Your guy couldn't ask for a better trail angel." He hoped the boyfriend appreciated her. She was really looking out for him.

"Thanks." She was blushing. There was something about a blushing woman. Always got him thinking about sex. He bet she got a full-body glow going when she—Not what he should be thinkin' about. He was working here. He wanted to break his sales record again today. And he thought she'd just asked him something.

"Sorry. What was that?" He didn't offer an explanation for zoning out. It wasn't like he could tell her the truth.

"Can I put other things beside food in the drop? I wanted to send some socks."

"Clean, dry socks. Doesn't get much better than that on the trail." Gavin led her over to the display he'd made. She laughed when she saw the "These'll Blow Your (Old) Socks Off" sign. Gavin loved making a woman laugh, and her laugh was an especially good one, throaty and full. And somehow, he was thinking about sex again. "If you want to really spoil your guy, get him a silk bag liner," he said, after she'd added a few pairs of socks to the basket.

"Already did. Present for him starting this summer's section of the hike."

"How about one of these little massage rollers. Only three inches around, but it really kneads out the muscles, and if he's getting plantar fasciitis pain, like most hikers do, this thing really helps."

"I'll take it. Hopefully, he won't toss it and complain that it was a waste of space. I usually do pretty well choosing things, but there have been some that he handed off or trashed immediately."

She didn't sound put out about it. If Rebecca had bought him—He shoved the thought away. They were over. Why waste time thinking about her?

"I guess I shouldn't get anything else. Too much weight. Unless you can think of anything vital I'm forgetting."

Every ounce counted out on the trail, and Gavin wasn't going to load her order with stuff that would just end up getting tossed. Making sales was one thing. Wasting someone's money, that was something else. "Not unless you want something for yourself. We have some killer chocolate. My fave is a milk chocolate bar with nuts and dried cranberries covered with a dark chocolate shell."

"Sounds amazing. I'll take one." She pulled the edges of that loose button-down she wore closer together. Had he been staring again? He turned away and headed for the cash register—and the display of chocolate beside it.

"Would it be okay if I add in something for the drop that I didn't buy here?" she asked. "I know some places don't allow that."

"That's not a problem."

"Oh, good." She dug around in her bag and pulled out a pale green envelope. The name *Owen* was written on the front in penmanship that looked like it belonged on a fancy invitation. "Nice handwriting," Gavin commented as he took it from her.

"Thanks. I perfected it writing the name of my crush on all my notebooks back in the seventh grade." And there was the blush again. "And I can't believe I just said that."

"I wish a girl like you had had a crush on me back when I was in the seventh grade. Although, I probably couldn't have worked a girlfriend into my packed schedule of smoking pot and Legend of Zelda marathons. Got turned on to that one by my dad. Actually, the pot too. Him and my mom. They gave me a bong on my thirteenth birthday."

"What?"

He'd shocked her. To him, his parents were just his parents, and he'd always found them pretty dang cool. But they weren't exactly conventional. "They were of the do-it-at-home-where-we-can-keep-an-eye-on-you school of thought." Sort of. They also just really liked to party. "So, what happened with this crush of yours?"

"Nothing. I'm not sure he even knew my name. If he'd ever spoken to me, I'd probably have had to race straight to the bathroom." He raised his eyebrows. "I always have to pee when I get nervous, and talking to him, talking to any boy back then, would have made me extremely nervous. And I *really* can't believe I just said that."

"If it'll make you feel better, I'll tell something embarrassing about myself. Okay, I told you I played Zelda, but I played tons of other stuff too, and I unlocked the Snake Beater achievement in Metal Gear Solid 2. Which means nothing to you." He used his fingers to rake his hair away from his face. "Okay. Uh, in Metal Gear you play this character called Snake, and at one point Snake's looking through some lockers. In one there's a poster of a woman wearing not so much of anything. I, as Snake, took a good long look, and, uh, not at her face." She started laughing. Loved that laugh. "And that's how I unlocked the achievement. What can I say? I was, like, eleven. I was curious. Now that's way more embarrassing than getting so nervous you have to pee, right?"

It took her a few seconds to stop laughing enough to speak. "Thank you for that glimpse into male adolescence. I didn't have any brothers, so . . ."

"Sisters?"

"An only."

"Me too. Always wished I had a bro." His parents let him do pretty much whatever he wanted, but staying up till two on a school night probably would have been more fun with a brother. Although, there were lots of nights his dad kept him company. Together they'd unlocked the Horde of Hoofbeats achievement in WoW, and that would never be embarrassing.

"Might have been nice having a sibling." She slid her card into the reader, and he realized in a few seconds she'd be leaving.

"So, what are you going to be doing while you wait for your boyfriend to make it into town?" What was he doing? It wasn't like he could ask her out.

"So far, I've just been looking around the town. I met a couple other trail widows. We're getting together for dinner tonight."

"Sounds good." Because what else was he supposed to say. He handed her the bag with her chocolate bar and her receipt. "We'll make sure all this will be waiting for him at White House."

"Perfect. Well . . . bye."

"Bye." She headed out of the barn, and he let himself enjoy the view for a moment, then started transferring her purchases from the basket to one of the Boots Camp drop buckets. He hesitated with the pale green envelope in his hand. It wasn't sealed. The flap was just tucked in. He carefully pulled it free and removed a sheet of matching paper.

"You're not thinking of reading that," Banana called from over by the coffee maker, "without letting me see it too." He joined Gavin at the register and looked over his shoulder as Gavin read:

> *Dearest Owen,*
> *I love you. I love you. I love you. I love you. I love*
> *you. I love you. That's one for every day I haven't been*
> *able to say those words to you. I'm counting the days,*

hours, minutes until you arrive here in Fox Crossing. My arms ache for you. My lips burn for you.

I think about you almost every moment of every day, at least those moments I'm awake, and even some when I'm asleep, because I dream about you almost every night. I love imagining you out there in the Maine woods, making your dream come true.

I want you to know how proud I am of you. When you get here, you'll be through the hardest stretch of the entire trail. Not many people have the mental and physical strength that you do. I know exactly how hard you've worked. I'm honored to have a small part in helping you reach your goal.

I love you! (I had to say it one more time!) So, so much!

Your Lillian

Gavin folded the letter and replaced it in the envelope.

"Nice letter," Banana said.

Gavin wondered if any woman had ever felt that way about him, had cared so much about his dreams. Although, he couldn't think about a dream that felt big enough, at least right now. He'd hiked the Wilderness with Niri, and done all the rest in sections, by himself sometimes, sometimes with friends. But if he hadn't gotten in every mile, he didn't think he'd care all that much. It had been fun, but he wasn't one of those hikers who saw it as some kind of quest or life test. Was there something other than hiking the AT that he felt that way about? Not getting a specific job, or going to a particular place, or anything that he could think of. Maybe just 'cause he'd always been able to find what he needed to be happy wherever he was.

"Nice letter," Banana repeated.

"Yeah." Gavin put the letter on top of the supply bucket. "Wonder if he knows how good he's got it."

Banana laughed. "Jealous? It seemed like you were liking what you saw."

"Come on. What man wouldn't? It's not like I was going to do anything about it." Gavin put the top on the bucket and wrote Owen's name and the delivery date on the side. "You ever have someone write you a letter like that?"

Banana scratched the salt-and-pepper scruff on his chin. "Letter? No. But Lea felt that way about me once. When I wanted to open the bar with a friend, she was behind me a hundred percent. She was up for moving to Fox Crossing, even though there was only one other black family here, and she worked as many hours as I did when we were getting the place up and running. She really did make my dream her dream. Then it went south. But for a while, yeah I had that."

"Must be nice." Gavin heard a strain of bitterness in his voice, which he hadn't been quite aware he was feeling.

"It was. But maybe that's why it went south with me and Lea. Maybe it wasn't good for her to be so focused on a dream that wasn't hers. She wanted the bar for me. But maybe we should have found something we both wanted. Or at least found a place where she could have something she wanted as much as I wanted the bar."

Gavin hadn't thought about that part of it, the downside for the person who was supporting the person with the dream. "You think that woman, Lillian, feels that way?"

"Didn't sound like it. It's different when it's for the short haul. It's not like she has to give up her life to be his trail angel."

"Yeah, just some months of it. Hey, I was wondering, does that barmaid, the one with the freckles, does she have a boyfriend?"

Banana gave his haw-haw-haw of a laugh. "Tell me again. How long ago did you split with your girlfriend?"

"Don't make it sound so—I'm not looking for a replacement girlfriend. I'm new in town, okay? I just thought maybe she'd want to have dinner with me some night." And possibly also have a little summer fun with him, but he wasn't sure Banana would want to hear that.

"As far as I know, Erin is unattached. She's just home for the summer. So you know, she's still in college."

"Hey, so am I. Are we talking freshman or senior?"

"Going into her senior year. But she worked full-time at the bar for a year before she started."

"And you're saying you think she's too young for dinner?"

"For—None of my business. But she breaks things when she gets mad. She worked for me last summer too, and she almost bankrupted me when she was going through a breakup. That happens this year, and I'll be sending you the bill."

"I'm not planning on breaking any hearts, so I won't be paying for any dishes." The last thing he wanted was drama. Light and easy summer fun. That's all he was looking for.

CHAPTER 3

Lillian snuck a quick look at the tracker app on her phone after the waitress finished taking everyone's orders. Miss Violet had decided to join Lillian, Bailey, and Ginger for dinner at the local barbeque place. Owen was still moving. It looked like he had about five more miles before he got to the lean-to. That meant he'd be doing some hiking after sunset. She hated when he did that. It was way too dangerous. He was going to be exhausted when—

"Caught ya!" Ginger playfully pulled the phone out of Lillian's hand. "Put it away, just until after dinner. I'm starting to feel guilty. I have the app too, but just in case Bryan gets in trouble out there. I don't think I've even looked at it since yesterday."

Lillian didn't understand that. If Owen stopped for an unusually long time she wanted to know as soon as possible so she could get him help. But more than that, she liked being able to picture where he was, filling in details from the maps she'd studied, the hiker blogs she'd read, and the YouTube videos she'd watched. "Checking in on him makes me miss him less."

"Aww, that's sweet," Ginger said. "How long have you two been together?"

"About three years." Lillian actually knew exactly how long, down to the day, but she'd feel a little silly saying so, so she kept it to herself.

"Still in the honeymoon phase then." Ginger looked over at Bailey. "How often do you check in on Stan?"

"Hardly at all," Bailey admitted. "But he has a couple hiking buddies. If something happened to him, one of them would get in touch."

Miss Violet clapped her hands twice. "Ladies, I must interrupt. I am in desperate need of inspiration. I must hold auditions for my play in less than two weeks to have it on the boards by the third week in August, as it must be. And every great play must have romance." She rolled the *r*, so loudly and for so long that a few diners at other tables turned to look. If Lillian had done anything to attract so much attention, she'd be wishing the floor would turn to goo and envelop her, but Miss Violet clearly loved it.

"I want to help, but I took one creative writing class in college and almost flunked it. My brain just doesn't work that way." Ginger picked up one of the crayons from the mason jar in the center of the table and began to draw on the butcher paper table covering. "If you need help with an art project, I'm your girl. Writing, no. No, no, no." With several quick strokes, she had the beginnings of a princess.

"I need raw material. No writing required. Tell me how you met your men. Talk to me of love." Miss Violet sang the last word, getting more looks, most of them amused, one annoyed.

"Sorry," Lillian mouthed to the annoyed woman.

"You should go first, Lillian. You're clearly a romantic." Ginger added a bluebird flying above the princess.

"It's not really an interesting story. I met him using a dating app. We had coffee. I wasn't expecting anything to come of it. I only went because my mother wouldn't stop haranguing me. She thinks single women are . . ." Lillian searched for the right word. Pathetic? Inadequate? Both of those were accurate, but they made her mother sound too harsh. "She thinks that every woman is happier with a man. Unless the woman is gay. She has no issue with that."

"I myself am gloriously single and wouldn't have it any other way," Miss Violet declared.

"So, you met for coffee," Bailey prompted. "And did you know right then? Was it like—bam! Not that that means love. I've had several bam moments that led to disaster."

"There wasn't a bam." Lillian didn't really have bams. It was her fault. She was just so stupidly self-conscious. When she met a guy, all the ratty thoughts came at her, and no matter how many times she tried to zing them with that imaginary sparkle wand, they wouldn't leave. All she could think about was if she was saying something stupid, or if she was wearing the right thing, or if she was being boring. She got so distracted it was like she could hardly focus on the other person. But there was something about Owen that settled her. He made her feel like everything was okay. If there was something she was doing that was wrong, he helped her fix it. Being with him was like letting out a breath she hadn't realized she'd been holding.

She didn't think these women would understand, because to understand you had to know about the thought-rats. "It was slower," Lillian finally said. "We realized we had a lot in common. We're both teachers. We're both—" She couldn't think of one of the other things off-hand. She gave a helpless shrug. "It's hard to explain why you fall in love, isn't it?"

"Bryan made me laugh. It's not like he cracks jokes or anything like that, but his worldview is just a little askew. He can find something funny in almost every situation, and that makes life just so much better." Ginger started sketching a prince to go with the princess. "Having to watch the *Lord of the Rings* movies is a small price to pay for his company."

"Especially since you sleep through them," Bailey teased.

"He even finds that funny."

Miss Violet clapped again. "This is not helping. Friendship and laughs are fine, but I need thrills. I need passion. I need— Oh, my." Lillian followed Miss Violet's gaze and saw the man from the Boots Barn walking into the restaurant. "Speaking of thrills. Speaking of passion. Now, he has leading man quality, am I right? Not classically handsome, but *s e x y* sexy."

Miss Violet, being Miss Violet, made her pronouncement loud enough for everyone to hear, including *him.* He turned and inclined his head toward her, a smile tugging at his lips. Then his gaze fell on Lillian, and the smile stretched into a grin.

Lillian felt her pulse pick up. Her stomach felt like it had gotten on the world's fastest elevator, going down, down, down. Which was exactly the way she'd felt when she walked into the Boots Barn and saw him. She thought Bailey might call the feeling a bam. Even so, she'd been able to talk to him with no problem. That was because she was with Owen, and she'd made that clear right away. That made all the difference. She didn't have to worry about what the Boots Barn man was thinking about her. It didn't matter. She didn't have to "put herself out there," because she already had somebody, somebody wonderful.

The man ambled over to the table. "Ladies," he said, then winked at her, adding, "Twinkle."

"You two know each other?" Bailey exclaimed.

"From the Boots Barn. He put in my food drop order. For Owen. My boyfriend." Just in case he'd forgotten.

"Ah, Banana's friend Gavin from New Jersey, who is working at Boots for the summer." Miss Violet looked him up and down. She seemed to approve of his collar-length sandy hair, hazel eyes, cleft chin, and that grin.

"You got it."

"I am going to cast you in my play." Miss Violet said it like it was the greatest honor imaginable.

"Is that right? You're going to make me a star?" Gavin batted his eyelashes, and a laugh started deep in Lillian and came spilling out. He was a goof. That story he'd told her about looking at a video game girly picture had been so unexpected that she'd had trouble getting her giggles under control.

"I most certainly am."

"Well, it's my policy never to turn down a new opportunity, so I accept."

Lillian wished she had a little of that adventurous attitude. New things usually stressed her out.

"Splendid." Miss Violet fingered one of the many purple Mardi Gras beads she wore. "I'll be in touch."

"Ladies, Twinkle, enjoy your dinner." With that he headed for an empty table across the room.

Miss Violet started to hum, then la-la-la, eyes still on Gavin. Clearly, he had sparked her creative spirit.

"Care to explain the 'twinkle'?" Bailey asked, leaning toward Lillian.

"It's the perfect name for my princess." Ginger wrote *Twinkle* under the girl in her drawing.

"Oh. That. It was because of my toes. I have these little rhinestones on my toenails."

"Seems you made an impression. That smile he gave you . . ." Bailey waggled her eyebrows.

"Me? No. I was the only one in the place, so we chatted a little."

"I think he was looking as well as chatting. I doubt he notices the toenails of every customer who walks in."

"And I bet the toenails weren't all he noticed." Ginger added some stars around the word *Twinkle*.

Was that supposed to mean her breasts? Lillian started feeling uncomfortable. "It would be impossible for him to notice most customer's toenails because most customers are probably wearing hiking boots." She stood. "I'm just going to run to the ladies' room."

She was relieved that she didn't have to walk by Gavin's table on the way to the bathroom. Thinking about the bam, and then Bailey and Ginger talking about how he was looking at her was giving Lillian the squirmy feeling. Which she hadn't had when she was actually with him and he was actually looking at her. She'd chatted with him like he was one of her teacher friends, telling him embarrassing stories about herself and everything. That wasn't like her. She should start telling every guy she met that she had a boyfriend, just so she would feel more comfortable.

She pushed open the restroom door, and it knocked into a teenage girl with short hair that was a deep burgundy, shading to orange toward the front, then going full golden blond when it reached the edges of her side-swept bangs. "I'm so sorry. I should have opened it more slowly."

"It's okay."

Lillian realized she'd met the girl. It was Honey's great-niece. She looked so different. "Kristina, hello. We met at Vixen's the day you arrived."

The girl looked down, and Lillian got a glimpse of the shy girl she'd met. She'd done a complete makeover on herself. Lillian couldn't remember what she'd been wearing the day they met, but she knew she would have remembered if it had been anything like Kristina's current outfit—a short skirt with three flirty little tiers in a cheetah print, a white tee, and white high-top sneakers with platform soles. She could be the before-and-after in one of those articles Lillian's mother was constantly reading. Lillian's mother gave herself makeovers every few months, usually right after a breakup.

"It's good to see you. I like your haircut." Lillian didn't say anything else about the transformation. If she gushed, it might seem as if she didn't think Kristina had looked good before.

And that wasn't true. She'd been just as pretty the day they met, but in a different way. Some people might not have looked twice at her then and might have missed her lovely skin, big brown eyes, and shiny hair. Nobody was going to overlook her now.

"Honey took me to Vulpini as a late birthday present." Kristina ran her fingers through her bangs, ducking her head. Then she lifted her chin and straightened her shoulders. "And, actually, it's KiKi. Everybody calls me that. Not Kristina. Honey just must have forgotten."

"KiKi. Got it." Lillian could see the shy girl was still in there, and she was sure that girl was waaay out of her comfort zone. Good for her for being so brave and putting herself out there.

"I think you said something about buying me a drink." Gavin slid onto the barstool across from Banana and put his blue mug down.

"Guess I'll have to make it two, since the mug gets you your first one. I've been experimenting with a new brew—malt, caramel, toffee, brown sugar, with a little kick of citrus. Wanna try it?"

"I give it four dead Buckys," an older man sitting a barstool away said.

"Then how can I turn it down?"

Banana took Gavin's mug and turned toward the taps. "You know the tragic story of Bucky, so can I assume you're a regular?" Gavin asked the man. The bar's logo was a donkey, presumably dead, with all four legs in the air. Banana claimed it was in honor of a donkey he once owned, a brilliant donkey. Banana said he'd taught Bucky the donkey all kinds of tricks and had been in the middle of teaching him the most impressive one—how to survive without eating a scrap of food. Banana said Bucky had been making real progress, then had suddenly keeled over. Completely unexpectedly.

"Never been here before. I had a friend, acquaintance anyway, who told me about it."

"Gavin, meet Simon. Simon, Gavin." Banana set Gavin's full mug down in front of him. "Simon's staying over at Violet's boardinghouse, nursing a knee injury, probably be in town a couple weeks."

"Is that all he got out of you?" Gavin asked Simon. "Banana usually gets everyone's life story before they finish their first drink."

"Simon remains a man of mystery," Banana answered.

"Which means you've been doing most of the talking, which is how Simon has learned the story of Bucky." Gavin took a swallow of Banana's latest. "Nice. I like that little citrus spin. What's this one called?"

"I'm thinking maybe Brown Is Beautiful Brew. And, yes, I did tell Simon the story of my beloved, deeply mourned Bucky."

"Did he tell you the part where the donkey gag comes from the oldest joke book in the world?"

"He didn't get that far."

"A Greek anthology called *Philogelos*. Probably fourth or fifth century," Banana explained.

Simon smiled. "I got the story behind the donkey on your sign. Now I understand why your place is called Wit's Beginning."

"Just so you know, 'wit' is a generous way of describing some of the stuff," Gavin told him. "I remember Banana telling me one about a young wife farting while sitting on her husband's lap."

Banana gave his haw-haw-haw of a laugh. "Gets me every time." He slapped the top of the bar, and turned to Simon. "Vi must have taken a shine to you. She has a rule that only trail widows—or widowers—can stay at her place. She has almost a phobia of hikers. She was engaged to one, and was staying in town while he hit the Wilderness. By the time he came back to town, he'd decided he was going to live on the trail, just go off the grid, doing odd jobs in trail towns when he needed cash. That's when Miss Violet bought that crazy mansion and turned it into the boardinghouse."

"Maybe she took pity on me because of my knee."

Or maybe she liked the look of him. He was about her age, Gavin figured, around sixty, and was what his grandmother would call a silver fox, although his thick hair was white, worn long and swept straight back off his forehead.

"Sounds like you two have known each other for a while." Simon traced the donkey on his mug with one finger.

"We met on the trail about three years ago, and stayed in touch off and on," Gavin said.

"Gav's one of the instructors at Boots Camp, the place I was telling you about where I do some teaching."

"Instructor at Boots Camp, and soon to be star of the stage." Gavin turned to Simon. "When I was over at the local barbeque joint, I ran into your Miss Violet. She took one look at me and saw star quality. Then she informed me she was casting me in her play."

"With Miss Violet, casting is more like conscription," Banana said. "I've been in several of her productions."

"Could be fun. I always say, I'll do anything once." Gavin picked up a couple pretzels from the bowl on the bar and tossed them in his mouth. They had a honey mustard bite that he wasn't expecting. He took a swig of his drink, then ate a couple more. "You better watch yourself, Simon, or you'll end up as my co-star."

"Dude, no. If she wants me to add up the box office receipts, I'm there. Other than that, no." Simon smiled, deepening the creases at the edges of his dark brown eyes.

"Another of the same?" Banana jerked his chin toward Simon's empty mug.

"Well. Hmmm. Possibly." He stared into the mug, like the answer might be written in the bottom.

"Or would you want to try something different?"

Simon shrugged, then pushed the mug toward Banana. "Surprise me."

The barmaid with the freckles, Erin, came through a pair of swinging doors carrying two towering platters of nachos. Gavin smiled at her, but she didn't seem to notice.

"This one is heavier on the citrus. I put orange peel and juice in when I brew it." Banana set a fresh mug in front of Simon.

He took a swallow and gave an appreciative nod. "Tell me something. That person I told you about who'd been here before, he told me a tall tale about a fox that had saved the settlers and was still wandering around the woods a couple hundred years later. Do I have it right?"

"All true. Some people say it's just a descendant of the first fox, that there's some mutant gene that gets passed down, giving it the white sock and black tail tip, reverse of all the other foxes. But it's the same fox. I saw it myself last year, right outside the bar, and it brought me almost as much luck as it did to those settlers way back when. It gave me back my daughter, and my granddaughter."

Simon straightened up. "You saw it right out on the street? In town? I'd like to get a look at it, since it's the town mascot and all."

Gavin shot a glance at Erin. She was laughing with the three thirtyish women sitting in one of the back booths.

"You and everyone else." Banana shook his head. "I know from long experience that The Fox is only seen when she chooses to be seen."

"I saw her my first night." Gavin wanted to take another look at Erin, but told himself to hold off a little. Didn't want to look too eager. "The Fox crossed right in front of me. I had to slam on the brakes to stop from hitting her."

"Was that around the bar too?" Simon asked.

"Out by the sign when you first drive into town." Gavin

took a swig of his ale. "I've been thinking that we should offer fox walks over at Boots," he told Banana. "The way that outfit over in Guilford gives moose tours."

"I don't know if making money on The Fox is right."

Gavin snorted. "Come on. Annie's grandparents have that store that's one big fox-a-palooza."

"I'd sign up, if you had them." Simon's words came out so fast they almost ran together. "It could be a nice way to do a little gentle conditioning while my knee heals," he added more slowly.

"Talk to Annie and Nick," Banana told Gavin.

"Will do." Gavin's attention was snagged by the sight of Erin striding back across the room, heading for the kitchen. He swung around on the barstool to face her. "I've been hearing some good things about you from Banana, Erin."

She shot him a grin, but didn't slow down, continuing to stride toward the kitchen with those long legs. "There's lots of that to hear," she tossed over her shoulder before disappearing through the swinging doors.

"I like that girl," Banana said.

"I'm liking her myself." Gavin liked her sass and confidence, and her freckles, and those legs. When she reappeared, carrying another nacho tower and a burger, he said, "How 'bout if I tell you some good things about me? I might not have as many as you, but . . ." He didn't finish, because she was already halfway across the room.

Banana shook his head. "You seem like someone who'd have game. I'm disappointed."

"I can only give your technique one dead donkey," Simon added.

"I need another mug."

"You're already reduced to two-fisted drinking? You only got shot down twice."

"Once," Gavin protested.

"I'm counting when you gave her that smile and she breezed on past you."

"Just give me a mug." Banana put one in front of him, and Gavin put it about five inches away from the one he already had. "Oh, I need a piece of paper too." He thought maybe he could get her to stop walking for at least a minute or two if he intrigued her with a puzzle. What you did was put the piece of paper over the two beer mugs, then bet someone that you could make the paper support a saltshaker. Most people didn't think it could be done, but all it took was some accordion folds.

"You're not going to try that paper bridge bar bet."

"You know it?"

"I know them all. So does she. Because we work in a bar."

"Dude." Simon laughed.

Well, damn. Of course she'd seen it. He'd even seen other guys do it. And here she came. Before he could decide what to say, she'd already passed him. She paused at the kitchen doors and glanced back at him. "What? That's all you've got?" Then she pushed her way inside.

"*Is* that all you've got?" Banana asked, clearly enjoying himself way too much. Simon looked like he was finding the show entertaining too.

Gavin stood up. He needed to mix things up a little. He wasn't going to be sitting right where she left him when she came back out. He walked out into the center of the room. "Anyone up for a game of Never Have I Ever, Westerosi style?" He sat down at an empty table, a big one near the center of the room. "Just grab your beverage and come on over."

"You had me at Westerosi," one of the women Erin had been laughing with answered. She headed over along with the two friends she'd been sitting with. "I know you like games, Yvette. Grab the husband and the chow and come on," she called to a couple at a two-top, and they started for Gavin's table too.

"Simon, you've got to get in on this," Gavin called.

Simon slid off the barstool, then hesitated, mug in hand. "Come on. It'll be fun," Gavin urged. Simon joined the group, and, just like that, Gavin had a circle of friends. He quickly got everyone's names. "Okay, everyone played regular Never Have I Ever?"

"Yeah. You say 'never have I ever done X,' then all the people who have done X have to take a drink," Jen, the *Game of Thrones* fan who'd been the first one to respond to Gavin, said.

"Right. So in Westerosi style, instead of saying something about yourself, you say something about another player. If it turns out to be true, the person the statement was about has to take a drink. If it's not true, the person who made the statement has to take a drink."

"I'll supply one round," Banana called. You could always count on Banana to have your back.

"Okay, since this whole shebang was my idea, we can start with me. Jen, you come up with a statement about me, and I'll let you know if you're right."

Jen narrowed her eyes at him, then had a whispered conference with her two friends. "You have hiked the entire Appalachian Trail."

"True. But I call foul. You can clearly see I have one of the mugs that Banana only gives to 2000-milers."

"It's called gamesmanship, my friend. It's called strategy." Jen turned toward the bar. "Banana, this man needs a drink."

"All right. It's my turn. I'm going to go with Simon. He has been called a mystery man, and I like a challenge." Gavin made a show of studying the man. No clues from his clothes, just basic dad jeans and a plaid button-down. He waited until Erin was nearby, then said, "I say, you collect belly button lint, and keep it in specially made glass vials." That got a nice laugh from the group, and that's what he was going for. He wanted her to see him as the guy who made things fun. Which he was.

"False," Simon said. Which meant another drink for Gavin.

"Okay, now you pick someone and make a guess," Gavin instructed Simon.

"Hmmm. Well . . ." Simon paused, thinking. "I don't know . . ."

"Just take a guess. Try Yvette," Gavin encouraged. "It doesn't matter if—"

"It's that song. Again! That 'Down in the Deep Dark' song," Jen exclaimed. "It's like it's eaten all the other songs."

"I love it. Don't you love it?" one of her friends asked. "I've heard it a million times, but I could hear it a million more."

"My mom told me she had a poster of Shane in her bedroom from back when he was part of a duo—Shane and Ryker. They had a one-hit wonder back in the day, then nothing, then Shane made a solo comeback. I don't even know what happened to the other guy. My mom used to kiss Shane's picture every time she walked in the door. He has to be, what, sixty by now? And still putting out the hits." Yvette looked over at Simon. "So, what have you decided to say about me?"

Simon stood up so abruptly that he almost knocked his chair over. Gavin reached out and steadied it. "Are you okay?" There was sweat coating the man's upper lip and forehead, and the hand that held his mug was shaking.

"Fine. Low blood sugar." Simon strode toward the door, breaking into a trot before he reached it.

"I'm gonna go check on him." Gavin hurried after Simon and found him on the sidewalk, bent over, hands pressed on his knees, pulling in gasping breaths. This was definitely more than low blood sugar. "Maybe you should come back in. Sit down for a while."

Simon slowly straightened. "I'm fine. Really. I'm going to head back to the boardinghouse. The fresh air will feel good." His breathing was becoming more regular, and, after he wiped his forehead with his sleeve, it looked like he'd stopped sweating.

"I can run you over there, no problem. My car's right around back."

Simon clapped him on the shoulder. "Thanks, but I'm good. Hope to see you on the flip side."

"Small town, so it's very likely." Gavin watched Simon until he'd reached the end of the block. He looked steady on his feet, so Gavin went back into the pub.

"He okay?" Banana called.

"Think so. I offered him a ride, but he wanted to walk." Gavin sat back down at the table.

"My husband just lost for the second time. I don't think he's even trying. I think it's all about the beer. Fortunately, we walked over here, so we can keep playing. I'm going to do you," Yvette told Gavin. "I know everybody else too well."

Gavin flung his arms out wide. "Have at it." He did a quick scan of the room. Erin was just disappearing through the swinging doors to the kitchen. He wondered if she'd seen him checking on Simon. He hadn't done it to get points, but if it had earned him some, well, that was all good.

After a few more rounds, a hand came down on his shoulder. "I'm joining in. I say this man hasn't had sex in way too long and is desperate."

Gavin tilted his head back and saw Erin looking down at him. "So, so true. Does that mean you'll go out with me?"

She held his gaze for a moment, smiled, then said, "Nope."

There was that sass again. He really liked it. And he liked a challenge. He'd change that "nope" to a "yes." Might take a little time, but he'd manage it.

CHAPTER 4

Lillian watched the green dot that showed Owen's progress as it moved closer and closer to the spot where she stood waiting for him. She'd gotten there too early, but better too early than late. She sat down on a boulder near the sign marking the beginning of the 100-Mile Wilderness, then stood back up. She was too excited to sit. She was too excited to stand. She began to pace, checking the tracker probably every thirty seconds. She figured he should be there in about fifteen minutes, if he kept up the same pace. Fifteen minutes! It had only been ten and a half days since she'd seen him, but it felt like months.

She did another tracker check, then called the inn to check on their dinner reservation. All good. She pulled out the elastic band holding her hair back, brushed her hair, then put it back in its ponytail. She was so nervous. No, not nervous. Excited. So excited. By the end of the night, she and Owen could be engaged. She thought about shooting her mother a text, telling her she thought this was the night, but no. If it didn't happen, she didn't want to have to deal with her mother's reaction. She'd probably make it Lillian's fault.

Lillian heard a rustling sound. Was that him? She rushed a little way down the trail. No one in sight. Of course it wasn't him. She'd just checked the tracker, and it couldn't possibly be him. She turned around, and felt her breath catch in her chest. A fox stood there, looking at her. Not just a fox. Lillian did a quick check—one white sock, one mostly white ear, black tail tip. It was The Fox. The magic fox! The magic fox who brought luck to anyone who saw it.

"Hello, beautiful," Lillian whispered, one hand drifting up to the pendant hanging at the base of her throat. "I've been wishing I would see you, wishing so hard." One of The Fox's ears twitched, as if she were listening closely to every word, then she turned and disappeared between two of the pine trees that lined the trail.

Lillian didn't move for a moment, just stood there, staring at the spot where The Fox had been. She felt like she'd been drinking pink champagne and was filled with happy bubbles. It was going to happen. She knew it for sure now. Owen was going to ask her to marry him. She gave herself a little hug, then checked the tracker. He was so close now.

She forced herself to return to the trailhead and sit on the boulder near the sign. She didn't want to look too eager. Although she didn't understand why that was a bad thing. If it were reversed, she'd love it if Owen were so eager to see her that he'd walked partway to meet her. And probably he would be, but just in case, she'd listen to the advice her mother always gave her about always holding back a little. Maybe that note she'd sent with his drop was a little too much. She'd admitted that she thought about him constantly. Her stomach tightened, and now she felt like she'd had too much champagne, a little nauseous.

Stop, she told herself, then sent a zing at all the rat thoughts that had started to head her way. You don't have to follow your mother's rules anymore. Owen loves you. He wants to marry you. He'd practically said so, even asking about rings she liked. That was almost a proposal. It was happening. It was only a matter of when and where. And now she'd seen The Fox! It had to be tonight.

Forget rules. Forget seeming too eager. Lillian jumped back up and started down the trail. She heard a rustling sound again. The Fox? No. Owen! Coming around the bend in the trail. He looked grubby and tired, but wonderful. She gave a little bounce on her toes, then rushed toward him.

"Hold up." He put out one hand, like one of the crossing guards at her school. She stopped. "The trail's full of roots and rocks. You've got to watch where you're going or you'll land on your butt."

"Oh. Okay." She took one careful step toward him.

"Just wait."

Lillian's toes dug into her sneakers as she forced herself to be still. "Congratulations! You made it through the Wilderness." She sang the last few words. Her mother had raised her on Madonna. Owen didn't even smile, while she couldn't stop smiling. How could she stop smiling when he was right in front of her?

When he finally—finally, finally, finally—closed the distance between them, she threw her arms around him. He backed up a step. "I stink, Lil. You don't want to be touching me right now."

"I don't care about a little stink."

"Well, I do. I didn't even brush my teeth this morning. I can hardly stand to be near myself."

She nodded. She got that. She wouldn't want to kiss him with a sour mouth. He'd feel better after a long, hot shower. "Let's get you home. I checked us in. Our room is beautiful. The shower is even one of the fancy ones with multiple heads, and there's a Jacuzzi tub." She'd checked out of Miss Violet's and into the best room the inn had to offer a few hours earlier.

"How does that sound?" Maybe after he got a shower, he'd want to soak in the tub with some Epsom salts—she'd picked some up at the Mercantile that afternoon—and her. "I'll call the pickup service."

"They aren't already here? Why didn't you have them wait?"

He sounded cranky. In addition to the shower, he probably needed a nap. He had to be exhausted. "I wasn't sure exactly how long you'd be. It won't take long for them to get here. They're just in town." She pulled out her cell and quickly asked for a pick up at the trailhead.

"They'll be here in fifteen."

"You knew how close I was, and you had them drop you off, didn't you?"

"It's hard to estimate exactly how long it would take you to get here. You always say it depends on the terrain. Here. Sit down on that boulder. It's nice and warm from the sun." He shrugged out of his pack and sat. "You'll want a snack, I bet. I brought some of this amazing chocolate with caramel and nuts and—"

"Even chewing feels like too much of an effort. I just want to move as little as possible until the ride gets here."

"Of course."

He closed his eyes. He wasn't even going to talk to her or look at her? It had been almost two weeks since they'd seen each other. And almost two weeks of grinding hiking, with probably really bad sleep and not-so-good food, she reminded herself. She'd tried, but it's not like instant mashed potatoes were ever going to taste like something you'd actually want to eat.

"What do you think you're going to order tonight? A big steak? Lobster since we're in Maine? Three desserts?"

Owen groaned. "I can't even think. My brain, along with the rest of me, is mush."

"Of course." Lillian checked her cell. Still at least ten minutes before the pickup could get there. "Oh! I have an amazing story for you!" He didn't answer, so she rushed on. "I saw a fox."

Owen gave a snort of laughter. "They're all over the woods."

"But this is a special fox. It's magic."

"A magic fox. Only you would believe in a magic fox."

He sounded a little . . . patronizing. Yes, she liked stories. She wouldn't want to live in a world without them. "Actually, not true. A lot of people in town think there's something special about this fox. I met a woman who said her granddaughter's boyfriend would have died if The Fox hadn't revealed itself to her granddaughter. It got her granddaughter to go looking for him in time to save him from dying from hypothermia."

Owen didn't open his eyes. "What was it now? A woman whose granddaughter's boyfriend this fox saved. How did you meet her?"

"She owns the most amazing shop on Main Street. Everything in it has a fox on it. It's called Vixen's. It's—"

"Lil." He finally opened his eyes. "Are you listening to yourself? A woman who has a shop filled with merch that has foxes on it told you a story about a magic fox. Now think. Is there any reason she might somehow benefit by creating a story like that?"

Lillian tried not to sigh, but she did, just a little. Owen was being just so Owen. He couldn't watch a movie or a TV show that had even a smidge of fantasy in it. His favorite show was just two guys fishing, for hours, mostly without saying anything.

"The store exists because of the lucky fox, not the other way around. The whole town wouldn't even be here without it. The settlement was about to die off. The people were starving. But then this woman saved The Fox, and the town's luck changed. It was a miracle."

"You're talking about something that happened a couple hundred years ago. The town was founded in like 1800, and the incident with the woman's granddaughter's boyfriend was recent, I'm assuming."

"Last year. But that's where the magic comes in. The Fox that I saw had exactly the same markings as the one the woman saved. She described it in her diary. And I saw it, Owen. It just stood there looking at me, so I didn't get just a quick glance. That means I get good luck. Which also means you get good luck. Because if something good happens to me, of course, it would be good for you too."

"How do you figure?"

Shouldn't it be obvious? "Because we're together. Because, say if I won the lottery tomorrow, of course I'd share it with you. I can think of lots of ways that luck for me means luck for you. Can't you?" Something like us getting engaged, she added silently. Please, please, please. She wished she had one of her lucky pennies and a wishing well. The evening star and a fluffy dandelion too. But she'd seen The Fox. She really didn't need any more good luck.

"Like I said, mush brain. When is that ride getting here? I've been thinking about getting into a nice soft bed for at least the last ten miles. I should be there by now. I can't believe you let them leave."

"Just didn't—" She stopped. There was no point in explaining again. She had to remember that, unlike her, he'd been hiking with the flies and the rain—there'd been three days of rain while he was out there—and his right hip had been aching before he'd even started. Of course, he was looking forward to bed. "I think I'd enjoy a nice soft bed this afternoon too." She tried to put a suggestive spin on the words, but even with Owen, she was bad at flirting. He didn't even register the invitation she'd been giving.

"Do you think you'd have time to do some laundry while I sleep? Everything reeks."

"Sure. Yes. Not a problem."

The Fox used her paws to dig a hole, then deposited the mouse there, and used her snout to cover it with earth and grass. Perhaps she would never need to return to the spot for her kill, but her long life had taught her that her world was unpredictable. Satisfied, she turned her attention to the humans. Though they were near, she knew they did not have the ability to sense the food that she had hidden. She would not have to defend it against them.

There was cord between the two, but it was not right. In places it was bright and pulsing almost as if it had life of its own, so dazzling The Fox could not look at it for long. In other places it was as if rot were eating at the cord, snuffing out the light. There was a wrongness there that she did not understand. But there was still much she did not understand about humans, even after observing them for so many years.

"Hey, Twinkle. How ya doing?" Gavin asked as he walked into the laundromat. Something was off. The last time he'd seen her, she really had kinda twinkled, her blue eyes bright, smile pretty much constant. Today she looked, well, tired maybe, maybe just tired, but more like some of the juice, some of the life, had been drained out of her.

"Oh, hi." It had taken her a few seconds too long to answer.

Gavin opened the top of the closest washer. Yesterday, his had made a sound like a garbage disposal eating a couple forks and died on him. He dumped everything in his laundry bag in.

It was just jeans and shorts and T-shirts, some underwear. Nothing good enough to bother with separating. He threw in a couple laundry pods, fed the machine some quarters, slammed the top down, and took the empty seat across from Twinkle. Lillian. Lillian Smith. Part of being good at sales was remembering people's names. And the boyfriend? He had to think for a sec, then it came to him. Owen. He did a quick calculation. "Did Owen make it back yet?"

"Just a few hours ago."

Okay. Something was definitely off here. She'd been so excited picking out things for him. And then that note. But she didn't look like somebody who'd just had some lovers' reunion. None of his business. "Did he like the stuff?" None of his business, but Gavin was curious what was going on with her.

"I guess." She sat up straighter. "Of course, he liked it."

"Good. So, what's next? When's he going back on the trail?"

"He's just stopping in town for the night. We're going to meet up every week or so. I'm going to try to convince him to spend a day with me in Story Land when he's going through New Hampshire. When I was eight or so, I read a book where a family visited there. Actually, I read it more than once. I just think it would be so wonderful to see it in person."

There, now. Some of the twinkle was coming back. At least it did for a minute, then it started to fade away as she continued talking. "Probably walking around an amusement park after days on the trail wouldn't be too fun. It's just . . . It's just that I didn't just read that book more than once. I read it at least a hundred times."

"A hundred? Must have been a hell of a book."

"It wasn't that as much as that it comforted me. I used to have nightmares, and I hated to fall asleep. I'd read until my eyes closed on their own."

"You gotta go there." Hell, he wanted to drive her there right now, seeing that look on her face when she talked about it getting her through those hard nights. Where had her parents been? They were supposed to be checking for monsters under the bed. His dad had done that for him. He'd made a big show of it, gotten Gavin laughing. Nights when his dad had been having a little too much fun and wasn't up for monster-hunting duty, Gavin would grab his sleeping bag and put it next to the couch—his dad didn't usually make it all the way to bed those nights—where he could fall asleep to the sounds of his father snoring. That was enough.

"Have you hiked the part of the trail that goes through New Hampshire?"

"Hiked the whole enchilada." She didn't look all that impressed, the way most people did. Although those people were mostly hikers.

"Where do you think we should go between here and Harpers Ferry? Owen won't be coming off the trail in every town, but we'll be able to spend at least a day together every week or so."

"There's a legendary hotel you gotta hit in Pennsylvania, little town called Duncannon. The place was built back in the 1770s. The couple who run it? Best people you'll ever meet." Suddenly, Gavin was remembering that the hotel wasn't exactly the cleanest, and there was kind of an odor. Might not be Twinkle's kind of thing. "Maybe don't stay in the hotel, but go for lunch. Get the jambalaya. Dickens is supposed to have stopped in. Can't miss a place with that much history."

"I'll make sure we get there."

"I would have said you had to go to the Gypsy Joynt when you were going through Massachusetts for sure, but it's been closed for, wow, six years or thereabouts. Moved to Galveston. I gotta make a pilgrimage sometime. Keith, who co-owned the place, was such an Arlo Guthrie fan that he decided to open the restaurant right there in Great Barrington. I stayed a couple extra nights when I was hiking that way, just to catch some more music. Every band wanted to play the Joynt."

"Maybe we could go to the Guthrie Center. Owen's a fan of folk music."

"Not you?"

"No, me too. My first love is opera, but Owen introduced me to folk, and now I'm a fan."

"Opera? Gotta admit, I've never seen one."

"I love the stories, all the drama and emotion. You should try it."

"Hey, I'll do anything once." That was kind of his motto. It had gotten him a lot of great memories. Some bad ones, but many more of the good kind.

"I wish I was more like that. I tend to stick to the safe, which means sticking to the familiar." Lillian looked down at her feet. Gavin noticed her toes were painted a pale pink today, no sparkles.

"You've got a perfect chance. You're road-tripping it from here to Virginia. Lots of new things to try along the way."

"I somehow never framed it as a road trip. I've just been thinking of it as driving to places where I can see Owen. But you're right. I'm spending my summer vacation on a road trip! That's so not like me. And there's no reason I can't stop and see some sights on the way."

She didn't sound completely sure of that last bit. "No reason at all. The great thing about driving is the detours," Gavin told her. "You said summer vacation. Does that mean you're a teacher?"

"Mmm-hmm. Kindergarten."

"Seriously? I have never met a kindergarten teacher. Well, back when I was in kindergarten, but not since then. Do you have a contract that says you're not allowed to go out to bars or something?"

"Yes. It's in the fine print. I didn't notice it right away, but it was right under the part about mastering the basics of puppetry, which I haven't. But I can do some good voices when I read stories."

"Do one for me?"

"No!" She sounded horrified.

"Come on. I want to hear one." Lillian shook her head, and one of her curls escaped from her pony. He wanted to smooth it back in, but—boyfriend. And he'd managed to convince Erin to go out with him that night. "Why not? Sounds like you do them all the time."

"But that's at school, so it's only in front of kids."

"I have, on numerous occasions, been called a big kid."

She looked at him for a long moment. Her eyes were the color of bluebells. He'd gotten lucky and seen a field of them once in Virginia. They only bloomed for a week or two.

"Okay. But don't laugh."

"Aren't I supposed to laugh at a funny voice?"

"All right, you may laugh, but I'll know if you're laughing at me or the voice." Lillian cleared her throat. "What do elves learn in school?" she asked in a low, gravelly voice. "I don't know. What?" That time her voice had been high and squeaky. "The elf-abet." She'd switched back to the low voice.

He laughed, applauding so hard his hands hurt. "That was awesome."

"Thank you," she said in the gravelly voice, then said "thank you" again in the squeaky voice. Now she'd gotten her full-on twinkle back, but within moments, her expression turned serious again. "Can I ask you something?"

"Shoot."

"Is the Wilderness that much harder than other parts of the trail?"

"It's tough, but so are a lot of other stretches. There's this one place, Lehigh Gap, that almost killed me. There's a rock scramble that feels like it goes straight up. Made the mistake of tryin' that the day after it rained. But I lived to tell the tale. I assume there is a second part to your question." Something that had made that sparkle dim.

"I just—" She twisted her hands together. "I—"

"Whatever it is, I've probably heard it before. I get around." He winked at her, but didn't get a smile.

"It's just that usually, in the past, when Owen got off the trail, he'd be tired, and hungry, and all that, but he'd want to be with me. *With* me with me."

"Got it."

"He barely—He just wanted a shower, then sleep. He was sleeping when I left. We're supposed to have dinner. He usually likes to go someplace nice when he gets off the trail, and, before he got on the trail, he had me make a reservation at the inn's restaurant. But he was acting like he might want to just sleep through the night."

And she wanted to know if the Wilderness was the cause of that change. Gavin didn't think anything would make him too tired to be *with* with Lillian, especially if he hadn't seen her for a week and a half. "Some days, you feel like lying down in the dirt and never getting up, just let everybody use you as a stepping stone. He's probably had one of those days. Don't take it personal, Twinkle."

The guy didn't know what he had. Gavin hoped Owen would get his butt out of the sack and take his girl out tonight. Especially because he'd bet anything she was here washing his reeking hiking clothes, and he knew she was going to spend her entire vacation being his trail angel.

"You're right. I'm being selfish. I—"

"Hey, now. I didn't say anything like that." He'd been thinking she was the opposite of selfish.

Lillian gave a dismissive flip of her hand. "Never mind. Guess what? I saw The Fox today. The one from the town legend."

"That means your life is about to change. At least according to Banana. He's the guy who was at the barn the day you were in. He teaches some classes, owns the local microbrewery, and generally has his nose in everybody's business, usually in a good way. He's sure I have some big luck coming my way."

"You saw her too?"

Gavin noticed that Lillian was one of those people who didn't say "it" when she was talking about an animal. "Right when I was coming into town. Pretty little thing."

"Do you believe in the luck?" She leaned toward him. Clearly this was important to Lillian, but he didn't want to bullshit her.

"I should say yes. It's good for business. But I don't know. Banana got some good luck after he saw it. He was pretty much estranged from his daughter and granddaughter. Post-fox, they're tight. They're even coming out here for vacation later this summer. And my boss swears he'd be dead if his girlfriend hadn't seen The Fox. It somehow made her think to look at the tracker app on her phone, and she saw he was in trouble."

"Oh, is that Honey's granddaughter?"

"That's her. Small-town living is a trip. There are connections between everybody. Don't tell her husband, but Honey's been flirting with me nonstop since the moment Annie, that's the granddaughter, introduced us."

"I'm not surprised. When I met her, she told me she still had it. Sex appeal."

He laughed. "And she does."

"I wish I was a little more like her. I am pathetic at flirting. I guess it doesn't matter now. I mean, as we've established, I'm not going out to bars trying to meet men. At least not anymore. Owen and I have been together for almost three years. Maybe it's more her confidence I wish I had." Lillian pressed one hand over her lips for a moment. "I can't believe I just said that. Why am I telling you things I should only be telling, I don't know, my mom?"

"Cause I'm just some guy you'll never see again. There's no pressure."

"Maybe that's it."

"So, what kind of luck are you hoping our Miss Fox will bring you?"

"Honestly—and why stop now, since, like you said, it's not like we're ever going to see each other again—I was hoping seeing The Fox meant Owen was going to propose."

Maybe it would be luckier if he didn't, Gavin thought. This Owen didn't necessarily seem like a prize.

"I'm not just basing that on nothing." She was misinterpreting the doubt she must have seen on his face. "Owen pointed out some engagement rings in a shop window and asked which one I liked. It's not really a question of if, it's just when. You don't just casually ask about engagement rings. And the inn seems like the perfect spot. And it's the perfect time, right before we spend my vacation together. And I've seen The Fox, so how can it not happen?"

She sounded like she was trying to convince herself. "Well, if you've already talked rings, sounds like you're right." Any guy would know asking a woman about the kind of engagement ring she liked was a commitment. "He was just beat after all those days on the trail. When he wakes up, he'll make it up to you."

She smiled, a good one that reached all the way to her eyes.

"He will. I know he will. He really is the most wonderful man."
Now she had her full-on sparkle back, and then some.

Gavin felt that twinge of envy, like he had when he'd read
that letter she'd written to Owen. He doubted any woman he'd
been with had sparkled like that just thinking about him. Not
even Niri when he asked her to marry him. Although that wasn't
so much asking as the two of them almost daring each other. He
really hoped that guy of Lillian's knew what he had. Although
if he did, he'd probably already have put a ring on it.

CHAPTER 5

Lillian zipped up her dress, then gave a little twirl. She couldn't help it. The full skirt was made for twirling. She'd bought the dress special for tonight. She knew Owen would love it. He always said he liked her best in pink.

Lillian glanced at her watch. She was just one of those old-fashioned people who still wore a watch, and she'd found the perfect one, vintage with a bangle cuff, in a thrift shop. She hadn't mentioned that detail to Owen. He only liked things that were brand-new. Their reservation at the inn's restaurant was in four minutes. All they had to do was go downstairs. They still had time, just.

The bathroom door was still closed, even though she'd heard the shower turn off probably twenty minutes ago. Should she remind Owen what time it was? He might think she was being naggy though, but she just wanted to make sure that he knew what time it was. Was that naggy? And there they were. The ratty thoughts coming at her, pointed ratty teeth bared. Zing! She squeezed her eyes shut, imagining all those rodents turning equine. And there they were. The beautiful gray horses, prancing away across a meadow.

If Owen wasn't out in another minute, she'd just call and ask to push their reservation out a little. There. Problem solved. They could have a drink in the bar, relax, visit. They'd hardly had a chance to talk. He'd still been asleep when she got back from the laundry, then, as soon as he'd woken, he'd gone straight into the bathroom for a bath. Going in a little later to dinner would actually be a good thing. This was, she thought, she hoped, going to be a special night. Why not draw it out? She picked up the phone, but before she could dial the extension for the restaurant, the bathroom door opened, and Owen stepped out.

"You look wonderful!" He really did, even with welts from bug bites swelling one half of his face and his nose sunburned and peeling.

"Shaving hurt like hell." He gingerly rubbed his swollen cheek.

"Oooh. Sorry. You should have stayed stubbly."

"I know you like me clean-shaven."

"That's so sweet. But you really didn't have to. We should get downstairs. I've read raves about the inn's restaurant." His lips tightened, the way they did when he wanted to say something but was holding back. "Is everything okay?"

"Fine." He did the thing with his lips again. "Just—"

"Just?" she prompted.

He shook his head. "Let's get downstairs. I'm starved."

"Did you like the pork rinds I sent? I wasn't sure if they'd be worth the space they'd take up, but Gav—but the guy at the outfitters said a lot of hikers like them and that they have a ton of protein."

"I already told you—" He did the thing with his lips one more time. "They were great. Everything you sent was great."

He still sounded a little grumpy. Maybe going to dinner the same day he came off the trail was a bad idea, even though he was the one who had asked her to make the reservation. He was probably still exhausted and achy. Maybe this time he just wasn't in the mood to go out. "Would you rather just get room service? It might be more relaxing." She didn't want him to say yes, but if he said yes, that just meant tonight wasn't the night. It didn't mean it wasn't going to happen. He'd asked her what she thought of those engagement rings in the window. It was going to happen, but maybe those ten and a half days on the trail had just been too rough. Maybe he wasn't in the mood.

"Lillian—" He sighed. "It's okay to do something you want to do. Everything doesn't have to be about me."

"But you're the one who's doing the hiking. I've just been lolling around, shopping, going out to eat. We should do what you—"

"Let's just go downstairs." He held the door open for her.

Did that mean he wanted to go? Or was he just doing it because he knew she wanted to? Because if that was why, then they just shouldn't go. She didn't want to sit there trying to eat while she knew he'd rather be in the room. Should she ask him— She could almost hear the little ratty nails as the rats moved closer. No. No rats tonight. She gave a preemptive Zing! Owen said they should go downstairs, so they would, and they would have a good time. She'd make sure of it.

She linked her arm through his as they started down the wide staircase leading to the lobby. As soon as she stepped into the restaurant, she felt the tightness in her chest ease a little. It was beautiful, the tablecloths with a delicate floral pattern, different for each table, candles in silver holders, and dozens and dozens of glass globes with lights inside hanging from the tall ceiling, making Lillian feel like fairies could appear any second. The host led them over to the perfect table, tucked away in a corner, but with a gorgeous view of the setting sun. She'd told the woman who took her reservation that it was for a very special night.

"So, what have you been drooling over in your dreams out there on the trail? Are you thinking steak or salmon?" Those were his usual go-tos.

"I haven't even opened the menu."

"True. We should listen to the specials too. I bet they have some amazing ones."

He gave a little grunt in response. Clearly, he wasn't feeling talky. Well, she'd give him some silence. When you were close with someone, you didn't need to talk all the time. She opened her menu and began reading the description of every single offering, even the ones she knew she'd never order. When she reached the desserts, she took a peek at Owen. His eyes were still on his menu, even though he had to have gone all the way through it.

"A tarn of raspberry sauce. Did you see that Owen? The chocolate cake is served with a tarn of raspberry sauce." Usually, he got a kick out of the overblown descriptions of food. "I don't even know what a *tarn* is."

"It's a small mountain lake," he said, without looking up.

"Ah." Lillian started reading the descriptions of the appetizers again. Before she reached the end, their waiter came over.

"Hi. I'm Dale. I'll be your server. What can I get you to drink?"

"Do you have pink champagne?" For her, pink champagne was the most festive beverage. Maybe it was because she'd listened to that Ariana Grande song so many times when it first came out. She'd been a teenager, and it had sounded so fun to go wild and dance in the streets. Not that she'd been the kind of girl who would dance in the streets. But she liked dreaming about being a girl like that, with a life like that.

"I think I'll stick with water," Owen said.

Not festive. But it wasn't like it mattered what they ordered.

They were finally getting some together time. Except now Owen was looking at the menu. Again. And it wasn't one of the ones with multiple pages.

"What do elves study in school?" she asked, doing the voice she used for the monster when she read *I Will Chomp You!* to the kids, making them squeal and giggle. She'd never done any of her voices for him before, but Gavin had laughed at this one, and she thought maybe doing something a little goofy might shake Owen out of this mood he was in.

He didn't laugh. He just looked at her like they'd never even met. She dropped the silly voice. "The elf-abet. That's the answer. Because they are elves." She gave an apologetic little shrug. "Just a joke. For kids. I do that voice sometimes. At school."

"Cute." And there he was, looking at the menu again.

"Having trouble deciding?"

"I guess I'll go with the steak."

'Then I'll get the salmon. That way you can have both your favorites."

"Why do you do that? Why don't you just order what you want?"

"You know I never finish, so I like to order something that you'll like too." This was nothing new. It was their thing.

"What I'd like is for you to think for yourself. You're a doormat, Lillian."

His tone was harsh, leaving Lillian feeling like she'd been slapped. Where was this coming from? "It's just dinner. And I like salmon." She tried not to show her hurt. She didn't want to make a big thing out of the way he'd spoken to her.

"It's not just dinner. It's everything. It's this whole summer. I'm hiking the Appalachian Trail." His voice was getting louder, loud enough that they were getting some looks.

"Owen, shh."

He ignored her. "And what are you doing? You're following

me around while I hike the Appalachian Trail. Do you think that's what I want? I want my match, Lillian." More people were looking now, looking and whispering. Lillian knew she should be doing something, saying something, but she couldn't. Her lips felt frozen. Her whole body felt frozen.

He stared down at her. When had he stood? She hadn't even registered him standing.

"You're the most passive person I've ever met. I want someone who has her own dreams and her own plans. I want someone wild. I want someone adventurous."

Now he was walking away. He was walking away. Owen was walking away. From her. From her. Owen was walking away from her.

Lillian stared after Owen until he disappeared from sight, then she kept staring. He was coming back. He had to be coming back. He'd realize how irrational he'd been, and he'd come back. Because she hadn't done anything, or, at least, nothing that she hadn't done dozens of times before. She always got something he liked, so he could share with her. But not because she was a doormat. It was just that she didn't have as big of an appetite as he did, so she wanted to get something that he could finish for her. She never ordered something that she didn't like too. That was just . . . it was just not being wasteful. It was . . . Why wouldn't she get something he could share? Her thoughts kept looping in her brain. This didn't make sense. It didn't make sense.

Slowly, she realized that their waiter was standing at her side. He'd asked something, but Lillian wasn't sure what. "I'm s-sorry. I d-didn't . . ." She realized her teeth were clacking together. Then she realized her whole body was trembling. "I-I—" Her teeth wouldn't let her get words out.

She had to get out of there. She just had to get out of there. She reached for her purse, but her hands were shaking too hard to work the zipper. The waiter laid a hand on her shoulder, and

Lillian knew the man could feel the tremors coursing through her. She tried to open the zipper again.

"It's okay. You don't need to pay anything. Is there someone I can call for you?"

Owen. She wanted Owen. Owen could make everything all right. But he hadn't come back. Was he really not coming back? She struggled to her feet, managing a stammered thank-you, then rushed from the restaurant. She paused in the lobby. Where was she trying to go? She couldn't go to the room. If Owen was there . . . If he was there and he looked at her the way he had a few minutes ago—could it only have been a few minutes?—she wouldn't be able to survive it. She'd shatter into a million quivering pieces.

She just needed to get away from here. It didn't matter where. She managed to get herself out the door and down to the sidewalk. Left foot, right foot, left foot, right foot. Just keep moving, she told herself. Just keep moving.

When she saw Honey working on a display in the big front window of Vixen's, she stopped. She barely knew the woman, but . . . Honey looked up, dropped the sweater she was holding, and two seconds later, had Lillian wrapped in her arms. "What happened? What is it?"

Lillian's teeth still wouldn't let her get out words. "Owe-Owe. I-I—"

"You need to sit down." Keeping one arm wrapped around Lillian, Honey opened the door and steered Lillian inside, then through the shop to the back room. She guided her down onto a chair in front of the worktable and put a fleecy fox throw over her. "Tell me."

Lillian shook her head helplessly. "I-I—"

"I know what you need. We just got in some Copper Fox whiskey." Honey poured some into a shot glass and pressed it into Lillian's hand, then helped Lillian raise her hand to her lips. "Drink it down."

Lillian took a swallow, then coughed until she felt her stomach heaving. "One more. Slower." Honey guided Lillian's hand to her lips again, and this time Lillian managed to swallow the rest.

"He's gone. He just left. I don't know why. I don't know. We were just ordering dinner, and then he was yelling because I ordered salmon." Now that she was able to speak, her words were coming too fast, tripping over one another, tangling.

"Your boyfriend who was on the trail broke up with you. Is that right?"

The words sucked the air out of her body. When she was able to breathe again, she was crying. Or maybe she'd been crying all along. She wasn't sure.

"I don't know what to do. I don't know where to go. All my things are in our hotel room, but I can't go there. I can't see him. I can't."

"Of course, you can't." Honey poured another shot and handed it to Lillian. "I'm going to call Vi, see if she has a room. If she does, I'll get Steven, he's the manager of the inn, to send your things over. Leave it to me. And drink that."

By the time Lillian managed to get the second shot down, Honey had everything arranged. "Charlie's bringing the car around." Honey took Lillian by the hand, as if Lillian were one of her kindergarteners, and led her back outside.

"You shouldn't—You don't have to—"

"Hush. You just do what I say. I like being bossy. Everyone knows that. I'm taking you to Vi's and putting you straight to bed. Everything will look better in the morning."

That wasn't possible. She'd ruined everything. Owen was disgusted with her. He couldn't even look at her. He'd had to get up and leave.

She felt paralyzed, only able to move with Honey's help. Into the car. Out of the car. Up the steps of the boardinghouse. Miss Violet was saying something about hikers, damnable hikers. Then with Honey on one side and Miss Violet on the other, Lillian was moved up to her room and bundled into a plush purple robe.

She knew the robe was warm, but cold was emanating from inside Lillian. She didn't think she'd ever feel warm again. It didn't matter. The rats were on her now. Yellow teeth bared. Eyes red. Lillian tried to imagine her sparkly wand into her hand, but it wouldn't come. Owen didn't love her anymore. The rats were going to devour her. There was nothing she could do to stop them.

"And that's when I joined the circus. I started selling peanuts, but then worked my way up to aerialist. I loved—"

"Wait. Back up," Gavin said. "Did you say circus?"

"I did." Erin took one of his fries and popped it in her mouth. "That was something this history teacher I had in seventh grade used to do. We'd all be taking notes, writing down everything he said, and then he'd start saying more and more outrageous things until we stopped. It took a while, sometimes."

Gavin shoved his hair off his forehead. "Sorry."

"What were you thinking about when you should have had all your attention on me? The woman who, in addition to being beautiful and charming, scored you a free meal at the nicest restaurant in town."

Erin's cousin was a sous chef at the inn's restaurant. He'd finagled them a table by the kitchen door, and the chef had made them these amazing lobster dumplings, something she was thinking of adding to the menu.

"I was thinking about that woman whose boyfriend turned psycho. I know her a little. She came into Boots to arrange a food drop—for the boyfriend. I was wondering if she was okay."

"She isn't. She couldn't possibly be."

"True." Even from across the room, Gavin had seen the devastation on Lillian's face. For a moment, he hadn't been sure she'd be able to walk out of the restaurant without help. He'd wanted to go to her, but Erin—And anyway the waiter had it covered.

"She was actually thinking he might propose tonight."

"Sounds like quite the conversation you two had."

"I'm a friendly guy. People tell me things."

Erin nodded. "Yeah, you made friends with everybody at the bar in about two minutes. It was impressive."

"Good." He tried to return all his focus to Erin. There was nothing he could do for Lillian, and, anyway, they barely knew each other. But to be thinking she was going to be given a ring, and then getting that— Criminal, what that guy had done to her. "I wanted to impress you."

"Well, it worked." She took another fry. "I don't get how she could be so clueless. That woman. How could she not realize there were problems between her and her boyfriend? And she was thinking they were about to get engaged? That's delusional."

Gavin shook his head. He'd been known to miss some clues in his relationships, but he wasn't telling that to Erin. "It sounded like they had all these plans for the summer, meeting up at places along the trail. He's hiking to Harpers Ferry. Seems like he was acting like he wanted to be with her."

"So, she's clueless, and he's a wuss. He obviously wanted out, but couldn't find the balls to tell her. Then it just came barfing up. That's what happens when you keep pushing things down."

She didn't sound very sympathetic. But, hell, why should she. She didn't know either of them. "I hope she has a friend she can call." He hated thinking about Lillian trying to deal with what had happened all by herself. She had to feel like the world had gotten yanked out from under her.

"I'm sure she does."

What was Lillian even doing right now? he wondered. It wasn't like she could go back to the room she and the boyfriend shared. Not his problem. He leaned closer to Erin. "So what were you telling me, before the circus."

"When you weren't paying attention?"

"Yeah, then."

"I forgive you since you were worried about that poor lady. What I was saying was that I'm trying to get an internship at American Cheese, you know, the gaming company. They're developing a spin-off of Rat Trap, and I want in. But I've heard that interns don't really get to have much input. I don't know if I want to spend a year getting coffee, although maybe even getting coffee could help. I could at least meet some people."

"Let them see your charm and beauty."

She grinned. "The charm. The beauty is for me on my own time. Anyway, I put in an application. No point in thinking about if I want it or not when no one has even offered it to me."

She was a go-getter. Gavin was going to be a senior too, and how many internships had he applied for? That would be a big goose egg. But he needed to work at a job that actually paid, unlike Erin, who was living in a dorm paid for by her parents, as far as he could tell. Not that there was anything wrong with that. He wouldn't have minded a little parental assist when he'd started school, but he'd made it work.

"You want to head over to the lake? Some of my friends are having a bonfire."

Lake. Bonfire. Beautiful, charming woman. Life was good. "Sounds great. You ready?" He pulled out his wallet.

"I told you, my cousin hooked us up."

"Gotta take care of the server." He put down a ten.

She nodded her approval. "You can tell a lot about somebody by how they tip. I'm thinking you're probably a good guy."

Gavin stood. "Probably?"

"One swallow does not a summer make."

"What now?" He had to stay on his toes with this one.

"My roommate was writing a paper on intelligence and the ability to understand metaphors. She was always throwing them at me. I'd never heard that one before. It means don't jump to conclusions. A good tip and a bar game do not a good man make. Not necessarily. Hence, the probably."

"Fair enough. I'll just have to make sure you spend enough time with me to see some of my other stellar qualities."

They started for the door, passing the table where Lillian had been left sitting alone. "I don't think I could end up in a situation like that woman. I don't think I could be with someone day after day and not notice they were losing interest. They say love is blind, speaking of metaphors, but I think it's good to keep one eye at least a little open."

Gavin flashed on Lillian's letter, where she'd written "I love you" over and over. She didn't hold back. And that's how she had gotten hurt. She'd loved the boyfriend so much she hadn't seen the truth about him.

"You know what? I forgot I need to put in some time planning the first fox walk before tomorrow. How about an ice cream and we do the bonfire another night?"

"How about an ice cream and I still go to the bonfire."

"Fair enough," he said again. He wondered if Lillian had checked into another room here at the inn. He could check at the front desk. You barely know her, he reminded himself. Let it go.

CHAPTER 6

Lillian looked like hell, her bluebell-blue eyes all puffy from what had probably been a long night of crying. Why wouldn't she cry? That bastard had KO'd her the night before.

"Hey, Twinkle." Gavin made sure to keep his voice upbeat. She didn't know he'd witnessed the breakup scene, and he didn't want to embarrass her by letting it slip.

Lillian walked up to the desk. "I want to sign up for the Boots Camp."

"That one goes for six weeks and meets five hours a day. Monday through Friday, with a couple weekend hikes thrown in. It's hardcore." And he'd seen those cute little toes of hers. Going to the Boots Camp would be like going from zero to sixty in 1.7 seconds.

"I know exactly what it involves." Brrr. Her voice was a little chilly, but Gavin didn't take it personally.

"Have you read about the other courses we offer? I'm not sure you want to spend your whole vacation doing—"

Her chin jerked up. "I don't need your permission. Sign me up."

"O-kay."

Lillian gave her head a few fast shakes. "I'm sorry. That came out wrong. Yes, I read the descriptions of everything on the website, and the Boots Camp is the one I want. And when I'm done with the six weeks, I'm planning to hike the Wilderness. Can't get more wild and adventurous than that."

And there it was. Wild and adventurous. The exact words the loser had thrown at her last night. Crap. Clearly, the plan was to twist herself into what he said he wanted and then try to get him back. Why the hell would she want him after what he'd pulled?

"What? You think I can't do it?" Her tone was half defiant and half defeated.

"After we put you through your paces for six weeks, you'll be ready. But—"

"But what?"

"Okay, listen, I was at the restaurant last night. Table over by the kitchen. You probably didn't notice me over there."

She took a step back, and a red that looked almost painful coursed up her neck, then stained her cheeks. "You were?"

He'd already gone there, so he might as well keep going. "Yeah. And I heard what Owen said about wanting someone wild and adventurous. You want to train and hike the Wilderness? Great. But don't do it because of that son of a motherless goat." He'd been about to say asshole, but she just didn't seem like someone who'd appreciate swearing. She was a kindergarten teacher, fer chrissake.

"He was right though. I am passive, a doormat. I've always been like that. I just— Half the time I don't even know what I think about . . . about anything. Like if you asked me if I wanted a blue water bottle or one of the purple ones, I'm not sure I'd even know which one I preferred."

"Maybe because it doesn't matter. I mean, who cares? They both hold water and keep it cold." He didn't like to hear her bad-talking herself.

"Last night, at dinner, I ordered salmon, because I knew that Owen liked it. That's what I was thinking about when I looked at the menu. What would Owen like—because I never finish everything, so I knew he would eat some. I do stuff like that all the time. Not just with Owen. With my mom. I just, I'm tired of it. That's why I want to do the Boots Camp. Not for Owen. For me. I'm tired of being myself."

Tired of being herself? Gavin didn't buy it, not entirely. She might be feeling like she wanted to change some things about herself, but it wasn't just because she had decided to do some self-improvement. She might say it wasn't for the guy, but it was for the guy. She'd used his exact words—wild and adventurous—when she'd talked about signing up for Boots Camp. But, none of his business. Gavin could tell she was determined to do this thing. "All right, let's get you signed up."

"I guess I need some hiking stuff too. I have sneakers. Do I need boots?"

"Not necessarily. There are some trail runners that are good, and lighter. You'll need to get some moleskin, because no matter how good the shoes, you're gonna get blisters."

"I'm being stupid. I know all this. I know exactly what I need, because I've gone shopping with Owen about a—" She gave her head a hard shake. "I'll need some socks. Do you have Darn Tough Hiker Micros? Those are the ones Owen—" She shook her head again.

Once they got her outfitted, Gavin rang her up. The gear, not including the course, was more than seven hundred, but she just handed over her credit card. "Okay. Well, I guess I'll see you on Wednesday morning. For Boots Camp. It's going to be great." Her voice didn't match those upbeat words, and tears shone in her eyes. He did not want to deal with her crying. He needed to stop that now, before it got started.

"Why don't you try out those trail runners right now. I have a fox walk booked. It's a new thing I came up with. I take people out to look for the town's legendary fox. Nothing strenuous. Just some nice scenery, and, possibly, a peek at The Fox."

"I saw it already, remember? Yesterday, which turned out to be the absolute worst day of my life."

Gavin thought maybe it would turn out to have been a good day. She deserved someone much better than that Owen. Not that he was going to tell her that. She'd bite his head off, then eat it. "Come anyway. Start breaking in your shoes. There'll be some nice scenery and some excellent company." He grinned. "That would be me. Although there will be three other people in the group." She hesitated. He didn't want her leaving. She'd probably just spend the day going over every detail of the breakup, making herself crazy. "Your feet will thank you."

"No time like the present, right? If I'm going to do this, which I am, I might as well start right now."

"Great. Just maybe don't mention your feelings about the luck of The Fox, since everybody on the walk is probably hoping for a little luck."

"I won't. I don't want to ruin it for them."

"We'll be heading out in about a half an hour. And what I like to do when I have a free half hour—hammock. Come on." He walked to the back of the barn and stopped in front of an orange-and-white-striped double-wide. Not that he was planning to share it with her. That would be . . . not good. She was a walking, talking lump of vulnerability. "I'll hold it steady for you."

Lillian eased herself into the hammock. The pillow resting on it fell on the floor. Gavin grabbed it and positioned it under her head, his fingers briefly tangling in her curly hair, then climbed into the hammock across from her.

"Ah, hammock time. Can't touch this." He crossed his ankles and put his hands behind his head. "My dad used to do the MC Hammer dance when he was really happy about something."

"I don't know it."

"What? No. That is so wrong. It's a classic. There are about a million gifs of it. I would stand up and do it for you right now, but I'm too lazy."

"Just so you know, what you saw last night, that's not Owen. He's never acted that way before. Never."

What was Gavin supposed to say to that? He wasn't going to encourage her to make excuses for the guy. But he couldn't tell her what an asshole he thought Owen was. She was not even close to being ready to hear that. "Huh," he said, to acknowledge that he'd heard her.

"I wish he'd said something before. I didn't know. He always seemed to appreciate it when I ordered something that I knew he'd like to share with me. He always seemed happy to help me make decisions. I didn't know he found it frustrating."

"Huh," Gavin said again.

"He seemed happy that I was going to be spending the summer with him too. He never told me he didn't want me to follow him from here to Virginia. If he'd told me, I wouldn't have come."

Sounded like Owen had it good. Someone to organize drops for him. Someone to wash his stinky clothes. Someone to write him love notes. There had to be something else going on. Hiking hookup. That had to be it. Sounded like when she dropped him off at Baxter, all was hunky dory; then ten-and-a-half days later—boom, it was over. Yeah, he met someone. Gavin knew how it was. Out on the trail, everything was intensified. Ten-and-a-half days out there could feel like a year of a regular relationship. Should he mention the possibility to her? It might make her stop trying to figure out all the ways she was to blame. But maybe it would just make her feel worse. Yeah, adding getting cheated on to the mix wasn't going to help anything. Maybe doing the Boots Camp would turn out to be a good thing. It would at least give her some distraction, and, at the end of the day, she'd be too tired to think about much of anything.

Subject change time. "You might know one of the people on the hike. Simon Reiser."

"He's staying at Miss Violet's. I saw him at breakfast a couple times."

"He's the one who gave me the idea for the fox walks. He wants to see her bad, was asking all kinds of questions about where she'd been spotted. The other two people coming with us are a couple, Stephanie and Ford. They saw the blog posts I got Nick and Banana to write. I figured getting their fox stories out there would help get people interested."

"Do you have anything on the site that gives the town history? It's such a lovely story, how Annabelle Hatherley saved The Fox and nursed it with her own milk, then the same fox saving all the people in the settlement." Lillian gave a snort. "Listen to me. I can't stop wanting to believe in fairy tales, even when I have hard proof they aren't real."

"Never know. Banana thought seeing The Fox was going to give him the luck he needed to finally make it through the Wilderness. He'd failed so many times that he'd lost confidence he'd ever be able to do it. As soon as he saw her, he was going to head straight for the trail. But before he could, he got a call from his daughter asking him to take his granddaughter for the summer. He was his daughter's last option. He's convinced that call came because of The Fox. And, now, like I told you the other day, he and his family are close, after years of almost no contact. Maybe you have some luck coming, just not the luck you were looking for."

"There's nothing else I want." He saw tears clinging to her bottom lashes. What Gavin wanted was a chance to punch Owen in the gut. Owen wanted to be with someone he'd met out on the trail? Fine. But he'd made Lillian feel like there was something wrong with her. Wanting to make her smile, Gavin stood, planted his feet wide, bent his knees, then started scooting back and forth across the floor, getting some shoulder action. She just stared at him. "The Hammer dance." He kept going, and a reluctant smile began to tug on her lips.

"Dude! Can't touch that!"

Gavin turned and saw Simon walking in. "Time to strap on those new runners," he told Lillian.

Fifteen minutes later, Gavin was leading his little group of good-luck hunters—and Lillian—across the meadow behind the Boots Barn. He'd decided to walk them through the woods to the sign at the edge of town where he'd seen The Fox, then loop back around and end with a stop at The Wit's Beginning where Banana had seen the vixen. Banana was going to give everyone a post-hike beverage, which might ease the disappointment if they didn't see The Fox, because odds were they wouldn't. Still, it was a beautiful summer day, not too hot, so there was always that.

"So, what kind of luck are we hoping The Fox brings?" he asked, shooting Lillian a wink to let her know he hadn't forgotten how she felt about the critter.

"I'm mostly here for a little exercise while my knee is healing up," Simon answered. "But I wouldn't say no to a little luck."

Gavin wasn't buying it. He'd seen the hungry look on Simon's face when he was asking about The Fox that night in the bar. Gavin wasn't going to push it though. None of his business. His business was making sure everybody had a good time and ended up feeling like their money was well spent.

"Wait! Wait, wait! I see something orange!" Stephanie exclaimed, stopping abruptly. "It's The Fox."

Gavin followed her gaze and saw a clump of flowers. "Uh, nope. Those are orange ditch lilies. Kind of an ugly name for something so pretty." Gavin had made sure to study up on all the local flora and fauna. "Each bud only opens for one day, then the petals fall off and are replaced by a new bud." He felt pleased with himself for remembering that tidbit. He'd always been a decent student. When, as Rebecca liked to remind him, he put his mind to it.

He wondered what Rebecca was up to. He hoped she was doing okay at her sister's. She and her sister didn't always get along, and sharing a place for the summer might not be fun. Too bad he and Rebecca had sublet their place. He should check in with Bec and see if she was planning to move back in after the summer. He'd be happy to let her have it. She'd fallen in love with it when they were apartment hunting. He didn't really care where he lived. A soft bed. PlayStation. A few beers in the fridge. Life was good.

Stephanie laughed. "I just saw a flash of orange and I got all—" She flapped her hands around her head. He liked her vibe. She was probably mid-forties, but she was rocking pigtails and overall shorts, and, clearly, she didn't take herself too seriously.

"Pretty eager to see The Fox, huh?" Gavin asked.

"Actually, she wants me to see it," Milford, Stephanie's boyfriend, answered. "She thinks it's powerful enough to cancel out all my bad luck."

"Hey, it saved a whole town. I'm sure it can handle you." Stephanie gave Milford a playful shoulder bump.

He smiled and gave one of her pigtails a light tug. "My little optimist."

"You look like a pretty lucky man to me." The way the guy looked at his girl made Gavin think things had to be pretty good.

"Let's begin with my name. Milford Stank. Shall I repeat it?" He didn't wait for an answer. "I shall repeat it. Milford Stank. Which quickly became Milfart Stank after an unfortunate toot in the cafeteria on the first day of first grade. The name stayed with me for the next eleven years."

"Dude," Simon said.

Stephanie gave an exaggerated sigh. "Here we go. The litany. I keep telling Ford that, if anybody made a list of every bad thing that had ever happened to them, it would be long. The same way it would be long if it were a list of every good thing."

"That makes sense," Lillian agreed. Even feeling as bad as Gavin knew she did, there she was, trying to make someone else feel better.

"I am now going to jump ahead, but be assured, I am omitting a plethora of bad luck. Yet, I was still able to get a date to the senior prom."

"And she was beautiful," Stephanie added. "I saw her picture in his yearbook. So, I think that should go in the good luck column."

"Sadly, she contracted mono, and had to cancel."

"Something that had nothing to do with you," Stephanie was quick to add. "She really wanted to go with you. It even said so in what she wrote in the yearbook."

"My parents insisted that I would regret it forever if I didn't go to the prom. So, they forced me to attend. With my sister."

"Dude," Simon said again.

"That . . . maybe wasn't the best idea." What had his parents been thinking? Gavin's parents would have cracked open some beers for all of them and started up a Farrelly brothers marathon. They might not have been conventional, but when he really needed them, his parents usually came through.

"Let's just say my luck, or lack of it, continued. You don't need all the gory details."

"He means it continued until, at age forty-eight, he met me." Stephanie gave him another shoulder bump. "Wait! Is that orange! Is that her?"

It took Gavin a second to figure out what she'd seen. "Wild strawberries," he told her. Not exactly orange. "Our fox might eat them. Next time, maybe give the 'orange' alert a little more softly."

"Oh! Right! Duh!" Stephanie slapped her forehead.

He led the way onto a narrow path that ran into the woods, narrow enough that they had to walk single file, and took a deep breath of the Christmasy smell of the balsam fir that ran on either side.

"Sorry I got so loud. It's just that Ford has to see that fox. I'm not going to get him to marry me if he doesn't."

"That makes it sound as if I don't want to marry the most wonderful woman I've ever met."

"Which is true. You don't." Gavin could hear the pain in her tone.

"I don't want to bring my bad luck down on her. If that weren't a factor, we'd already be married."

"We almost were. It was so close. It took me a full year to convince him that I wanted to be married to him, no matter what, and that any bad luck that came our way, if it did, we'd handle together."

"And then the day of the wedding, a sinkhole opened up under the church. I almost killed her and fifty-four of our nearest and dearest."

"Dude," said Simon, from the back of the line.

"He won't believe it wasn't his fault. When I read about The Fox, I knew that was the answer. If Ford sees it, I know it will counteract any bad luck he thinks he has. And he's agreed if he sees it, we can get married. Remember, you promised, Ford."

"I did. And nothing would make me happier. But I don't believe Milfart Stank is someone who will see a magical fox."

This was life and death to both of them. Or at least happiness and unhappiness. Gavin hadn't thought there would be desperate people on his little fox walks. He hadn't thought it really mattered one way or the other if The Fox showed. Come on, vixen, he thought. You're needed.

The Fox breathed in a scent she recognized. It came from the human female bound to the human male with the unnatural cord that held both brilliant light and rot. She moved closer, and saw that one end of the cord was still connected to the woman, but it was flapping loose on the other end, the edges there raw and ragged.

Connections between those The Fox lived among were simple. There were cords between the hunter and the hunted, the mother and the kit, the mated pair. Over the years she had lived on the fringes of the human dwellings, she had seen the humans begin to lose some of the connections they once had. Some still had cords reaching out to almost everything in her world. Some had few cords at all. The Fox did not think it was possible for any that lived in her woods to have a cord as damaged as the woman's. Only humans could create something so unnatural.

She let her gaze rest on the cord between two humans who walked with the first. She could feel heat coming off it, as if it were a living thing. She closed her eyes, and allowed herself to soak in the warmth, the sensation that of lying in the meadow, basking in the sun.

The fox hadn't put in an appearance, and Milford and Stephanie were mostly silent as they had their free drink at Banana's. Simon didn't even stay for his, deciding to walk back to the boardinghouse.

Gavin drove Lillian, Milford, and Stephanie back to the Boots Barn in Banana's yellow Jeep. "I'm sorry it didn't work out for you."

"Oh, we'll be back. We don't give up that easily," Stephanie told him. But Milford shot Gavin a look that said he knew it was hopeless.

"Well, that sucked," Gavin said as he and Lillian watched them drive away.

"They've got to see The Fox. You can tell how much they love each other."

He wondered how much it hurt seeing a couple like Stephanie and Ford after her own relationship had imploded. "You don't believe The Fox is lucky."

"I know," she sighed. "But I want to believe, I *need* to believe that somebody can get their happy ending."

You're still alive, Lillian told herself as she left the boarding-house the next morning. Your heart is still beating. Air is still going in and out of your lungs. That means you're surviving.

Except that it felt like every heartbeat hurt, and every breath made her chest ache. Didn't matter. Who knew, maybe it hurt terribly for a caterpillar to turn into a butterfly. And that's what she was trying to do. What she *was* doing. She was transforming. The first step had been signing up for the Boots Camp. Now she just needed a way to pay for it. She'd saved all year long to be able to afford spending the summer on the road with Owen. She could use that money to pay for her room at the boardinghouse and food, but the six-week course and the gear had taken a big bite out of her savings, and she needed to replace it. So, part-time job.

She'd go into every store on Main Street for starters, she decided as she walked. Maybe one of them would need help. First, the flower shop. While the woman working there helped her make up a bouquet, Lillian asked if they were hiring. They weren't. Well, plenty of other shops to try. But she had something more important to take care of before she continued to job hunt.

Less than two minutes later, one of the benefits of small-town living, she was opening the door to Vixen's, setting the little copper bells jingling. Kristina—no, KiKi, she wanted to be called KiKi—stood behind the counter, looking adorable in a baseball cap featuring a glittering fox. "Good to see you again, KiKi."

She heard a loud, disgusted snort, and turned to see Evie in a matching hat folding T-shirts at a nearby table. "KiKi." Evie's nose wrinkled. "Her name is Kristina. Tina if you don't want all the syllables."

"I think KiKi's a cute nickname. Is Honey around?"

"She's in the back. You can go in. She won't mind," KiKi said.

"Honey? Hi! It's Lillian," she called, before she swept back the curtain.

"I have been so worried about you." Lillian held the bouquet out to the side so it wouldn't get squashed as Honey gave her a hug. "If I hadn't known from my sources that you were all right, I would have been over at the boardinghouse checking on you yesterday."

"Sources?"

"I have many. Miss Violet, of course. And Banana. I heard from him and Annie that you'd signed up for the Boots Camp, so I know you're staying for the summer."

"You're all caught up. These are for you." Lillian handed over the bouquet. "Thank you so much for taking care of me the other night. I don't know what I would have done without you. I'd probably still be wandering the streets, sobbing." She tried to say the words lightly, but couldn't manage it. They felt like the truth.

"Well, so you know, everyone in town is ready to kill that man for what he did to you."

"Everyone?" The woman at the florist shop had been extremely nice and had given Lillian an amazing deal on the flowers, but Lillian had thought it was Fox Crossing friendliness. "Does everyone know?"

"Well . . ." Honey hesitated. "Yes. I think all the locals will have heard. Everyone knows someone who either works in the restaurant or was there having dinner."

Lillian's face grew hot. All those people hearing Owen, so loud and scornful, call her a doormat. Well, she was transforming. By the end of the Boots Camp, she wouldn't be that person anymore. "I can't believe I was in here nattering about how he was going to propose to me. I feel so foolish."

"There's nothing foolish about a loving heart. You just need to find somebody deserving of yours. Now, I know every single man in this town, and practically every one in the whole state. I can find—"

"No!" Lillian yelped. "No, please. Please."

"I got a little ahead of myself there," Honey said. "And as sweet and beautiful as you are, you wouldn't need my help anyway. I bet you have, why"—she gave a mischievous smile—"at least half as many beaus as I did when I was your age."

Lillian laughed. She hadn't thought she'd ever feel like laughing again, but there was something about Honey. "I'm sure you had many, many more gentleman callers than I've ever had. I'm not good at all the man stuff."

"Man stuff?" Honey cocked her head, causing her fox ears to slip a little.

"Going out, flirting, talking to strangers . . . Honestly, I get so nervous it makes me need to pee."

"You talked to me fine the day we met, and I was a stranger." Honey adjusted the ears and gave her blond curls a pat.

"That's different. With men, I always feel like they're evaluating me.

"It's you who should be evaluating them. They should be working to win your approval. You should just sit back and relax."

"Right now, I don't even want to get within a hundred yards of a man, at least not one who's single. I'll make an exception for unattached boys under twelve, and unattached men over ninety."

"I know a ninety-one-year-old who would be all over you like flies on molasses," Honey warned, which made Lillian laugh again.

"Over a hundred then. Do you think everybody's knowing . . . what happened will make it easier or harder for me to find a part-time job? Do you think I could get a pity hire?"

"I'll hire you. No pity. I need the help. The southbound herd won't hit until the end of August, but now that black-fly season is almost over, the NoBos will be coming through."

"I would love to work here. You're sure you really need me?"

"Ask me next week when I'm running you ragged. How about two nights a week and Sundays?"

"That would be—"

The curtain swished open, and KiKi rushed in. "Honey, you need to get out there. Evie is harassing a customer, and I can't make her stop."

Lillian and KiKi followed Honey into the shop and over to where Evie stood talking to Simon. "I know him. He's staying at the boardinghouse too. Simon, this is Honey. She owns the place. She's the great-aunt of these two young ladies."

"She doesn't like the 'great' word," Evie volunteered. "She thinks it makes her sound old. We just call her our Honey."

"I like it." Simon ran his fingers through white hair, mussing it a little.

Evie narrowed her eyes at him. "When you were hiking, I want to know if—"

Honey placed her hand lightly over Evie's mouth. "She's vivacious. She gets it from me. Now, Evie, I need your help in the back doing inventory. Start by counting all the fox mugs."

"You can take my phone and listen to music while you count," KiKi offered.

Once she handed the cell over, Evie started walking away, extremely slowly.

"What can I help you find? Or would you like to browse? I love a good browse," Honey told Simon, putting one hand on his arm. She definitely still had it, Lillian thought. Simon clearly found her charming.

"I was interested in the history of your fox. Do you have a—?"

Music started blaring from the back room. Evie must have the volume all the way up. "In the deep, in the dark, in the deep, deep dark," she began to sing, in a high, clear voice.

"Miss Violet has actually written a wonderful—Are you all right?"

Simon ran his hand through his hair again, and Lillian could see his fingers trembling. Sweat sheened his upper lip and forehead. "Come sit down," she urged, taking him by the elbow and trying to steer him toward a fox-print armchair in the corner.

He shook her off. "No, no. I just need a little . . . air." He staggered toward the door. Lillian and Honey followed him outside, Evie on their heels. "You're clearly not all right." Lillian watched as Simon struggled to pull in a breath.

"I am. Just a little stuffy inside. I'm fine now." He did look better, his breathing getting more even. He pulled a bandana out of his pocket, and, when he used it to wipe his face, his hand was steady. "I'll head back to the boardinghouse. Do some rocking on the veranda. A little rest is all I need." He started away from them,

"Are you sure I can't get you a drink?" Honey called. He didn't turn, just waved in response.

"He was limping on the other leg when he was in the store," Evie announced. "And he was lying about being a hiker. No fly bites, and too pale."

"Let's go back inside." Honey turned and opened the door, ushering Evie and Lillian into the store.

"Evie, I can't have you bothering customers with dozens of questions," Honey said.

"Maybe you need to Prudently Interrogate. Only ask a question or two," Lillian suggested.

Evie adjusted one of her many barrettes. "Prudently. That's a *P* I haven't used yet."

"Obviously," KiKi muttered. "Is he okay? I didn't want to crowd him, so I stayed inside."

"It seemed to me that he recovered once he was outside." Honey looked at Lillian, and she nodded.

"You said he was staying at the boardinghouse too. What has he said to you?" Evie asked. "I need to know everything."

Lillian decided Evie needed to be redirected. "That reminds me, as I was leaving Miss Violet gave me some fliers about auditions for her play. Would you put one in the window?"

"Of course. What's this one about? I haven't heard." Honey frowned. "Which is unusual. Violet usually talks up a storm about her productions."

"I don't think she knows. I don't think she's written much. This morning, she burned the cinnamon rolls, and only sang a few notes. She's putting a huge amount of pressure on herself."

"Usually she writes reams, and suffers when she has to cut out scenes and characters."

"Can I see the flier?" KiKi asked.

"Of course." Lillian handed it to her.

"Can I please just ask one question?" Evie gave a bounce on her toes. "That would be Prudently Interrogating."

"You may not," Honey told her. "I admire your dedication, but all people have secrets, and it's not your job to find out what they are."

"It says that kids and teens can audition," KiKi said. "I'm going to do it."

"You barfed on Joseph's feet when you were an angel in the Christmas pageant. And he was wearing sandals. It was so gross," Evie reminded her sister. "Stage fright," she added to Lillian.

"People change. I'm not that girl anymore," KiKi said. "I'm doing it."

"Lots of my kindergartners get a little scared when we do a show for the parents."

"She wasn't five when this happened. This happened last year."

"People can change. Take me. I've never been much of an outdoor person, but I signed up for the Boots Camp. I'm going to turn into an Amazon. I'm thinking of it as turning from a caterpillar to a butterfly. An Amazon butterfly." Lillian smiled at KiKi. "I say the two of us can be butterflies together."

CHAPTER 7

"Squats are your friend. One of the best training exercises for the trail. Which means—one more round!" Gavin called to the Boots Campers in the meadow by the barn. "Drive those heels into the ground on the way up." He scanned the group. "Carter, don't let your knees go that far forward. Don't let them go out past your toes. Spencer, don't think I don't see you cheating. Get those hands off your knees. Lillian"—he wasn't sure she'd like being called Twinkle in front of everybody—"you're rounding your shoulders. Remember, the motion is like sitting down in a chair."

A couple people had clearly spent some hard time in the gym, and they were breezing through this morning's workout. Others, Gavin figured, had done a lot of trail time, but hadn't done much cross-training. And then there was Twinkle. He was sure teaching a group of kindergarteners kept her on the move, but he doubted she'd done any kind of structured workout since gym class.

"All right. Three more." He counted it down. "Now planks." Everybody dropped to their mats. He waited until everybody got into position. "And thirty seconds." He walked through the group, checking postures. "Butt down. Keep your head in line with the rest of your body. You're building a strong core, and that's going to make carrying a pack a hell of a lot easier."

As he passed Lillian, he could see tremors running through her body and hear her ragged breathing. Her face was tight. She was using everything she had to hold the position. "Five, four, three, two, and one." She collapsed to the ground with a groan. "Great work, everybody. That's lunch. After that, you've got Annie for first-aid class."

"Need a hand?" he asked Lillian, who looked plastered to the ground.

"No. I'm just going to stay here . . . for a minute."

"All right. Nice job."

He headed over to the picnic tables where lunch, catered from Flappy's with cookies from Shoo Fly's bakery, was spread out. Eating with the group wasn't technically part of the job, but getting to know everyone made for a better experience for all of them, and he was all about delivering the goods. He sat down across from Spencer, a thirty-something who was in the middle of the group's fitness range.

Spencer added a second layer of pickles to his peanut butter sandwich. Gross, but whatever. "Don't knock it until you try it." He must have noticed Gavin's disgusted expression. " 'The vinegary snap of the pickles tempers the unctuousness of the peanut butter.' " He laughed. "That's a quote from Dwight Garner, guy who writes for the *New York Times*. He described it so perfectly that it stuck with me."

"I have no idea what unctuousness is," Gavin admitted.

"Smarmy. But in food it means oily or creamy." Spencer put the top on his sandwich. "Obviously, I'm a foodie. I'm not looking forward to weeks of fruit leather and beef jerky."

"You know what I'm not looking forward to?" A.J., clearly a gym rat, asked as he joined them. Gavin reminded himself to start giving him some variations to make the workouts more challenging. "Losing my muscle mass. I've worked too hard building it."

Gavin nodded. "It's almost impossible not to lose some. We'll be going over trail nutrition, and I can give you some tips on getting the most calories and macronutrients out of what you carry. You could also take some zeros and hit the gym."

"If I take a day off, I'm hitting a restaurant." Spencer took a bite of his sandwich and gave a little groan of pleasure.

Gavin glanced at the other tables. No Twinkle. He checked her mat, to make sure she wasn't still face-planting. Nope. There she was, over by the BOOTS CAMP sign, taking a selfie.

"Don't miss the junk-drawer cookies. They're different every time, but always outrageous. Shoo Fly, the guy who makes them, owns the bakery, but has a side gig as an instructor here. He's got a triple crown."

"I have no idea what that means," Spencer said.

Rene looked over her shoulder from her spot at the next table. "Somebody who's hiked the AT, the Pacific Crest Trail, and the Continental Divide Trail. Vertical gain of 1,000,000 feet. Almost 8,000 miles." She was one of the Booters who Gavin thought had done a decent amount of hiking—and reading about hiking—but hadn't put in a lot of gym time.

"Try the cookies. Seriously." Gavin stood and walked over to Lillian. "Put the phone away."

Her bluebell-blue eyes widened. "Are we starting again already? I thought lunch was an hour."

"It is." He shook his head. "I knew it was bull when you said you weren't signing up for Boots Camp to get that"—he skipped over all the words that applied—"guy back."

"I'm not." Her voice was way too high.

"Twinkle, please. Look at me and tell me you're not over here taking sexy selfies to prove how, what was it, wild and adventurous, you are." Her lips parted, but she didn't speak. What could she say? She couldn't deny it. "Haven't you ever heard of the no-contact rule?"

"The what?"

"The no-contact rule. If you want the guy back, which I don't know why you would, but none of my business, you can't have any contact of any kind for four weeks minimum."

"I'm not trying to . . ." Her words trailed off. "Where'd you come up with that rule anyway? You act like it's a thing everyone knows."

"Haven't you ever read *Cosmo*?"

"No. Why have you read *Cosmo*?"

"I had a girlfriend who always left it on the back of the toilet. But the rule is all over the web. Some people say you have to go sixty days, but I think thirty works. But it has to be no contact. None. No calls, no texts, no asking his friends how he is, no liking on Facebook or Instagram, no posting on social media either. Don't even go on."

Although, maybe she didn't need the rule. If he saw a picture of Lillian the way she looked right now, cheeks flushed, hair even more curly than usual from perspiration, T-shirt without that baggy shirt over it showing off her body, he'd want her back. But he wouldn't have been stupid enough to let her go in the first place. Maybe he'd ask her out, now that she was unattached. It wasn't like he and Erin had anything really going yet. Just one dinner. And he'd be doing Lillian a favor. He could be her transition away from the butthole.

"You really think it would work?"

Look at her, how hopeful. Nah, even if he could start something up with her, it wouldn't be worth it. When she fell, she obviously fell hard, and that meant drama. His plan was for summer fun, and it seemed like that was what Erin was in the mood for. She was going back to Champlain College in Vermont, and he was heading back to Jersey to get his last few credits done. Neither of them was looking for long-term.

"It works for a lot of people. There's other stuff you can do, but that can wait. For now, no contact."

"No contact. I can do that."

Look at that eager face. She'd be lucky if she made it thirty minutes, forget about thirty days. "You're coming out with me tonight. Me, Annie, and Nick," he added quickly. "It's bottomless nacho night at Banana's place."

"I'm going to be exhausted by the end of the day. I already am."

"Not too exhausted to send a text. You need protection from yourself. For starters, hand over the phone." She did, reluctantly, and Gavin deleted the selfies—definitely sexy. "You want him back, you do what I say. Be at Banana's at seven, and I'll make sure you don't blow the no-contact rule the same day you start it."

"Okay." She nodded. "I will." She nodded again. He could tell she was trying to convince herself that she really needed to break off contact.

"Good."

Lillian's calves, and thighs, and butt protested as she walked down the boardinghouse staircase. She hadn't felt sore right after that morning's workout, but now—ouch. Means it's working, she told herself. The transformation has begun. That last rep of planks, her whole body had been shaking. The whole time, she kept imagining Owen's reaction to the soon-to-be new her. He wouldn't believe how great she'd done today.

Except he wouldn't know, since she'd agreed to Gavin's no-contact rule. Thirty days seemed like so long. She paused, hand on the polished bannister. Checking on Owen with the tracker, which was still installed on her phone, wouldn't be getting in contact. Owen would never know, so that was still following the rules. She pulled her cell out of her bag and took a quick peek. He was getting close to Avery Memorial Campsite, right on schedule.

How could he do that? How could he just go on with his plans with no hesitation? They had been together nearly three years. They'd talked about marriage, well, almost. Even though the breakup had been his idea, didn't all that time together mean anything to him? She looked at the tracker again. He was actually a few miles ahead of schedule. If their breakup hurt him, even a little, it didn't show in the progress he was making.

Well, she was making progress too. Her aching muscles proved that. She continued down the stairs. Maybe at some point, Owen would want to talk to her, maybe even want to make sure she was okay. He had to still care about her, at least a little. And if he called her, that wasn't her making contact, so that meant—

A high, long wail pulled Lillian away from her thoughts. She raced toward the sound and found Miss Violet sitting in the middle of the kitchen floor, head in hands, shoulders shaking with sobs. "What's wrong?" Lillian sat down next to her. "Did you fall?"

"I've l-l-lost . . ." Miss Violet got out between sobs.

"Lost what? I'm great at finding things. What am I looking for?" Although this had to be something much worse than a set of missing keys.

"I-I-I've lost m-m-my muse."

"Your muse?" It took Lillian a second to understand what Miss Violet was talking about. "You're having trouble with the play."

Miss Violet hiccupped three times, then reached up and grabbed a tea towel from the counter and used it to blow her nose. "I'm not having trouble with it, because it doesn't exist! I have nothing. And auditions are this weekend! I'm doomed."

"Maybe you need a little distraction, a little break. I'm going over to The Wit's Beginning. Why don't you come with me?"

"Dudes! What's all this?"

Lillian looked over her shoulder and saw Simon standing in the doorway. "Miss Violet is struggling to write the play that she puts on every summer."

He sat down on the floor with them. "I know how bad that feels."

"You're an accountant. You can't possibly know the anguish of creative despair." Miss Violet clasped his hand, then she seemed to realize what she'd done and thrust it away, with a muttered "damnable hikers." She nodded at him. "But I do appreciate your sympathy. Writing is who I am. Without it, I'm a husk. My life will be dry and mundane from this moment forward."

"Miss Violet, please stop." Lillian could almost see the rats surrounding the woman. "You can't let all those negative thoughts take you over." She hesitated, wondering if her method for dealing with the ratty thoughts would seem ridiculous, but she had to help Miss Violet if she could. "Here's what I do when my bad thoughts are taking me over. I imagine the thoughts as rats, nasty ones with red eyes and sharp yellow teeth. Then I imagine myself with a sparkling wand, and I use it to turn the rats into beautiful horses, and then the horses gallop away across a meadow."

Simon rose to his knees, picked up a silver serving spoon from the table, and handed it to Miss Violet. "You could pretend this is your wand."

"Desperate times and all that," Miss Violet said. She squeezed her eyes shut and waved the spoon in the air.

"Is it helping?" Simon asked.

"I do feel a soupçon better. At least I believe I can get up off the floor." Lillian stood and gave Miss Violet a hand up. "You go on to Wit's and have a good time."

"I don't mind staying." Lillian really didn't feel like a night out. She was only going to the pub because Gavin had insisted.

"I'm in for the night," Simon told her. "Maybe Miss Violet will join me in a game of heads-up poker. Or gin rummy. Or, maybe something else."

"I adore poker. I'll get the pretzels. We can use them for chips."

"Have fun." Lillian took the short walk to the pub. She took one last look at the tracker—Owen was still going—then stepped inside. Gavin spotted her immediately and waved her over to the booth in the back where he sat with Nick and Annie. She'd met them both at Boots. Annie taught classes, and Nick had given a welcome talk in which he outlined everything they'd be doing during the six-week Boots Camp.

"You came! Wasn't sure you would." Gavin slid over, and Lillian sat down next to him.

"I said I'd come."

"You always a woman of your word?" He raised an eyebrow as he looked at her, and Lillian got the subtext—was she keeping her word about the no-contact rule? It had only been a few hours. Didn't he think she'd have been able to hold out that long? Yes, she'd checked the tracker, but that was simply observation.

"Yes, Gavin, I am a woman of my word." She forced herself to look directly into his hazel eyes as she spoke, finding it a little hard, even though she wasn't fibbing. The tracker absolutely was not contact.

"Good girl."

"What did I just hear you say?" Annie demanded.

"Uh . . ." Gavin looked over at Nick. "Help me out here."

"I believe my lovely companion objects to the word 'girl' being used on an adult."

"I didn't mean anything by it. It's kind of affectionate. I—"

"Making it worse," Nick said.

"O-kay." Gavin looked from Annie to Lillian. "Good woman?"

"Marginally better, although I don't see a reason for you to be judging her as good or not good at all."

"It's okay. He didn't mean—"

Annie cut Lillian off. "It's not okay. I don't want to hear that paternalistic bull from anyone who works at Boots."

Nick flexed a bicep and gave a grunt. "*Harrh.*" He smiled at Lillian. "That's a thing Annie does to show how little she needs men. She got it from her mother."

"I was raised by a single mom. She wanted to be sure I knew she didn't need a man for anything." Annie leaned in to Nick. "They may be exceedingly nice to have around, but they aren't necessary."

"It was so the opposite for me. My mom was on her own, too, but she hardly had any time between boyfriends. If some one broke up with her, she'd get almost panicky, and start going out every night to meet someone new. Maybe that's why I . . ." Lillian shook her head. This was not the time or place to start analyzing her issues with men. She barely knew any of them.

"It actually turned out that Annie's mom had a long-term relationship going," Nick said.

"But she would have been fine if she hadn't." Annie did the flex and "*harrh.*"

"Fine, yes, but you have to admit that Shoo Fly has brought a lot of joy into her life. Just as I have brought joy into yours."

Annie rolled her eyes, then wrapped her arms around his neck and kissed him. Lillian felt a sharp jab of pain. She didn't have anyone to kiss anymore. No one to talk about her day with. No one to laugh with. She slipped her hand into her bag and wrapped her fingers around her cell, feeling an overpowering need just to see the little dot that was Owen.

Owen. She couldn't seem to go more than a few minutes without thinking about him. If she could just get a redo of that night in the inn. She knew he had been exhausted. She should have just canceled the reservation, ordered room service, then put him straight back to bed. After just a few hours of exercise that morning, she was aching. She couldn't imagine how he must have been feeling that night. No wonder he—

Gavin nudged her. "Drink?" He angled his chin toward the server who was waiting for her to order.

Lillian pulled in a breath and released her grip on her phone. She'd been holding it so tightly that her fingers cramped. She flexed them a few times. "I'll have a beer."

"Asking for a beer at Banana's is like asking for a piece of chocolate at Willy Wonka's. You have a spectacular array to choose from, all handcrafted," the server, whose nametag read "Erin," told her.

She had no idea what to order. She knew nothing about beer. Owen was the connoisseur, and, when they went out, he always chose one he knew she'd like. The thought brought tears to her eyes. She quickly blinked a few times, hoping no one had noticed. "Do you have a suggestion?" she asked.

"Sure. I'm great at this. I'm like a beer matchmaker. For you . . ." Erin studied Lillian for a moment. "I'd say a Berry Manilow. That's 'berry' as in picked a berry off the bush. Banana names all his concoctions, so don't blame me. It's a pale ale, creamy, really low bitter, with nice berry and citrus notes."

"Perfect."

"On me."

"Oh, no. You don't have to."

"On me," Erin repeated. And Lillian got it. Erin knew. She must have been at the restaurant, or heard the story from someone. Shame flooded Lillian. What must Erin be thinking after seeing how disgusting Owen found Lillian? She struggled to keep a pleasant expression on her face.

"Same again for everybody else?" When Erin got nods from the rest of the group, she headed back to the bar.

"You both know too, don't you?" Lillian asked Nick and Annie.

Nick glanced away, but Annie met Lillian's eyes. "Yes."

Lillian felt her stomach shrivel into a ball. "I feel so stupid."

"He's the one who showed his butt, not you." Annie must have seen Lillian's confusion. "It's a Honey expression. It means he was the one who behaved badly. He did you a favor. You would have figured out who he really was eventually. This way, you get to move on faster."

"He's never done anything like that before."

"Well, it wouldn't have been the last time."

"Annie, can be . . . direct. She means well," Nick said.

"I don't need you to be my interpreter," Annie shot back. "But he's right. I was actually trying to be comforting. You deserve better, is what I was trying to say."

"So much better." Erin had returned with the drinks just in time to hear Annie.

Annie and Erin didn't know Owen though. They didn't know how he'd made her feel safe and wanted, in a way no other man had.

Lillian's fingers slipped into her bag again, wrapping around her phone. If you want him back, you have to follow the rule, she told herself. Gavin knows a lot more about how a guy thinks than you do. She slid her hand free. Thirty days. She just had to get through thirty days.

Erin handed out the drinks. When she set down Gavin's glass, he caught her lightly by the wrist. "I know you deserve better than me, but do you think I could take you out again?"

"Make me an offer and I'll consider it." Erin sauntered off without waiting for him to reply.

Now, she definitely wasn't a doormat. And look at Gavin, grinning as he watched her walk away. He obviously liked her attitude. Annie clearly wasn't someone who struggled to make decisions either. Hand her a menu, and Lillian was sure she'd order whatever she wanted without a thought about Gavin. And look at Nick—he obviously adored Annie.

Lillian needed to be more like those two women. And she would be. In thirty days, she'd be more than halfway through Boots Camp. When she was finally allowed to get in touch with Owen, she'd be his perfect woman.

CHAPTER 8

The Fox had thought to spend a few moments soaking in the warmth of the cord between the two humans she had observed once before. The cord still held the heat, but the humans stank. The odor was similar to that of the green liquid left behind by a frightened possum. She turned and trotted away.

Damn fox, Gavin thought. Show yourself!

When he'd come up with the idea for these fox walks, he thought they'd just be a nice little money-maker, and that, fox or no, everybody would have a good time. Maybe that was true for most of the people in his group today. But Ford and Stephanie were back, and the desperation coming off the two of them was almost strong enough to knock him over. Simon was back too. He acted like all he was interested in was a little light conditioning for his knee, but every question he asked was about The Fox, and every time Gavin looked at him, which was pretty often because he wanted to make sure the guy hadn't fainted on him, Simon had a hungry look on his face.

He heard a low *ooh-aah* sound, and held up one hand to get everyone to stop. "Fox?" Stephanie whisper-shouted. Gavin had been working on getting her to keep the volume down, because yelling "fox" would make any fox in the vicinity hightail it out of there.

"No," he said softly. "But something you'll all want to see." He pressed his finger to his lips, then led the group forward. They rounded a curve in the trail, and, yeah, there it was, a bull moose. Gavin had recognized the sound a bull made to call a lonely cow.

"Dude." Simon's voice was low, and there was a little wonder there. Gavin got that. The moose stood at almost seven feet, and had to weigh close to 1,500 pounds, with a massive set of antlers, an impressive sight. But wonder or no, Gavin knew that a moose sighting wasn't what Simon wanted. People over in Guilford were paying good money for moose hikes and moose kayak trips. If they had been here right now, mission accomplished. But there were around 75,000 moose in Maine, and, far as Gavin knew, only one fox with a white ear, a white sock, and a black tail tip. Made it a lot harder to deliver.

The moose lowered its head to drink, and Gavin and his group continued down the trail that rimmed the lake. They'd be back at the Boots van in another ten minutes. It didn't look like it was going to happen. Not today. He felt like a snake oil salesman. He'd known from the get-go that seeing The Fox was unlikely. But he hadn't realized that some of his customers would be coming on these walks looking for a miracle. At least that's what it felt like.

He wondered if he should pull aside Stephanie, Ford, and Simon when they got back and tell them that he'd seen The Fox, and that it was cool and all, but not a life-changer. He didn't know if that would make it better or worse.

On the ride back to Boots, most of the group chattered on

about their favorite parts of the hike, but not his miracle-hunters. Still, all three of them handed over tips and told Gavin thanks, same as everybody else. Gavin felt relieved when they all started to their cars, and he could get back to the barn. Annie was behind the register. It didn't look like any of the customers needed help, so he walked over. "So, what do you think? Do you think The Fox saved Nick's life last year?"

Annie shoved her hands through her short, dark brown hair. "I know for sure that if I hadn't gotten to Nick when I did, he'd be dead. It was a really close thing. And it's true that I got out my cell to take a picture of The Fox, and then, while I still had it out, I used the tracker to check on Nick and figured out he was in trouble. Is it possible I would have checked anyway? Yes. I didn't think he was ready for the Wilderness, so I checked on him periodically. Would I have checked in time without The Fox?" She shrugged.

"I like things rational." She ran one finger over the fox sticker on the side of the register. "I'm not like one of those people who wants to see a ghost, and I'm not entirely comfortable with a world that has a magical fox in it. Who knows what else is out there then? So I tell myself what I saw is a descendant of that long-ago fox that carries some of the same mutant genes, and that the same thing might have happened if I'd had my phone out because I'd gotten a call from a friend or some guy wanting me to change insurance. Nick though, he believes. And you know Banana does."

"There are a few people who have gone on two of the fox walks who want to believe, badly. There's this couple—" Just as Gavin was about to start talking about Stephanie and Ford, Stephanie came into the barn. "I told Ford I wanted to use the bathroom."

"It's right over—"

"But that was a lie. Can I talk to you?" she asked Gavin.

"Sure." Clearly, she wanted to talk to him alone, so he led her to a corner in the back. "What's up?"

"Ford is serious about not marrying me if he doesn't see that fox. He's sure he's going to ruin my life by tainting me with his bad luck. It took everything I had to get him to agree to marry me this spring. When the church went down in that sinkhole, that was it. It took me a whole month to get him to even talk to me on the phone." She swiped at her eyes with her shirtsleeve, but he'd already seen the tears.

"I love him. He is the best man, best person, I have ever met. He always pays for the person behind him in the Starbucks drive-thru. Always. And when one of his neighbors lost her husband, he'd put grocery store gift cards in her mailbox anonymously. And it's not just money. You're broken down on the side of the road? He stops. He won't be able to fix the car, but he'll wait with you until the tow truck comes. You need help moving? There. You need someone to kill a spider? There. Except he won't kill it, he'll take it outside, but far enough away that you won't worry it will creep back in. Because he is just the best guy."

Gavin nodded. "From what you're sayin', can't think of a better one." What was he supposed to do here? He couldn't make The Fox appear. There was no pattern to the places it had been seen. "I feel bad—"

"No. It's not your fault. Listen—there is something you can do for me, though. You might not like the idea. I don't like the idea. But I'm desperate."

He listened, then, god help him, he agreed to what she'd asked. He was still shaking his head after she'd walked out of the barn.

"What was that?" Annie asked.

He hadn't even noticed her coming toward him. He glanced

at the register. Nick had it. "I was only spotting him while he was in the bathroom. I'm not welcome as part of the Boots sales force, which is fine by me. The classes are great. I hated it when I was running Hatherley's and I'd have to sell people stuff I knew they'd use to go out on the trail when they weren't ready and probably end up hurting themselves. Now I get to teach first aid, and get people in shape, so they are as prepared as possible. So much better. Now what was that?"

"That was someone who believes our fox is her last hope."

Annie shook her head. "Even if there is a fox that brings luck, most people are never going to see it. People have to take charge of their own lives."

"Actually, I think that's what she's planning." Whether her plan would work or not, Gavin wasn't sure.

"I'm going to head out. I want to check out the bike route for Tuesday." The Booters could use a little cardio cross-training.

"How's Lillian holding up? I decided to take Banana's yoga class, and I could tell she was hurting."

"She's hanging in there. I've had to give her modifications on some of the exercises, but she never quits." Sometimes doing reps, she'd have her eyes squeezed tightly shut, and Owen wondered if she was picturing the boyfriend, the ex-boyfriend, and if that's how she managed to keep going. They'd already had one guy drop out. "Have you ever thought of us taking on a masseuse? I bet you could keep one busy, at least part time. Wouldn't be hard to get a treatment room set up in the loft."

"Not a bad idea. There's a guy in town, Monty, with a portable table that he'll bring to the rooms of people staying at the inn. I bet we could get him to dedicate some time over here. I'll check into it."

"Great." Unlike some people Gavin had worked for, Annie and Nick were open to suggestions. He snagged one of Shoo Fly's cookies on the way out, then drove over to the bike rental place. He confirmed they were good to go for Tuesday's trip, then rented a couple bikes for him and Erin, loaded them onto the Boots van, and drove over to the old farmhouse just outside of town that Erin was sharing with six—or was it seven?—other people for the summer. She was waiting out front, looking cute in biking shorts that had a crazy mix of flowers and stripes.

"Hey." He leaned over and gave her a quick kiss when she climbed into the front seat. "I wanted to check out the Four Seasons Adventure Trail. I don't want to take the group out on the road. Too many cars during tourist season. I'm thinking around ten miles. That work?"

"I'll have no problem keeping up with you."

"The path we're taking used to be an old railway, so it has some nice long stretches."

"Who are you talking to? I'm the one who grew up here, remember? I've biked this trail easily fifty times."

Gavin laughed. "I was just practicing for the Boots trip. I like to give out a little info about the area. I was reading up on the trail last night."

"Good for you. I didn't have you pegged as the conscientious type."

Unfair. She barely knew him. "Why not?"

Erin shrugged.

"No, really. Why not?"

"I guess because you're twenty-seven and still haven't finished school."

"School takes money. I work almost full-time every semester." He didn't mention that, yeah, he'd taken a few semesters off. Anyway, it was different for her. She only needed money for fun stuff. She was doing dorm and dining card. He didn't bother pointing out that school took longer when you had to earn enough for rent and food at the same time.

"The other night you said you worked a couple shifts at the campus rathskeller, so that's what, eight hours a week?" he asked.

"Pretty much. The tips are lousy too."

Yeah, he didn't think she worked many hours, but he didn't call her on it. "That's why I try to work in town. Students are always broke."

"Banana said you were supposed to be moving here with a girl." O-kay. Gavin hadn't seen that comin'. Had Banana been trying to give Erin some kind of heads-up? He didn't have to worry. There wasn't going to be any bad breakup between Gavin and Erin. The summer would end, and they'd go their separate ways. No breakup needed.

"Is that a question?"

"Yep."

"I was, but she decided to hang with her sister this summer." That was true. Deciding might be pushing it. But Rebecca *was* at her sister's right now.

"Wait. Are you still together?"

He'd hoped Erin would let the whole thing slide. "No. We broke up."

"And then she decided to hang with her sister."

"Right. What about you? Do you have a guy waiting for you to come back to school?"

"Oh, lots, I imagine. But I'm not together with anyone." She flipped down the visor, looked in the mirror, then flipped it back up. "So why did you break up? It must have been recent, if she was supposed to come out here with you."

Gavin was definitely not going to get into an analysis of his and Rebecca's relationship. "She thought Maine would be a fun vacation, and that she could find a summer job here. Then she found a job she wanted there." Lie. "We ended up deciding to go our separate ways. We weren't that serious." Bigger lie.

He was relieved they'd made it to Dover-Foxcroft, allowing for a natural subject change. "You can park at the—" Erin began.

"Filling station on the right near the trail crossing," Gavin finished for her.

She grinned at him. "Were you a Boy Scout by any chance?"

"Not even close. But I wouldn't drive a bunch of paying customers out here without knowing where to park." He found the station, no problem, and there were a couple of empty spots. "You want anything before we head out?"

"I brought water and some snacks."

"Water. I didn't think about water." Gavin smacked his forehead, then grabbed his backpack. "Oh, right. It's in here. And some protein bars and fruit." He unloaded the bikes. "Since you're the local, why don't you take the lead?"

"I was planning to."

He still liked that sass, he thought as they started biking out of town. Wind in the face. Sun on the back. Girl in bike shorts up ahead. Life is good.

Lillian paused outside Hatherley's Outfitters, looking at the display of protein bars, jerky, and food packets. Owen would be running low on almost everything. He'd have to stop at the next town for supplies. But her research had told her the town was tiny and only had a limited selection of trail food. Her plan had been to stock up and bring fresh supplies with her when she met up with him there.

She didn't like the idea of him trying to hike on peanut butter and crumbly bread, the kind of thing he'd be able to buy in that town. He hated peanut butter. Lillian hurried into Hatherley's. She'd buy a few things and send a package to the hostel where she was sure he'd be staying. It was the only place to stay. It didn't count as contact. Not really. She wasn't going to put a note in or anything. She wouldn't even put her return address.

He'll know it's from you, though, she thought. There's no one else who would have thought to send it. Didn't matter. It was just food. It didn't mean anything. Quickly as she could, as if she were doing something shameful, she went inside, gathered up all his favorites, and, when she paid, she got the guy behind the counter to give her a box. She'd have just enough time to pop over to the post office before work. It was Sunday, but she could use the postage machine in the lobby.

Lillian made it to Vixen's with five minutes to spare. She did a quick scan of the shop. Honey was showing two ladies the hand-knit fox sweaters. KiKi was ringing another woman up. A hiker clearly straight off the trail was studying the three-foot fox in the front window. Lillian got a whiff as she passed by. Hikers who'd been out for days lost the ability to smell their own stink. Yesterday, there had been a couple who complained, loudly, about the stench coming off two hikers, and it had gotten . . . tense. Honey had managed to defuse the situation in seconds. There wasn't anyone she couldn't charm.

"I'm just going to put my bag in the back," she told KiKi on her way past.

"Wait. Can you show me how to open the drawer when I didn't make a sale? I know Honey showed me, but I can't remember."

"She gave me the wrong change." The woman was acting as if KiKi had done it just to annoy her.

"It happens." Lillian said. She stepped up next to KiKi and quickly entered the code. The drawer slid open. KiKi grabbed thirty-five cents and handed it to the woman. "I'm sorry."

"That's still not right."

"Sorry!" KiKi yelped, and gave her another dime.

The woman raised her eyebrows, with an I'm-waiting expression. "Well?"

"Is it still not right?"

"You didn't give me my package."

"I didn't? What did I do with it?" KiKi looked around wildly.

Lillian gently pulled the bag out of Kiki's hand and handed

it to the woman. "Thanks for visiting us." She waited until the woman left, then asked, "Are you okay?" KiKi was usually fast and competent on the register.

"*Kristina* is definitely not okay." Evie appeared from behind a curio cabinet, duster in hand. "She woke up before me this morning, and she never wakes up before me. I heard her talking to herself in the bathroom. She didn't eat anything for lunch, and we had pizza, which is her favorite. It's because the auditions are today. She's afraid she's going to puke."

KiKi glared at her sister. "You are being P.I.—Putridly Irritating. You're supposed to be making bags of the gummy foxes. Go."

Evie made an elaborate show of ignoring her sister and focusing all her attention on Lillian. "I want to ask you a few more questions about Mr. Reiser. I made a list." Every day Evie had had at least one question about Simon. She pulled out a notebook. "I've been gathering evidence. I observed him while he was having lunch at the BBQ yesterday, and I have also been interviewing secondary sources, like you."

"I've told you absolutely everything I know." Which wasn't much. He was one of the few people who didn't eat Miss Violet's cinnamon rolls. He liked sitting on the veranda in one of the rockers. He'd gone on a few of the fox walks. He'd started playing cards with Miss Violet every night. That was pretty much it. Not that she would have told Evie anything that was truly personal.

"Evie. Go. Now." KiKi's voice was low, but Lillian was sure she wanted to scream. Evie huffed and slowly headed toward the back. Kiki looked at Lillian. "Do you have any sisters?"

"I'm an only. But sometimes my mom felt like a big sister. We'd paint each other's nails, try out new hairstyles. When she came home from a date, she'd wake me up and tell me all about it. My parents got divorced when I was little. That's why she was going out on dates."

"All Evie wants to do is keep me under surveillance, since she doesn't have any actual P.I. jobs. Obviously. Like today. What was she doing? Standing with her ear pressed against the bathroom door? I can't even have privacy in the bathroom!"

"Was she right about you being stressed over the auditions?"

KiKi let out a long, shaky sigh. "It's making me crazy. That's the third time I've messed up on the register today. What do you think I'll have to do?"

"I think usually you'd have to read a scene from the play, but I don't think Miss Violet has any scenes finished." Lillian thought Miss Violet was at least as anxious about the auditions as KiKi was.

"I don't know if I can do it. Evie's right. I might puke."

"What about doing something backstage? Maybe working on costumes or sets?"

"You don't think I can do it."

Lillian realized she'd said exactly the wrong thing. KiKi had needed a confidence boost, not someone basically saying she was right to be afraid. "That's not true. I was being protective of you. I saw how anxious you were, and I didn't want you to be feeling that way. I was wrong. Avoiding something you're anxious about isn't a good solution. I'm bad about doing that myself."

"You are?"

"Uh-huh. Like last night, I almost went out to dinner alone, but I started feeling super anxious. I have this thing about eating in a restaurant by myself. But instead of pushing through it and doing it anyway, I grabbed a frozen dinner at the Mercantile and ate in the boardinghouse kitchen."

Had she said too much? She hadn't meant to make it about her. KiKi didn't need to know about her issues. Lillian didn't want to be like her mom, who had overshared on a regular basis when Lillian was a kid. "You know what? I'm going to do it tonight. Maybe I'll be anxious the whole time, but if I do it enough, I'll get used to it. I'm missing out on too much fun by staying home if I don't have someone to go out with." There. Maybe her oversharing could turn into motivation.

"The auditions are any time between now and seven. Honey said it was okay to go once you got here."

Lillian just nodded. She'd pushed enough.

"I could go and see what it's like."

Lillian nodded again.

"So, I guess I'll go. Will you tell Honey that's where I am?"

"Sure. See you in a bit." Lillian realized she was still holding her purse. She headed to the back room where Evie sat at the worktable, listening to music on KiKi's phone and making up bags of gummy foxes.

"I know why Kristina wants to be in that play, even though it makes her feel like puking." Evie tied one of the bags closed with a piece of orange-and-white dotted ribbon, then straightened one of her barrettes. "And why she suddenly wants to be called KiKi and dyed her hair."

Lillian hung her purse up on one of the wall hooks. "Those bags look great, Evie." She wasn't going to encourage the little girl by asking questions.

"Look." Evie scrambled up from her chair and held the phone out in front of Lillian. "See that girl. See her hair?" The girl had almost the exact haircut that KiKi had gotten. Her hair was dyed in shades of blue, in a way similar to the red, orange, and gold of KiKi's. "And her name is GiGi. *And* she's in the drama club at KiKi's school. KiKi's trying to turn into her."

It certainly looked that way. Lillian remembered buying a top because it was almost exactly like one she'd seen Tiffani Amber Thiessen wearing in *Teen* magazine. What KiKi was doing was a little more extreme than that, but it was the same kind of thing. "I think Kristina's—KiKi's—hair is cute. I need to get out front."

"But this girl, GiGi, she was really mean to Kristina. She and these other girls made fun of her all the time. Kristina started hating to go to school."

"I'm sorry to hear that anyone was mean to your sister." There had to be some deep pain there. Lillian hated thinking of KiKi's turning herself into a girl who'd hurt her, but it wasn't something she was going to talk about with Evie. Or with KiKi, unless KiKi brought it up. Lillian returned to the front of the shop and refilled the oil in all three diffusers. They put out a warm, woodsy scent that made it feel like you were in a place a fox might like. They also combated, to some degree, the hiker funk. She helped a man choose a pair of earrings for his girlfriend. Helped a little girl decide between a fox-in-the-box and a stuffed fox. Told an abbreviated version of The Fox legend three times. She loved doing that. She rang up eight customers. Finally, when the fox bells jangled, it was KiKi coming back.

Lillian checked her face, trying not to be obvious about it. KiKi wasn't smiling, but she didn't look shaken or disappointed. "How'd it go?" Lillian had wanted to sound interested, not concerned, and she thought she'd pulled it off.

"It was scary, but okay. Miss Violet read a scene with me, not from her play; she said she has to finish it up." And start it, Lillian thought. "I kept focused on her, and tried to forget anyone was watching. She's really dramatic, so that helped."

"What happens next?"

"She said that she's going to give everyone who auditioned a part, even if it's a little one. We're all supposed to be at the Palace of Performing Arts—she calls the theater POPA, like how they call the Museum of Modern Art MOMA—at six thirty on Wednesday."

"Were there any other kids your age auditioning? Am I asking too many questions?"

KiKi pushed her bangs out of her eyes. "It's okay. There were a few." She smiled in a way that made Lillian think there might be one particular person who had caught KiKi's eye. "I want to go tell Honey. And Evie, I guess, unless she's bugged the place and already knows." KiKi started toward the shelf where Honey was restocking fox socks, then turned back. "Are you still going to go out to dinner by yourself?"

"Definitely. You're my inspiration."

Which was why that evening she stood in front of Amore, studying the sign, which had two foxes sharing spaghetti à la *Lady and the Tramp*, trying to force herself to walk inside. KiKi's going to ask you about it next time you work together, she told herself. Are you really going to tell her you chickened out?

No. She decided she'd just pretend that Owen was with her. Thinking of Owen was getting her through Boots Camp. When she didn't think she could do one more rep—like when Annie had them do rows using their backpacks as weights—she would picture herself striding down the trail, all wild and adventurous and in fabulous shape, and running into Owen. She imagined the expression on his face when he'd see her, full of admiration and wonder and desire.

Tonight, she'd imagine that she'd already been reunited with Owen, and he'd asked her out to dinner here, at Amore. With that decided, she opened the door and walked inside, picturing Owen holding her hand.

CHAPTER 9

Gavin biked across the bridge, enjoying the bump-bump as he rode over the wooden planks, then it was back to the gravel path running between what was almost a tunnel of trees. Getting paid for this? Ridiculous. He should be paying Nick and Annie.

He rounded a curve and saw a horse and rider coming toward him. He slowed his speed and gave them a wide berth. The trail was getting a lot of use today. He'd already seen three ATVs and lots of people out for hikes. The tree tunnel opened up to farmland, and he could see the spire of the Dover-Foxcroft Congregational Church. He led his convoy of Booters into town and over to Dottie's.

"The great thing about Boots Camp," Gavin called when everyone in the group had come to a stop, "is you burn massive amounts of calories, which means you need massive amounts of fuel. Have at it. I'll stand watch over the bikes." He flung one arm toward the bakery. "Don't miss the whoopie pies. The town has a whoopie festival every year, and the ones at this place shouldn't be missed," he added as the group headed past him.

Lillian returned about ten minutes later with two iced teas and two of the whoopies. "I got chocolate. I hope that's okay. I could go in and trade yours if you'd rather have pumpkin or—"

"Anything but chocolate is practically sacrilegious. Thanks, Twinkle." She really was a sweetie. For probably the hundredth time, he wondered why any man would break up with a woman like her. "You know the story about how these got their name?"

She shook her head. He'd just discovered the story when he was doing his due diligence for today's outing. "It's supposedly Amish women who invented them. They didn't like wasting cake batter, so they'd make little mounds with whatever was leftover and bake them, then cut them in half and stick 'em together with frosting. Supposedly, when one of the Amish farmers would find one in his lunch box, he'd shout, 'whoopie.' "

Lillian laughed, that husky laugh, then took a bite. "Whoopie!"

"Now, I can't be mad at you, since you just brought me this." He held up his whoopie. "But you told me you were a woman of your word and—"

She didn't let him finish. "I didn't put in a note. I didn't say who it was from."

"Yeah, but you knew exactly what I was talkin' about, now didn't you?"

"How did you even find out?"

"You know Hatherley's is owned by Annie and her family, don't you?"

"I didn't really think about it."

"We needed a couple more hydration packs at the Boots Barn, and Hatherley's had extra, so I stopped by to pick them up. Jason, the kid who works behind the counter, asked if we needed any protein bars, jerky, that kind of stuff. I told him no, and he said he thought we might, because one of the Booters was in there buying food. I asked him for a description, although I was already pretty sure it was you. You're going to need to restart your thirty days of no-contact."

"I was passing the store, and thinking that the little town Owen will be stopping in next hardly has any variety of trail food. He'd been planning on my bringing him supplies. I didn't want him to go without. You don't expect me not to care about him, do you? Because that's not possible."

Gavin pulled the bandana off his head and wiped his face with it. "I don't get why you want him back. I just don't get it. Not after the way I saw him treat you that night."

"I told you—"

"That he's not usually like that," Gavin finished for her. "Tell me this. Has he apologized?"

"He's out on the trail."

"And he's probably had cell service some of the time. Also, it has been more than a week. He's come off the trail someplace by now. He could have called or, hell, shot you a text."

"You know how exhausted—"

"Don't even. If he's a decent guy, like you say, he wouldn't treat you that way, and then say nothing."

"Not usually. He's never acted the way he is right now. I don't understand it, and I need to understand it. I'm not willing to abandon everything we had."

Unless the guy had a tumor pressing on his brain, Gavin didn't think there was any acceptable explanation. But he could tell nothing he said was going to change her mind. "Okay, well, like I said, you want him back, the big thing is the no-contact rule. Your new thirty starts now, and it includes any kind of contact, including care packages with no notes. And we're going to add in something new."

"What?" Lillian started anxiously nibbling on her iced tea's plastic straw, drawing Gavin's attention to her mouth. He forced his eyes away. She was trying to get some other guy back. He had his summer thing going with Erin. And even if neither of those things were true, Gavin wasn't ready for any kind of serious thing. No moving in with someone, nothing like that. He was keepin' everything casual for a good long while. And, even though he'd only known Lillian a little while, he knew her well enough to know she didn't do casual.

"I'll pick you up at Miss Violet's tonight after dinner, say eight."

"But what about Erin?"

"Erin's working tonight." He was pretty sure she'd said she was working tonight, and, anyway, they didn't have to get together every time one of them had some free time. "Be ready. Wear something pretty."

Lillian felt a flutter of anticipation in her belly. What exactly did Gavin have planned for tonight? Why was she supposed to wear something pretty? Was this pretty? She had on a pencil skirt covered with frolicking foxes. Honey had given it to her, because she liked everyone to wear things sold at the store. Lillian had told Honey that she thought pencil skirts made her look hip-y, something Owen had mentioned once, but Honey had said that hips were good, and that Lillian had an hourglass figure and that it was borderline criminal not to show it off.

Lillian studied herself in the cheval mirror. She still wasn't sure. . . . But it was three minutes to eight, so she grabbed her clutch and headed downstairs. Gavin was already in the foyer, obviously flirting with Miss Violet. She couldn't hear what he was saying, but Miss Violet was giggling. Giggling was the only word for it. It was the first time Lillian had heard her laugh in days. She was still struggling with the play, and the first rehearsal was only one night away.

"I was just tellin' Miss Violet here, that all she has to do is put her and me up on stage, and no one will care what we're saying. They'll just be dazzled by the sight of us."

"I agree." Gavin was sweet, taking time to give Miss Violet a boost. He was like that at Boots too. When she thought she couldn't do one more of any of the many torturous things Boots entailed, he'd be there, making her laugh or giving her inspiration. And not just her. Everybody.

Lillian held out her arms wide. "Am I acceptable?"

"What kind of greeting is that?" Miss Violet exclaimed.

"You're perfect." He turned to Miss Violet. "I'm taking Lillian out so she can meet some men."

Something between a gasp of horror and a squeak of terror escaped Lillian's lips. If he'd told her what he'd had planned, she never would have agreed. Which was exactly why he hadn't told her. She could tell by that smirk on his face.

"A wonderful plan." Miss Violet's wide smile faded. "And now I must hie myself off to my computer." She turned and walked out of the room. The first few days Lillian had been at the boardinghouse, she'd never seen Miss Violet simply turn and walk. She'd always been whirling, striding, twirling, prancing, and the like. Lillian hoped she'd make some progress with the writing, so she could get back to her old self.

"I don't know how you think I can make Owen jealous, if you won't even let me post pictures on Instagram. And even if you did let me, I'm a kindergarten teacher. I don't post pictures of myself out with men."

"This isn't about Owen. It's about you."

"I don't want to meet anybody new. You know that."

"It's not about that either. It's about you having more confidence. You need to get it into your head that you are a woman lots of men would be interested in."

"I don't think that I'm . . ." What? She tried again. "I don't think that I'm unattractive to men."

"You don't think that you're unattractive to men? What was I thinkin'? You have enough confidence for two or three women." He walked to the door and held it open for her. "Let's go."

A car packed with teenagers drove past, stereo blaring. Lillian wished KiKi had a group of friends here to go out with. KiKi was the one who needed a confidence boost.

"Are you okay?"

"I'm still not sure—" Lillian realized that Gavin wasn't talking to her. He was looking over at Simon, who was leaning forward in one of the rockers, head between his knees. His shoulders were heaving, and his breaths were coming out in wheezes.

"I'm okay," Simon answered, without straightening up.

"Like hell you are." Gavin crouched down next to him.

"I'll go get some water." Lillian rushed into the kitchen, filled a tumbler, then hurried back out. Simon looked much better. He was upright and had even started slowly rocking.

"No way is that low blood sugar," Gavin was saying.

"I never said it was."

"You did the night you had one of these spells at the bar."

"Dude, it's low blood pressure, not sugar. A medication I'm on makes it drop sometimes, but it's not serious. I'm fine. Go on. Have fun."

Lillian handed Simon the water. "We're happy to stay out here with you for a while. I love this veranda. I could sit out here all night."

"I bet you could," Gavin muttered, low enough that only she could hear him.

"Go on. Go have fun."

"Call Miss Violet if you start feeling bad again," Lillian told Simon, and he nodded.

Gavin started toward his car. "We're not walking?"

"Didn't think you'd be up for walking to Greenville after a

day at Boots, but if you're up to it, we could. It's only fourteen miles, give or take." He opened the door of the Porsche, and she got inside.

"Why are we going to Greenville?" she asked as he pulled out onto the street.

"I figured you'd be more comfortable picking up guys if you weren't surrounded by people you know."

"I'm not picking up guys."

"Okay, not picking up. I'm not expecting you to take somebody home. You're just going to do a little flirting, and buy at least one man a drink."

"I don't flirt. I can't."

"You mean you don't want to."

"No, I mean I can't. When I try . . ." She let her words trail off. She couldn't talk to him about this.

"When you try—" he prompted.

He wasn't going to let it go. "I just feel silly." But it was so much more than that, so much worse. She felt excruciatingly self-conscious, and everything she said and did felt stupid and wrong. Then, of course, the ratty thoughts came for her, telling her the guy thought she was pathetic.

"You're just out of practice, because you were part of a couple for—what was it?"

"Almost three years."

"That's what I'm talking about. You're a little out of practice."

"Gavin, stop. I'm not doing it. Let's just go back to town." Her voice came out shrill and shaky.

He pulled over onto the shoulder of the road and turned off the car. The branches of the pine grew so low they brushed the windshield, but they still let in the light of the setting sun. She wished they didn't. She didn't want him to look at her. He must think she was crazy, getting so upset over nothing. Because it was nothing. Women flirted all the time. "Sorry I overreacted."

"No, I'm sorry I kept pushing you. You said you didn't want to. That should have been that."

"It's not that I'm out of practice. I've never felt comfortable flirting. Before Owen, I had a billion coffee dates that went nowhere, because I was always so stiff and awkward."

"You're not stiff and awkward around me."

True. From the beginning, she'd been at ease around him. "Because there's no possibility of anything romantic between us. You know I want to get back with Owen. And I know you're already going out with someone."

"So, maybe you should practice flirting with me. Then you can move on to other guys. But only if you want to. No pushing here."

"Why do I have to do this again? I don't see how it helps me get Owen back."

Gavin scrubbed his face with his fingers. "Think of it like a negotiation. Like you're trying to, say, buy a car. You don't tell the guy selling the car that it's the perfect car and you'll do absolutely anything to get it. That's the way to get taken advantage of. You want to give the impression that this car is one of many you're looking at, and that you're not even close to making up your mind. That's when you get a great deal."

"So, I want Owen to think he's not the only car I want."

"Exactly. And to do that, you've got to walk the walk. You've got to know in your gut that you can have your pick of cars. That's why I thought you should do some flirting, to pump up your confidence. Cause, Twinkle, I get the feeling that you feel lucky this Owen guy decided he wanted to be with you, when he's the lucky one."

She did feel lucky, so lucky. "I told you. I met so many guys. They weren't interested. Or they were interested for a couple dates, then they disappeared."

"Guys are jerks. They want to think everyone wants the woman they're with. It's all about ego. And for some reason, you aren't putting out the vibe that you know what you're worth and you expect whoever you're with to know it too."

"And that's about flirting?"

"When you flirt, you're putting yourself out there. That takes confidence. You don't put yourself out there if you feel like no one is going to be interested."

"You know who is great at flirting? My mother," Lillian told him. But was her mother really confident? She pretended she was. She always acted like she was better than any other woman in the room. But at home, Lillian had watched her obsess about the lines around her mouth or an extra five pounds. Sometimes it felt like just by being younger, Lillian made her mother feel bad. "But she's had a lot of bad breakups."

"If being good at flirting equaled being good at relationships, then I wouldn't have rolled into town by myself this summer. My girlfriend, my ex, was supposed to come with me, but the whole thing blew up on the day we were supposed to leave."

"You broke up with her?"

"She broke up with me."

"I'm sorry."

"Don't be. It wasn't working. We were always fighting, mostly about stupid stuff. Even if we'd made it through the summer, it wasn't going to last."

"Are you really that okay with it? How long were you together?"

"Just about a year."

"Don't you feel like—Isn't there a hole left?"

"You know what, there probably should be. But I haven't even been thinking about her much. Like I said, things weren't great between us. She thought I was always doing things to push her away."

"Were you?"

He didn't answer for a long moment, then finally said,

"Maybe." He raked his hair through his fingers. "There were some things I did that I knew bugged her, but I didn't think they were that big of a deal. Maybe I should have realized that to her, they were that big of a deal."

"Oh."

"You can say it. I'm a . . . son of a motherless goat."

"Maybe now that you're aware of it, it will be different. Like with Erin."

"Maybe." He turned toward Lillian. "Tell me that my shirt makes my eyes look so green."

"What?" Where had that come from?

"Just tell me."

"Your shirt—"

"Wait. Look me in the eye when you say it."

Lillian raised her gaze to his, and she got a little *bam*. He was, as Miss Violet had said, s e x y. He probably gave lots of women little *bams*, meaningless little *bams*. "Your shirt makes your eyes look really green."

"Now give a little smile."

She smiled.

"There. That's your flirting practice for the night. Let's go get ice cream."

CHAPTER 10

When The Fox closed her eyes, she could feel the radiance from the moon and stars brush against her fur. When she was younger, she hadn't been able to feel the light touch, but as the years passed, her connections grew stronger.

A human, a female, moved through the forest, her steps so loud that for a moment, The Fox's communion with the night sky was broken. The woman let out a long, high cry that sounded almost like the ones The Fox's kin gave to let the males know they were ready to mate.

The sound came again, and The Fox felt drawn to respond. She stepped into the moonlight, looked at the woman, then tilted her head back and let out her own cry.

"Hey, KiKi." Gavin took a seat next to Annie's cousin in the last row of the town's little theater. He'd met KiKi the other night when he'd seen her and her little sis at a concert in the town square with Nick and Annie. It had come out that KiKi was going to be in the play too. Later, Annie had told him KiKi was a little nervous about the whole thing, as in nervous enough about being onstage that she'd puked when she was performing in a Christmas pageant. He'd promised to look out for her. "I thought I was going to be late."

"You are, a little. But Miss Violet isn't here yet. The guy who works in the barber shop next door unlocked the theater for us." KiKi brushed the bangs off her forehead. She was rocking the multicolored hair.

Gavin propped one foot up on the seat in front of him and surveyed the room. Most of the under twenties were sitting on one corner of the stage. "Looks like it might be more fun for you over there." He tilted his head toward the kids. "Not that I'm not great company, but I'm old, and we both know it."

KiKi didn't bother denying it. She let out a sigh, then stood up and straightened her shoulders, like she was preparing for battle. "If you don't like any of them, come back." She nodded, and walked straight down the aisle, and swung herself up on the stage. A guy around her age smiled at her. A girl around her age, with long brown hair down almost to her waist, looked from the guy to KiKi and back and then gave KiKi a little bit of a side-eye, but a couple of the other girls seemed to be welcoming her to the group. Cool.

He wondered what Twinkle had been like at that age. Would she have gone for it, the way KiKi just did, or hung back? Probably she wouldn't have been here at all. He bet she'd have been off by herself, reading a book. He remembered her telling him about that crush she'd had in what—seventh grade? eighth grade?—and how she would have freaked out if he'd actually spoken to her. And even now, at somewhere around his age, she couldn't handle the idea of doing a little flirting, when he knew for damn sure most men would want a woman who looked like her to pay them some attention. If—

Miss Violet burst through the set of double doors closest to him. What had she been doing? She had a smear of dirt on her face, and more on her purple-flowered skirt. There was even dirt in her hair, some twigs too. She climbed the four stairs up to the stage, positioned herself dead center stage, and flung out her arms. "Everyone, go home! There will be no play this year."

That got some confused mutterings going. Gavin got up. "What's going on, Miss V?" he called as he started toward her.

"Last night, there was a full moon, and I took myself out to the woods. I vowed I would not return until I saw The Fox, because only The Fox could bring me the inspiration I needed to write my play."

People in this town had to get a grip. They were giving that critter way too much power. He still couldn't believe Milford Stank wasn't going to marry a woman he obviously loved unless he saw it. And now here was Miss Violet, spending the night and most of the day in the woods, sleeping on the ground, by the looks of it, that is if she'd even slept at all, because she thought she couldn't function without the luck of The Fox.

He took the stairs two at a time and strode over to Miss Violet. He wrapped one arm around her shoulder and spoke into her ear, voice low. "Don't make any decisions right now. You need to go home, have yourself a bubble bath, a shot of, let's say, tequila, a nice dinner. You don't need to see The Fox. You have—"

She jerked away from him. "But I did see The Fox. She stood in a pool of moonlight. Beautiful, so beautiful. Then she tilted her head back and screamed. The sound gave me goose bumps. It sounded like a woman in anguish. As soon as she disappeared into the brush, I sat right down on an old log and pulled out my notebook and my favorite fountain pen, and— nothing." That last word was a shriek so high it made Gavin's ears ring. He bet The Fox and her scream had nothing on Miss Violet. "No words came. I stared at the blank page for hours, until I realized that, although I had seen The Fox, she had chosen not to gift me with her luck. Go home, one and all. I'm sorry to dash your hopes against the treacherous rocks, but I don't think I will ever write again."

One of the boys, the one who'd smiled at KiKi, jumped off the stage. He took a step toward the door. A couple of the adults stood and began gathering their stuff. "Wait!" Gavin called. "Come back here on Sunday. Three o'clock. We're not going to let this be the first summer in—how many years since Miss Violet started putting on plays?"

"Twenty-seven," Flappy, of Flappy Jacks, answered.

"Twenty-seven years. We're not going to let this year be the year that tradition ends." That got a few cheers.

"But I simply cannot—" Miss Violet began.

Gavin raised his voice, talking over her protests. "Sunday. Three o'clock."

"I'll be here," the boy answered. "Anybody want to go to the park since we're not rehearsing?" Gavin noticed that his eyes were on KiKi as he threw out the invitation.

"Me!" KiKi leaped off the stage. The girl with the long hair immediately joined them.

"This is madness! There is no play!"

"Sunday. Three o'clock." Gavin took Miss Violet's arm. "Let me walk you home. We're gonna come up with a plan."

"Even The Fox couldn't save me, and that means there is no hope in this world."

Gavin didn't bother trying to answer, focusing instead on steering Miss Violet out of the building and down the sidewalk. When they reached the huge white house, with enough massive columns for the Parthenon, he spotted Lillian and Simon sitting in rockers on the veranda.

Lillian jumped up and rushed to meet them, Simon a few steps behind, moving fast. His knee must be healing. "Miss Violet! You're back. Your note was so mysterious." Lillian looked at Gavin. "It said she was going on a quest, and that she would return only when she had been given the 'Gift of the One Who Dwells in the Forest.' "

"Also, that we should put the cinnamon rolls in the oven for fifteen minutes at three-fifty," Simon added.

"It was all for naught," Miss Violet said. "All for naught."

Gavin gave the explanation. "She spent the whole night looking for The Fox, and she actually saw it, but she still wasn't able to get any writing done on her play."

"Where did you spot it?" Simon asked.

"You were out all night?" Lillian began plucking twigs out of Miss Violet's hair.

"I should have stayed. There is no place for me in civilization if I no longer have the theater."

Gavin couldn't stop himself from giving a snort of laughter, which he tried to disguise with a cough. Miss Violet should wear a crown with all her drama queening. "Here's an idea," he said as they went inside. "How about this year you do a play that's written by somebody else? Just to give you a little break."

"No! The people expect a Violet Beauchamp original work. Anything else would be the equivalent of serving skim milk in champagne flutes."

"Dude!" Simon exclaimed.

Skim milk in champagne flutes. That was a nice turn of phrase. Miss Violet clearly still had the chops. Gavin was sure she'd get back to writing before long. He got her settled in a chair at the kitchen table, while Lillian filled up the teakettle.

Simon sat down next to Miss Violet, picked up the salt-shaker, and began turning it around and around. "There are so many legends about The Fox. I have to believe there's truth to them. Maybe your luck is still coming."

"It cannot be considered luck if I don't have it now, when my need is dire. We must begin to rehearse within days to be ready for the August premiere."

Gavin still thought his idea of doing a play by someone else was the best solution, but he knew there was no point in bringing it up again. "What about if we talk through some ideas together?"

"How about an adaptation of a fairy tale?" Lillian suggested. "There are so many wonderful ones."

Miss Violet shook her head, sending a twig Lillian had missed flying. "It must be something unique."

"Or what about using the story of The Fox? You've already written a book about her, so you'd be basing the play on something you've written." Lillian began setting mugs on the table. "Maybe that's your luck. Maybe instead of The Fox bringing you inspiration, she *is* the inspiration."

Gavin jumped in. "Tourists would love it. We started doing fox walks at Boots, where people come out with us, hoping for a look at her, and they're getting really popular."

Lillian put out a cherrywood chest filled with tea bags. "What do you think, Miss Violet?"

"There is some appeal. But it doesn't quite say Violet Beauchamp. It lacks my signature panache."

Simon put down the saltshaker he'd been toying with and selected a tea bag. He opened his mouth as if he were going to give a suggestion, then shut it.

"Do you have an idea?" Gavin asked him.

"Possibly. I've heard you singing in the mornings, Miss V. Have you ever considered writing a musical?"

Miss Violet pressed her hands to her chest. "A musical. I would adore producing a musical. And a musical about The Fox. Magical."

"See there?" Gavin said. "Trying something new is all the inspiration you need."

"Alas, I don't read or write music." She let her hands drop to her sides and lowered her head.

"I do some noodling on the piano. Maybe I could—"

Miss Violet was on her feet before Simon could finish. "I have a pianola in the parlor. Let us away."

"Dude," Simon mouthed over his shoulder to Gavin as he followed Miss Violet out of the room.

"I'd find all those emotional highs and lows exhausting, but she seems to thrive on them." The kettle squealed. Lillian grabbed it and began filling the mugs with hot water. "I can't believe she spent the night in the woods. That might be crossing the line from eccentric into dangerous."

"Doesn't seem to have hurt her." Gavin winced as Miss Violet began singing some la-la-las, her voice tremulous but loud. Very loud. Simon began adding in some chords.

"This may have broken her writer's bl—"

A crash interrupted Lillian. She and Gavin rushed to the parlor. Simon was backing away from the piano. The piano bench lay on the ground, clearly the source of the sound.

"What is it?" Miss Violet cried.

When Simon turned toward the door, Gavin saw that he was sweaty and shaky. What was going on with this guy? This wasn't low blood pressure or low blood sugar, that was for sure. "I can't do this. I thought I could, but I can't. I can't play for crap."

"Come on to the kitchen," Lillian said. "We'll sit and have our tea."

Simon nodded. When they reached the kitchen, Miss Violet went straight to one of the drawers and took out a large silver spoon. She presented it to Simon with a flourish. "Your wand."

"Wand?" Gavin asked.

Lillian returned to filling the mugs. "It's something I do. When I'm having a lot of . . . bad thoughts. I pretend the thoughts are rats, and I pretend I have a magic wand. I zing the rats with the wand, and turn them into horses, and then the horses run away. Bad thoughts gone. The other night, Miss Violet tried it, and she used the spoon as her wand."

"I don't think I'm the magic wand type," Simon told Miss Violet.

"Everyone is the magic wand type," Miss Violet decreed. "It doesn't have to be a wand. I use that because I love fairy tales. You could imagine any object you think of as powerful."

"My axe." Simon's hand was steady as he dunked a tea bag into the water. The spells he had never seemed to last for too long.

"Okay. Good. Now what thoughts were you having when you started to play?" Lillian sat down next to Simon.

"That I suck. That no one wants to hear me. That I'm delusional. That I suck. That I suck."

Lillian nodded. "Okay, now picture those thoughts as the most horrible creatures you can imagine, and swing your axe at them. Picture yourself chopping their heads off if you want to."

Simon shut his eyes, and began slashing the spoon through the air in wide arcs. Gavin leaned back to avoid getting axed.

"Is it helping?" Miss Violet asked.

Simon took a few more swings, then opened his eyes. "A little."

"Let's try again. Bring the axe."

Simon mopped his forehead with a napkin, then got up and followed Miss Violet from the room, holding his mug and spoon. Gavin studied Lillian for a moment. "What are your rats, Twinkle?"

She sighed. "Oh, so many. It doesn't matter."

"It matters."

She sighed again. "That I'm boring. That I'm always saying stupid things. That I'm not good enough, at anything."

"You don't really believe that." It was pure craziness.

"Sometimes, I do. Not always, but sometimes."

"Ah, hell. Who put that crap in your head? That guy?" Not for the first time, Gavin wished he could punch Owen in the gut.

"Owen? No! He never—Except that one night." She shrugged.

"It's always been what's in my head. I can't remember not having the rats, although there must have been a time when I didn't. It's not as if I were born with them."

Twinkle was a better person than he was by a damn long way, and he walked around feeling pretty good about himself most of the time. "Reality check. I have never found you boring. The only stupid things I've heard you say are the ones about being boring, saying stupid things, and not being good enough. And I've seen you be plenty good enough, just watching you at Boots. You've got more heart and guts than anyone out there. You go full-out, every damn day."

"Thanks." She smiled, but he could tell it was forced, and she couldn't bring herself to quite meet his eye. What had he thought, a few words from him, and she'd be over it? He wished it worked that way, but it didn't.

Once again, The Fox was unable to understand the behavior of the humans. They ran as though they were being hunted, but The Fox could sense no danger, and she would know there was something to fear long before the humans would.

They had shelter nearby. If there were a predator near, they should go there. They had let their connections to her world fade, and no longer understood what even the youngest who lived in her woods knew.

Lillian walked down the hill, gasping for breath, chest heaving. "Remember to take it slow coming down. This is your rest," Annie called, as if Lillian needed a reminder. "Okay, on three, turn and back up for thirty more seconds. Full-out effort. Leave nothing on the table. One, two, and three!"

Locking her eyes on the top of the hill, Lillian took off, pumping her arms. Go, go, go, go, she silently chanted. "And back down," Annie instructed. Lillian turned and slowly walked back down, calves burning, lungs burning, thighs burning. How many more times were they going to have to do this? In what felt like two seconds, although she knew they walked for thirty, Annie clapped her hands. "Okay, in three. Don't forget to breathe."

"Oh, that's what I was doing wrong. I've been holding my breath this whole time," Spencer muttered. Lillian laughed, then wheezed, and he flashed her a smile. At least she wasn't the only one struggling.

"One, two, and three!"

Go, go, go, go! Lillian knew she wasn't going as fast as she had been the first three rounds, but she was giving it everything she had.

"And back down."

"I'm thinking about using that cyanide capsule I have in my false tooth," Spencer told her, gasping between every word.

"I hope you brought enough for the class," Lillian gasped back. And then Annie was sending them back up the hill. It wasn't possible that was thirty seconds of walking. Was. Not. Possible.

"Stay strong and tall. Don't bend at the waist!" Annie yelled.

It was all Lillian could do to keep moving. She couldn't even tell if she was bent over or upright.

"And back down."

Please let us be done. Please, please, please. Spencer didn't speak this time. He had his head down, and she could hear him sucking in breaths. She felt like her heart was trying to bash its way through her ribcage. Please let us be done.

"Last time. One, two, and three!"

Lillian felt like her trail runners had turned to lead. It was so hard to pick up her feet. In her peripheral vision, she saw Spencer stop and heard him retching. Few seconds more, a few seconds more, go, go, go, go, GO!

"And you're done! Take a break, but don't sit down!" Annie called.

"You . . . okay?" Lillian managed to ask Spencer on their way back down the hill.

"Can you see me?" he panted. "I thought I was a ghost. I know I have to have died that last time up."

"Me too."

"No, you were amazing. You kept going." He fell into step beside her. When they reached the bottom, Lillian veered toward the spot where she'd left her backpack, giving him a wave. She pulled out her water bottle, and let some water spill on her face, before taking a long swallow. Her cell started to play "Mamma Mia." Damn. She'd been avoiding talking to her mom, sending her texts instead, but it had been too long.

"Hi, Mom."

"What have you been doing? You're panting."

"Running." Lillian still didn't have enough air for a lot of words. She sucked down some more water.

"Why?"

Excellent question. She hadn't told her mother about the Boots Camp, because that would mean telling her about the breakup, and Lillian had been afraid that would put her right back where she'd been the night it happened, barely able to function. But it had been enough time. She couldn't avoid the conversation forever. "I decided to take a course that preps people for hiking the AT, the Appalachian Trail. We've just been doing some conditioning."

"What about Owen? Aren't you meeting him every week?"

Here we go, Lillian thought, bracing herself. She knew her mother would have at least a hundred reasons why the breakup was Lillian's fault. She hesitated. No, she couldn't take her mother's reaction. Not yet. "We decided that wasn't a very fun way for me to spend the summer. And after this course,

I'll be able to go hiking with him." Her mother didn't respond. "Mom?"

"Your boyfriend decided it was a good idea to spend months apart? I hate to tell you this, but it's over."

"That's not true! We were only going to see each other a handful of times between now and the end of August. It didn't make sense."

"He's hoping it will peter out, and he won't have to tell you it's over. I've been seeing this coming. You've been together for almost three years. You'd be married by now if he truly wanted to be with you."

Lillian's heart rate started kicking up, even though she was standing still. Her mother was right. Owen had said he wanted to be with a completely different kind of woman. But that didn't matter. She was transforming. By the time they were both back home in Sylva, *she* would be a completely different kind of woman. Wild and adventurous.

"Did you hear me?"

She couldn't have this conversation. Not now. "Mom, we're about to start back up. I have to go. But don't worry. Everything's fine between Owen and me. I told you, he even asked me what kind of engagement rings I liked." She hung up before her mother could reply, and shoved the phone into her backpack, zipping the pack up even though the phone had started to ring again.

"Good work today," Annie said, stopping next to her. "HIIT training can take it out of you, but it's great for building stamina. It's like getting a high gear you can shift into."

"Thanks." Lillian's mind was still on the phone call. Had her mother really seen the breakup coming? If she had, maybe it was because she got broken up with a lot.

Annie pushed her sunglasses up on her head. "Are you feeling nauseous? Exercising this hard means more blood to your heart, lungs, and brain, which doesn't leave as much for digestion. Make sure you eat between one and three hours before working out, and—"

"I'm not nauseous. I was just talking to my mother."

"Sometimes, in my experience, the sensations can be similar."

Lillian put her hands on her hips, tilted her head back, and took in a long, slow breath, then looked over at Annie. "I love my mom."

"So do I. That doesn't mean I haven't on occasion wished I was an orphan."

"I just lied to mine, because I didn't want to listen to her tell me all the ways it was my fault that my boyfriend broke up with me," Lillian admitted. "But Gavin's working with me on a strategy to get him back, so she doesn't need to know."

Annie raised her eyebrows. "I didn't realize Gavin was in a position to be handing out relationship advice."

"It's more like he's helping me understand male psychology."

"The male psychology I'd want to understand, if I were you, is why the man broke up with you in the first place. I'd want to make sure he had his head on straight before I even thought of getting back together." Annie put her sunglasses back on. "I've been told I have a bad habit of thinking I know what's best for everyone. It's a trait shared by all the women in my family. No offense meant."

"None taken." All right, it was true that Lillian and Owen might have some issues to work out once they were back together. But before that could happen, she had to get him back. She unzipped her backpack, pulled out her phone, and took a quick peek at her tracker. Owen would reach the hostel tonight. When he found the care package waiting, he'd get in touch, at least just to say thank you. And that would be the beginning.

CHAPTER 11

"For this first number, Annabelle Hatherley will be singing to The Fox, who has her leg caught in a trap. The chorus will be the other woodland creatures. I will cast the production a bit later, once I become familiar with the vocal talent I have to work with. Simon, if you please." She stepped up behind him and gave his shoulder a squeeze.

Simon began to play, and Gavin was close enough to see the beads of sweat sprouting at his hairline and on his upper lip, but his fingers kept moving over the keys. Maybe he was imagining himself axing all the bad thoughts.

Gavin had heard from Lillian that Simon and Miss V had been hunkered down in the parlor till the wee hours every night, working, and that Simon was having to take fewer and fewer axe breaks. Day saved. Partly due to Gavin's refusing to let Miss V cancel the whole shebang, but mostly because of Simon. His idea of turning the play into a musical seemed to have cured Miss V of the writer's block.

Gavin glanced down at his sheet music and joined the chorus. He wasn't sure about the whole singing-animal chorus, but what did it matter? The show would go on! "Very nice, every-one," Miss Violet called when they finished. "But remember, you are seeing one of your fellow forest beings in excruciating pain, near to death. I need to hear that in your voices, and see it on your faces. For next time, I'd like each of you to write a diary entry from the point of view of the animal you are drawn to portray in this scene." Yeah, Gavin didn't think he'd be doing that.

"You're giving us homework?" one of the teen boys protested, clearly feeling the same way Gavin was about the assignment.

"The theater is a demanding mistress, Robert," Miss V answered, and a few of the kids snickered at her choice of words.

This Robert was the one KiKi had her eye on. She'd positioned herself next to him, but as they rehearsed, another girl, the one with the waist-length hair, had managed to squeeze between them.

"We'll take ten, then we'll move on to the starvation song. Those of you in the chorus will have many roles. This time rather than forest animals, you'll be the town settlers, each of you desperate for food."

"I'm surprised Annabelle Hatherley didn't eat The Fox when she found it in the trap," a woman behind Gavin murmured. Gavin laughed, imagining the hissy Miss Violet would throw if she'd heard. He glanced over at Miss V. She'd joined Simon on the piano bench and they were deep in conversation, heads close together, shoulders touching. Maybe Miss V and Simon would have a little summer fun of their own.

Gavin wandered outside and leaned against the building, taking in the sunshine. Robert, the long-haired girl, and a couple other kids came out a few minutes later and gathered at the benches in front of the barber shop. KiKi appeared a few moments after that, looked at them, but didn't make a move to join them. He decided to give her an assist, and pulled a twenty out of his pocket. "Why don't you go get some soda for everybody at the Mercantile," he suggested.

"I guess." She didn't sound too enthusiastic.

"Why don't you ask somebody to go with you to help you carry stuff back? Maybe that Robert kid." Gavin winked at her.

"No. You don't talk to boys. At least not first. Boys talk to you."

"You say it like it's a law."

"It's what this girl at school, a friend, says, and all the guys like her." KiKi was, what, fourteen or fifteen? And already she was thinking she had to play games to get a guy's attention. Okay, the thirty-day no-contact rule he was having Lillian follow was kind of a game, but different situation.

"I bet that's not why they like her though."

"When you ignore a guy, it makes him want to talk to you." She said it with absolute certainty. Dang.

"Or maybe they think that you don't want them to talk to you," he countered. "Anyway, all guys aren't the same. They don't all think one way."

"I'll go get the soda."

O-kay then. She clearly didn't think he knew what the hell he was talking about. Gavin pushed himself away from the wall and headed back inside. Miss Violet spotted him and waved him over. "You have a nice strong baritone. I'm thinking of you for the role of Celyn Hanmer, the man who discovered slate on Annabelle Hatherley's land. I'm thinking of a duet between Celyn and his horse, ending with the horse throwing Celyn. I'll have to discuss it with Simon."

"Speaking of Simon, the two of you are looking pretty cozy. Is something going on there? Enquiring minds want to know." He waggled his eyebrows at her.

"Never!" She sounded as if he'd suggested she French-kiss Celyn Hanmer's horse. "The man is a hiker. I do not consort with hikers."

Right. Now Gavin remembered. Banana had said that, way back when, Miss Violet had had a hiker boyfriend, and he'd left her to spend his life out on the trail. Sounded like he hadn't even done the decent thing and told her that they were over. "I kind of think what you're doing with him right now could be called consorting."

"Simon and I have a professional relationship. I drew up a contract agreeing to split all the play's profits sixty-forty."

Fair enough. She was directing, in addition to writing the lyrics. Although, they couldn't be talking about much cash.

Gavin batted his eyelashes at her. "I'm a hiker. Does that mean I don't have a chance?"

"Even if you weren't a hiker, I wouldn't take a chance on you. I know a heartbreaker when I see one."

Heartbreaker. Where was she getting that? He was the one who was always getting dumped, not the other way around.

"Lillian, meet Cujo." Gavin handed her the end of the leash and a tote bag. She laughed, looking down at the corgi with the wildly wagging tail.

"Is the name ironic or aggrandizing?"

Gavin laughed. "No idea. His owner's a friend of Banana's. I do know that Cujo loves his *b a l l* more than life itself. I have to spell it, because he'll go berserk if he hears the word. It's in the bag. I have it all set up for you."

"I want to help Stephanie. She and Ford seem like such a good couple. I'm just worried that this could go very badly."

"I feel you. But we're in it now, right?" Stephanie was the one who had come up with the plan. If it went south, she was the one who would have to deal with the consequences, so he figured it was her call. "You should get going. They'll be here soon."

Lillian nodded. "See you out there."

"But, hopefully, I won't see you." Gavin shoved his fingers

through his hair. This probably was a crazy stupid stunt, but he'd agreed to it. That day Stephanie had stood in front of him, all torn up at the thought of losing Ford, Gavin hadn't been able to say no to her.

"Come on, Cujo." Lillian led the little dog across the meadow behind the Boots Barn. Gavin sat on one of the picnic benches to wait for Stephanie and Ford. When they pulled up, it looked like Ford's Honda Civic had a fresh dent, a big one, in the front fender.

"Sorry we're late!" Stephanie called as she and Ford walked over to Gavin.

"Everybody okay? I don't remember that dent."

"Just happened," Ford ansdwered. "A bee got into the car and stung me on the finger. I jerked on the wheel, and tree met fender."

"And he never even kills spiders!" Stephanie brought her thumb to her lips and started gnawing on the cuticle. It looked like she'd given some of the other cuticles the same treatment. The one on her pinkie had a smear of blood on it. Gavin wondered if she was having second thoughts about the plan.

Ford tugged Stephanie's hand away from her mouth and kissed it. "She still expects fairness from the world. I don't kill spiders, so that means nothing in the insect kingdom should harm me. But my bad luck is Doug's good fortune."

"Doug works at the body shop Ford uses," Stephanie explained. "I think Ford single-handedly paid for his son's braces."

"And Brandon's teeth look perfect." Ford gave one of Stephanie's braids an affectionate tug.

"Ford knows because we were invited to Brandon's bar mitzvah."

"There was a small incident during the candle-lighting ceremony, but no real damage. I warned Doug that he was taking a risk having me there."

"It was hardly a thing." Stephanie brought her thumb to her mouth again, realized what she was doing, lowered it and twisted her hands together. Definitely some nerves there. "Should we head out?"

"Yeah. Let's do it. I want to try a spot in the woods where Miss Violet, who owns the boardinghouse, saw The Fox just a few weeks ago."

"It's just us today?" Ford asked.

"I forgot to tell you. I booked us a private walk. I thought maybe too many people were scaring away The Fox."

"Or maybe one person who tends to get loud when she gets excited." Ford smiled at Stephanie.

"Or maybe that. I'm going to try to control myself today." If her plan worked, it wouldn't matter how loud anybody was. "Has her luck already changed, the boardinghouse lady?" Stephanie asked.

"You know what, it has. She puts on a play every summer at the town theater, one she writes herself, and this year she had writer's block. It got so bad that she stayed in the woods all night, hoping to see The Fox. And after she did, she started writing like crazy." Gavin left out the part about Simon giving her the idea to do a musical. Although maybe Simon was part of The Fox luck.

"Did you hear that, Ford?" Stephanie nudged him with her shoulder.

"I heard."

They crossed the meadow and entered the woods. Not much sunlight made it through all the trees, which would definitely be helpful. "Over there, those stones, those are part of the foundation of an old farmhouse. There's part of a well over there too."

"Ford, don't go near it," Stephanie warned.

"Me plus something it's possible to fall into? No thanks." The guy sounded so cheerful when he made these pronouncements. As many bad things as had happened to him, he'd been able to maintain a good attitude.

"Looks like we might get rain later. See how the leaves on that maple are turning upside down, with the silvery side up. They do that when rain's coming." Gavin lightly touched one of the leaves.

"How come?" Stephanie asked.

Gavin wouldn't have brought it up if he hadn't known the answer. "The humidity goes up before a storm. That makes the leaves limp, and the wind is able to flip them over." Gavin paused, holding up one hand. "We're coming up to the spot. There's a clearing around that bend in the trail up there." He hoped he was speaking loudly enough for Lillian to hear him. He didn't want to get too loud, since in theory they didn't want to make enough noise to spook The Fox.

Stephanie pressed her finger to her lips and nodded, then Gavin started forward. Hope this works, he thought. They'd barely started around the bend when Stephanie let out a cry. "I see The Fox. Ford, look!" She pointed. A creature with a pointed snout and a reddish coat tore across the far edge of the clearing, here and gone in moments.

Ford stopped. "I saw it! I saw The Fox. I can't believe this is happening."

"Believe it." Stephanie hugged him, burying her head in his shoulder. "And now we can get married."

The grin that spread across Ford's face—pure joy. Gavin felt a spurt of guilt. But could it really be a bad thing to make someone so happy? "Congratulations!"

"You have to come to the wedding," Ford said, when Stephanie released him. "When should we have it, Steph?"

"I'd marry you right here, right now, if I could. But our families—"

"Cujo, no!"

The creature was running toward them now, Lillian racing

after it. Cujo slid to a stop in front of Gavin and dropped a saliva-coated ball at his feet. When Gavin didn't react, Cujo gave the ball a nudge with his nose, his narrow, fox-like nose. Cujo had the pointy ears and reddish coat too, and, at a distance, moving fast, he could pass as The Fox, especially when The Fox was what Ford had been primed to see. Gavin had thought he'd found a good fake fox for Stephanie, but up close, Cujo was unmistakably a dog. Gavin picked up the ball and threw it into the clearing. The dog could at least have some fun.

"I'm sorry. The fishing line broke," Lillian said as she reached them. Gavin had attached a length of fishing line to the ball, so Lillian could throw it, then pull it back toward her, with, in theory, Cujo chasing after it.

Ford stared at the dog running across the clearing for a long moment, then looked at Stephanie. "Did you arrange this?"

Stephanie tugged on the end of one of her braids. "Yes, but only because—"

Ford didn't let her finish. "This isn't going to work, Stephanie. I shouldn't have even agreed to try it. Every day that you're with me is another day you're at risk. I can't live with that."

"But I can't live without you. Don't you understand that? You make me happier than anyone ever. If some bad things come along with that, I don't care. The worst thing that could happen to me is losing you."

He started to reach for her, then clenched his hands together behind his back. "You could have been killed that day at the church. You could have been killed today in the car if I'd been going faster when the bee stung me. I don't even want to drive home with you. You take the car. I'll find my own way."

"Don't do this to me." Stephanie started toward him, and he backed away so fast he almost stumbled.

"I'm doing it *for* you." Ford's voice cracked with emotion. "I'm doing it for you. Let me go. Please." He turned and walked away from them. The path would take him back to the meadow. At least Gavin knew Ford wouldn't get lost.

"I'm sorry," Lillian said again.

"It's not your fault. It was my idea to have you fake a fox sighting for me. It was stupid. I just couldn't think of any other way for me and Ford to be together. There's no chance of that now." Stephanie looked down the trail, and they all watched as Ford rounded the bend and disappeared from sight. "Let's wait a little. He's serious. He's not going to let me near him."

"He loves you. It's so clear that he loves you." Lillian put her arm around Stephanie.

"He loves me too much. I had a little accident last week. Just stepped off a curb wrong and twisted my ankle. Nothing serious, not bothering me at all now, but he was with me, and he's convinced it was his fault, because of his bad luck. He just doesn't want anything else bad to happen to me. He's afraid the next thing might be big. And I don't care. Being with him is good enough to outweigh any bad, and I don't believe in his bad luck anyway. Or The Fox's good luck. I just thought if Ford saw The Fox and believed his luck would change, it would actually change."

Cujo returned with the ball and dropped it in front of Stephanie. She threw it for him. She was kind. Even now, with all that had happened, she didn't ignore the dog. She and Ford were a good match. Ford would have thrown Cujo the ball too.

"I have this friend who didn't drive for a long time because she lived in New York," Stephanie told them. "She went to visit her brother, and he told her she could drive his car to a restaurant or someplace if she could make it around the block without running into a mailbox. And what happened? She got in the car, and the third house she passed, she ran into a mailbox. I think it's like that with Ford. He has it in his head that bad things are going to happen, and he somehow makes them happen."

Gavin could see tears shining in her eyes as she continued. "He became convinced at such a young age that he has bad luck, so he sees it everywhere. I thought if I could just get it in his head that he had good luck, that maybe it would change the way he saw his life, which would actually change his life." She gave a harsh laugh. "Now he'll just have another item for his bad-luck list—the day the woman he loved betrayed his trust."

Gavin knew he should be saying something. But he didn't know what to say. He could offer to give her money back for the walk, but that seemed so small compared to the size of the pain she was feeling. Insultingly small. "He's probably far enough ahead." Slowly, they began to walk back down the trail, Cujo trotting ahead, holding his ball. When they reached the Barn, Stephanie actually tried to give Gavin a tip. "I hate that it went down this way," Gavin said, closing her fingers around the bills she was holding out to him.

"Not your fault. I knew it was a risk." Stephanie gave a little wave as she headed for the Honda. Together Gavin and Lillian watched her drive away. Alone.

"Do you think she did the right thing, trying to fool Ford into thinking his luck had changed?" Gavin asked.

"If he'd believed, it could have changed his whole life. I think Ford has as many ratty thoughts as I do. His are mostly about accidentally hurting people he loves." Lillian tucked a lock of hair back into her ponytail. "Even though I work on zinging my bad thoughts away with my wand, they still control me so much. Like I couldn't even go out and flirt, because the thoughts were too bad." Her chin came up. "But I can do it. I want to do it. Still want to be my wingman?"

The Fox watched the dog. Living with humans had broken so many of his connections to the world his ancestors came from. He chased the ball the way he should be chasing a rabbit, even though when the dog captured it, he received nothing for the effort. But the dog was willing to chase it again and again.

And the two humans with the cord that spread warmth wherever it went . . . They didn't seem to be able to sense its presence. They'd almost let it tear, but it had held. It wouldn't continue to if they didn't protect it.

So many had lost the ability to feel what was natural and right.

"Cujo will be an even better wingman than me." Gavin gave the corgi's head a pat. He couldn't return the dog to his owner until later that night, so they'd decided to go to the big patio off Shoo Fly's bakery, which was extremely dog friendly. They stopped at the park across the street, so Cujo could take a pee break, while she and Gavin talked strategy. "I'll go in separately, and be right there if you need me, but you'll be a lot more approachable if I'm not at the same table."

Lillian's stomach already felt tight, but seeing how Ford's life was controlled by ratty thoughts made her want to get past hers. Maybe she couldn't ever get rid of the ratties completely, but she could stop letting them control her. She hoped.

"Just pick a guy who has his dog with him, and you'll have something to talk about right off the bat," Gavin suggested. "I've got one other suggestion."

"I want all of them you have." Partly because then she could delay going over there and talking to guys—at least one guy— she didn't know.

"Take off that top shirt. It's plenty warm enough for just your tee."

"I like how the shirt looks with the tee, how the colors match." She felt like she was Linus, and he'd just asked her to throw away her security blanket.

"You have a good body. There's nothing wrong with showing it off a little."

She felt herself flush. "I just . . . I feel uncomfortable when people look at me."

"What? All people?"

"Kind of. I feel like they're judging me."

"So they look at you, and what do you think they're thinking?"

Her stomach was cramping now. "I don't know. That I'm desperate. Or that I think I'm better than everyone else. Or I'm slutty. Or that I'm trying to get their boyfriend. Or—"

"Whoa, whoa, whoa. All this, just from seeing you sitting someplace?"

"Sitting someplace and wearing a tight T-shirt." She knotted her hands in the loose fabric of the button-down she liked to wear as a jacket. "Not at Boots Camp. I'm used to wearing a tee by itself there, because it makes sense when I'm working out. But, like at a bar, by myself, or with girlfriends—" Although she never went to a bar with girlfriends. She'd never had those kinds of girlfriends. When she got old enough, she would go to bars with her mother sometimes, when her mother was between boyfriends. "When it seems like I'm trying to meet men is when I have those thoughts."

"Well, no wonder you don't want to do it." Gavin scrubbed the back of his neck with his hand. "As a guy, I can tell you, yes, we notice, and appreciate, your body. But then we're thinking things like 'don't be a jerk, don't stare at her boobs.' And 'does she have a boyfriend who is suddenly going to pop out of nowhere, because it would be crazy if she didn't have a boyfriend.' And 'I wish she'd give me some kind of signal that she's not going to shoot me down if I go over there.' See? Not really any judge-y thoughts. It's a lot about ourselves."

"I know I'm being conceited, thinking everybody is paying all that attention to me anyway."

"That is not even close to what I said, Twinkle. You manage to find every possible way to feel bad about yourself, don't you? You worry because you think people are thinking bad stuff about you. Then you get mad at yourself because you shouldn't be assuming people are thinking anything at all. You're putting yourself through a lot."

Lillian sighed. "And I feel bad about that too, because what kind of person makes themselves feel so bad all the time? I think that's why I like teaching kindergarten. When I'm with the kids, I'm not worried about what they're thinking about me. I'm not thinking about me at all. I'm thinking about them, and which one is about to have a meltdown, which one is about to smack someone, which one has stopped paying attention. I don't have time for any other thoughts."

"I bet you're a great teacher."

There was part of her that wanted to say, "I'm okay." Or, "Lots of people are good teachers." Instead, she said, "I think so," giving a little zing to the ratty thought about being full of herself.

Gavin pressed one hand to his chest in mock astonishment. "You took a compliment."

She laughed. "It was kind of hard." She looked over at the patio. "I guess I should get over there."

"Your mission—to talk to one guy. That's it."

"I don't have to flirt?"

"Don't think of it as flirting. Think of it as being friendly. Smiling back at someone who smiles at you, that kind of thing."

"Friendly. All right. You ready, Cujo?" The dog wagged his curly tail. She looked at Gavin. "I'm going in." She took two steps, then pulled off the button-down and tied it around her waist.

"I won't be far behind you. I'll be right there if you need me."

She walked across the street. Her mother wouldn't approve of her shorts and tee, or her makeup-free face, but Lillian had come straight from being out on the trail. And it was the middle of a Saturday afternoon in a town that catered to hikers. Having clean clothes made her slightly overdressed.

The patio had waiter service, probably because dogs weren't allowed inside. Lillian found a seat at a table next to a big pot of petunias and some little blue flowers that she didn't know the name of. She leaned over and scratched Cujo behind one ear, just to have something to do, then she forced herself to straighten up and look around. She always had trouble figuring out what to do with her face. She didn't want to grin like a lunatic, but she wanted to look pleasant. She turned the corners of her lips up in a small smile, but the tension of keeping them in that position made them tremble. Calm down, she told herself. Please just calm down.

She was relieved when a server, a teen girl, came over. Ordering gave Lillian something else to do. But too soon, the order was given. She looked around the patio again and saw that Gavin had arrived and found a seat several tables away. She was glad he wasn't close enough to hear her talk. It would make her too self-conscious, knowing he was listening.

Time to pick out a guy to approach. She let her eyes wander, without focusing too long on any one person. There. A man maybe a little older than she was, with a cute little pug wearing a red and yellow bandana.

She heard Gavin's voice in her head. All you gotta do is make a little eye contact, and give a little smile, he'd told her on the way over. But Lillian looked away, before the man looked back. It felt so . . . It was like she was just assuming that he'd want to talk to her. He might think—She closed her eyes for a moment and imagined using a wand on the approaching ratty thought.

"Here you go." The server set down her iced tea and scone, and the fire-hydrant shaped biscuit she'd ordered for Cujo. And an idea hit Lillian. Before she could kill it by analyzing it to death, she said, "Would you send the pug in the bandana a dog biscuit from me? Me and him." She patted Cujo on the head.

"Absolutely." The girl gave her a little wink. A friendly wink. See, she wasn't being judge-y.

Lillian took a sip of her tea, trying to look like a normal person instead of a breathing ball of anxiety. Her chest was feeling so tight, she was amazed she could pull in a breath. She kept glancing at the sliding glass doors leading to the patio, checking for the waitress. She was afraid to look at Gavin, even though it might calm her nerves. She was afraid the guy belonging to the pug might notice, and think . . . what? That she was flirting with every man in sight. Zing! Rat into beautiful gray horse!

Here came the server, with a dog biscuit on a pretty polka-dotted plate. She was going up to the man, and then they were both looking at Lillian. The man raised the biscuit in a kind of salute, then handed it to the pug, who seemed most pleased. Lillian smiled at the man, then took another sip of her tea, glad to have something to do.

Now the man and the pug were moving toward her. "Is he friendly?" the man asked before he got too close.

"I . . . I'm not sure. He's a friend's. We haven't spent a lot of time together. His name is Cujo, but I think that's ironic or maybe aggrandizing." Gavin had seemed to think it was funny when she'd said that earlier.

The man laughed. She'd made him laugh! "They're both wagging, so I think we're okay." The man came closer, close enough for the dogs to touch noses. Lillian pretended to ignore it when they started sniffing each other's butts.

"May I sit?"

"Of course."

Mission accomplished. And she didn't even feel like she had to pee!

CHAPTER 12

"I don't get why it was such a big deal." Erin took a swig of her beer.

"Everybody has stuff," Gavin answered. They were sitting on the porch of his cabin. Bright stars. Cold beer. Friendly woman. Life was good.

"True. I guess working at a bar has gotten me really used to talking to all kinds of people. I don't remember being nervous about it when I first started, though." Gavin wasn't surprised. Erin's sass and confidence were what had attracted him to her. That and the freckles. And the legs.

"What does make you nervous?"

"Hmmm. I'm thinking." She caught her lower lip in her teeth for a moment as she considered the question. He loved that move. He should remember to tell Twinkle to try it, once she was ready to move on to more advanced flirting techniques. Now that he knew the kind of things that were racing around that brain of hers, he understood why doing some easy-peasy flirting felt so scary to her.

"Noises on airplanes. Roller coasters. And scary movies. If I'm going to watch a scary movie, I have to have a solid six hours before I go to sleep."

"Why do you watch them at all?"

"The same reason I go on roller coasters. It's a thrill. What about you?"

He wasn't really the nervous type either, so he had to think about it too. He wasn't a fan of conversations where someone was spewing their guts, because why dig all that stuff up? But they didn't make him nervous exactly. "Bees. Needles—I'm a wuss about getting a shot." For a few years when he was a kid, he'd been nervous about his parents dying. He'd always say "see you in the morning" before he went to bed, like that would mean they'd always be there alive the next day. He definitely wasn't telling Erin that. "Heights. I don't mind roller coasters, because they're moving so fast, but I hate being stuck at the top of a Ferris wheel."

"So, if we go on one, I shouldn't rock the car if we're stopped at the top."

"You definitely shouldn't."

"Even though it might be fun to make you beg for mercy." She gave the words a sexy spin, so, of course, he had to kiss her. Several times.

"I heard from American Cheese, that gaming company I was trying to get an internship with," she said, when they came up for air. "They've narrowed it down to ten candidates, and they have three slots to fill. They invited us all up to Vermont in a couple weeks to tour the place and look at some of what they have in development."

"Hey, great!" She was a go-getter.

"They said we could bring someone. I know you're into gaming. You want to come with?"

There was one American Cheese game he played a lot, Tidal

Zone, that was supposed to be getting a sequel. Getting a look could be cool. But meeting these prospective bosses. Seemed like a couple thing. "What weekend is it?"

"Don't you always have weekends off?"

Pretty much. The Booters sometimes went on an easy hike on Saturday morning, but Banana usually led it. "It's possible I'll need to fill in at the Boots Barn. I think Nick was saying something about going to visit his parents one weekend." He hadn't said anything. But it was possible he might want to.

"It's weekend after next. Maybe we could spend a night at Pirate's Cove. My family went there for vacation a couple times, and I always wanted to go back." Gavin remembered driving past some billboards for the place on one of his road trips. Definitely a place for families. "They have, I think, eight pools and a great water park. They have a lot of things for kids, but I think it would still be fun."

Wow. Her family sounded like they belonged in a throwback sitcom. That kind of vacation was something the Tanners would take. Gavin had had a stretch when watching *Full House* reruns had been a secret pleasure. His parents would have laughed their asses off if they'd known he actually liked it.

"I'll check in with Nick about my schedule."

Erin stretched, sticking her legs way out in front of her. "Maybe I should head home." The way she said it made him feel like she could be convinced to stay. They hadn't gotten to that stage yet.

Maybe that hadn't even been what she was signaling. "Yeah, it is getting kind of late."

"Mr. Reiser was limping on his left leg again. But when I saw him at Hen House last Tuesday, it was his right." Evie consulted her notebook. "That's three times left, two times right. Are you sure you can't give me more data?"

"I honestly never paid attention," Lillian admitted as she wrangled a toddler T-shirt reading "Foxy" onto a stuffed fox for a new window display.

"I just don't understand how that's possible."

"I'm just not Purely Investigative." Lillian chose another stuffed fox and another toddler T-shirt.

"Will you please try to remember to watch him when you see him at the boardinghouse? There's something strange about him, and I have to find out what it is. I can't help it. I'm Perilously—"

KiKi interrupted with a squeal. "It's him! Robert! We're in the play together! He's crossing the street. What if he comes in here? Is he coming in here?"

"The store's not even open yet," Evie pointed out.

KiKi dashed to the door and flipped the sign from "closed" to "open."

"Hey. It's not time!"

"It's only six minutes early. Maybe he'll come in. Maybe he'll talk to me. At rehearsal, it kind of seems like he might like this girl, Riley. But maybe not."

"If you want, I could investigate him, and let you know. I wouldn't even charge you, since you're letting me use your phone for my business."

"No! I don't want you doing your weird P.I. stuff around Robert."

Evie got very busy studying her notebook. Lillian could tell KiKi's words had stung. "I'm always amazed at how much you can figure out about people, and so fast."

"Doesn't matter. He's not coming in. I think he's going to the Mercantile. I could go over and buy . . . something. Maybe he'd see me and talk to me." KiKi began twisting one of the rubber bracelets she wore. "Except maybe he saw me see him, and he'll think I followed him."

It sounded like KiKi also had some ratty thoughts. Lillian hadn't realized so many people suffered from them, but now she knew Miss Violet, Ford, and Simon all had them too.

"He'd think you were following him, because you would be following him," Evie muttered.

"He might not have seen me though." KiKi kept twisting the bracelet. "Do you think he saw me?"

"He might have seen you, since we were all standing in front of the window, but I don't think that means he'd assume you'd followed him if you went over to the Mercantile," Lillian answered.

"If he thought I followed him, that would ruin everything. I'm not going to go."

"Not that you want any of my Professional Intel, but he's heading back this way," Evie announced.

KiKi spun around and rushed to the back of the shop. "I'll be right back. I need lip gloss."

"I'm going to start tracking her behavior." Evie flipped to a fresh page in her notebook. "I think she's developing a psychological disorder. Hey! That gives me a new *P*. I can offer P.I., Psychological Inspection."

The fox bells jangled and a boy—*the* boy, Robert—sauntered in. His shirt made Lillian smile. It had a rabbit making a shadow puppet of a hand. She decided not to comment on it, figuring a teen boy wouldn't want a twenty-nine-year-old to think his shirt was cute.

Evie flipped the page in her notebook again and began scribbling away. Lillian shifted her position to put herself between him and Evie, who wasn't always subtle with her surveillance. "Anything I can help you with?"

"I wanted to get some gummy foxes, if you have any of the cinnamon ones."

KiKi appeared from the back room as soon as the question

was out of the boy's mouth. "I think there are still some." She walked over to the register and started checking the little bags of candy. "Yep." She held one up.

"Fire." Robert headed over to her.

"Three fifty-five," KiKi said.

Say something else, Lillian silently urged. Even though she knew how hard it could be to talk to a guy.

"They're showing *Beetlejuice* at the park tonight," Robert told KiKi. "It's a town thing. Everyone dances when that 'Jump in the Line' scene comes on."

He was going to ask her out. This was like one of Lillian's teenage daydreams come to life. Although if it had actually happened, she'd probably have been unable to speak and would have completely humiliated herself.

"*Beetlejuice*? Really?"

KiKi's tone dripped with disdain. What was going on? Lillian took a fast look at the girl. One of her eyebrows was arched, and her lips were curled into a sneer.

Robert took a step back. "Forget it." And he was out of there.

"What did I do?" KiKi wailed as soon as the door closed behind him. That's what Lillian wanted to know.

"You insulted the guy you like, and now he thinks you're evil." Evie kept scribbling in the notebook. "I think you're evil too, in case you care, which I guess you don't."

"He wasn't supposed to leave. He was supposed to try to make me change my mind. It was supposed to make him want to be with me more."

"I don't think I understand." Lillian put down the stuffed fox she'd been about to add to the display, and walked over to KiKi.

"I just—I don't—" KiKi twisted her bracelet so hard the rubber tore. She didn't seem to notice. "That's the way this girl at school is with boys, and they all love her."

"Are you talking about GiGi McAvoy?" Evie demanded.

"How do you even know about her? You don't even go to our school."

"I know she's the one who posted all those mean things about you. I know she's why you got a stomachache every morning when it was time to go to school. Why are you trying to be like her, with your stupid name, and stupid hair, and stupid stupidness?"

KiKi leaned on the counter, as if the strength had gone out of her legs. "It was working though. He liked me."

Evie snorted. "Not anymore."

"Maybe you could apologize to him," Lillian suggested.

"He hates me now." KiKi looked over at Evie. "I don't want you to hate me too. I'm sorry for what I said about your P.I. stuff."

"I'll make a note of your apology." Evie flipped back a page and began to write.

KiKi pushed away from the counter. "I need to see The Fox. That's the only way I can make this better. I have to see The Fox."

Gavin wondered if Lillian had any clue that Spencer, who Gavin always thought of as the peanut-butter-and-pickle guy, thought she was pretty cute. Gavin could see it from the parking lot, even though the two of them were over at one of the picnic tables. It was all in the body language, the way Spencer kept leaning in as they practiced tying knots.

Nah, Twinkle was oblivious. All those nasty thoughts of hers kept her from seeing what was right in front of her. Even if she did realize Spencer was interested, it wouldn't matter. She was still hung up on the butthole. Gavin knew Owen had to have received that care package by now, and she'd heard nothing. Gavin would have known immediately if she had. She would have gone incandescent.

Arms wrapped around his waist, soft breasts pressing against his back. Erin, of course. What was she doing here? They didn't have plans. He turned and saw she was holding a picnic basket, an actual wicker one, like something Martha Stewart would have. "Hey, baby," he leaned down to give her a kiss, feeling a little self-conscious. He was at work, although he was done for the day and about to head home.

She gave the basket a little swing. "I'm taking you to lunch."

Nice surprise. Beautiful girl. Lunch outside. Life should be good, but Gavin felt a little jab of irritation. What if he'd had plans? He didn't, but it wasn't impossible. "Lucky for me I don't have anything going this afternoon."

"I knew that. I asked Banana about your schedule." She looked pleased with herself, but if she wanted to know his schedule, he's the one she should have been talkin' to. "Come on. Let's eat. Over at the edge of the meadow would be perfect. We'll get some shade from the spruce."

"Sure." She grabbed his hand, and they strolled over to the spot she'd chosen. Erin put the basket down, pulled out a red-and-white-checked tablecloth, spread it out on the ground, then started to arrange dozens of little plastic containers on top. "I got lots of different things. We're eating tapas style."

"I've been thinking about BBQ all day, for some reason."

"Maybe we can do BBQ for dinner. I'm off."

It was too early to be thinking about dinner. And they hadn't even talked about going out that night. Gavin sat down, and Erin passed him a bottle of wine and two glasses—made of actual glass, not plastic. Who brought real glasses to a picnic? She'd brought real silverware too.

"You got a corkscrew in there?" He shook his head. "Why am I even asking? You obviously packed everything in your kitchen."

"Not quite, but I've got everything we need." She gave him the corkscrew, and he filled their glasses.

"I've always gone for paper plates. Even at home." He took a long swallow of the wine. "Is there an occasion I'm missing here?" He hoped she wasn't one of those girls who did one-month anniversaries. Even if she was, you didn't celebrate mini anniversaries when you were only planning on being together for the summer.

"Nope. Just a beautiful day."

"Oh, I talked to Nick about that weekend you have the intern thing. I can't get off." Lie. The idea of going with her made him itchy. He didn't want to meet a bunch of people who'd ask him questions about him and Erin.

"Maybe Banana could cover for you."

"Banana doesn't work too many hours. No time with the bar."

"Big Matt could cover for him at Wit's, if Banana didn't want to put in such a long day. I could ask them."

"I can ask myself." The words came out sounding harsher than he'd meant them to. He scrubbed the back of his neck with his fingers.

"Well, will you?"

"I said I would."

"Not exactly, you didn't." Erin spooned some lobster salad onto her plate—china, of course. What else, with the silverware and wineglasses.

"Well, that's what I meant." He was being a brat. "Thanks for bringing lunch." He took some of the lobster salad, some potato salad, and some kind of grain salad. "You really went all out."

"I thought it would be fun."

"You were right." He took another swallow of wine. "This is good." He looked at the label. Failla. Olivet Ranch Chardonnay. He'd seen it in the liquor store. It ran about forty-five dollars a bottle. He let out a whistle.

"I know, right? It was a present from my parents. The basket too."

"Must be nice to have a rich mommy and daddy." He'd known there was no way she was living like this on a barmaid's salary, good tips or no.

"Okay. That's it." She jerked the wineglass out of his hand, poured the contents on the grass, then put the glass in the hamper. She drained her own glass, and put it away too, then began jamming the lids on the containers. "Lunch is over."

"What? I was just kidding around."

"No, you weren't. You were being a giant butthead." She quickly stuffed everything else back in the basket.

Gavin thought he heard one of the glasses break, and winced. "Erin, I—"

"I don't want to hear it." She stood up, grabbed the basket, and walked away. He could have gone after her, but what was the point? She obviously wasn't going to listen to anything he had to say.

He stretched out on his back, realizing she'd forgotten her tablecloth, and closed his eyes. He'd just stay here a while. Give her time to leave.

A few moments later, he heard Erin come back, and felt her sit down next to him. "Can I have a new glass of wine?" he asked without opening his eyes.

"From the expression I saw on Erin's face, outlook not so good."

He knew that voice. Lillian. He sat up. "I had one of those Magic 8 Balls when I was kid. One night, during an episode of weed paranoia, my mom smashed it. Something about communicating with evil spirits."

"You say these things about your childhood like they're perfectly normal."

"I had a perfectly normal screwed-up childhood. Actually, most of it was pretty cool."

"I'm remembering how you told me your ex said you kept doing things to push her away." When he didn't comment, she added, "It looked like Erin just got pushed."

"Cannot predict now." This was not a conversation he wanted to have with Lillian.

"Signs point to yes," she countered.

"We were in the middle of a picnic, with excellent wine. I had no reason to want to push her away. I was joking around, and she got mad."

"What kind of joke?"

"Where is the girl who has trouble talking to men?"

Lillian pulled out a clump of grass and threw it at him. "What kind of joke?"

"Just something about how it must be good having a rich mom and dad, because the wine was way too expensive for her to afford. Nothing to get her panties in a twist about."

"I guess it depends on how you said it." Lillian pushed herself to her feet.

"You're leaving?"

"I have knots to tie, and you might have an apology to make."

He'd just been playing. But Erin hadn't taken it that way. She'd called him a butthead. Had he been a butthead?

CHAPTER 13

"I need to go on another fox walk." KiKi slumped down next to Gavin in his usual seat at the back of the theater.

"Keeks, you're killin' me. If I could, I'd hand you The Fox with a pretty pink bow around her neck, but I can't." She looked so dang miserable, and had at every rehearsal for a solid week. "Whatever's going on, I can guarantee that there's a better way to handle it. Are you ready to tell me yet? I give excellent advice."

She glanced around, then whispered, "I did something so horrible."

"You? I find that hard to believe."

"Believe it."

"Well, come on. Tell me. Whatever it is, there's a very good chance I've done worse."

Her big brown eyes filled with tears. For as much as he hated dealing with crying women, he seemed to attract them. "I was so mean to Robert."

Gavin hadn't seen that coming. She obviously had a huge crush on the boy. "Mean in what way?" A wave of red surged up her neck, then stained her cheeks. Whatever it was she'd done, it sure seemed like she felt ashamed of it.

KiKi took another look around, probably making sure no one else was in earshot. "He asked me if I wanted to go to a movie in the park. *Beetlejuice*. And I acted like he was a baby for even wanting to see it."

That made no sense. Unless . . . "Is this something else everybody knows, like how you can't talk to a boy first?"

"It's how the most popular girl at my school is with boys. And it works! They're always trying to get her attention."

"Looks like Robert is a different kind of boy, one who doesn't like games. And I don't think you really like playing them."

"He hates me now. He can't stand to even look at me. That's why I need to see The Fox."

"There's this thing you can do, that might work even better."

He waited until she asked. "What is it?"

"Apologizing."

She gave him a look that made it clear she didn't think Gavin had any idea what he was talking about. "You hurt someone, you've got to apologize," he continued. "I accidentally hurt my friend Erin's feelings, so I called her up and said I was sorry. Now we're going away for a weekend together." Family fun park and meeting the prospective bosses. Whoopie!

"What if he just tells me to go away?"

"It's still the right thing to do. And it'll make you feel better."

Miss Violet made one of her grand entrances, followed by Simon. She stopped in the aisle and pointed at Gavin and KiKi. "No. This is not acceptable."

Gavin looked at Simon, hoping he could help him out. 'Cause Gavin had no idea what Miss Violet's problem was. Simon shrugged. "Not sure what we're doing wrong."

"You"—she pointed at him—"are a chipmunk. She"—she pointed at KiKi—"is a raccoon. Chipmunks eat plants and fungi. And what do raccoons eat?"

"Uh, garbage?"

"Well, yes, but, also, chipmunks! I've told you I want you to get in character the moment you enter the theater. If you were in character, you would be trembling in fear sitting so close to her." Gavin heard a couple of the kids snicker. Great, just what KiKi needed. They were laughing at Miss Violet, but he'd bet KiKi felt like they were laughing at her.

Gavin stood up. "I guess I better scurry off." He moved to a seat several rows away. He still couldn't believe he had to play a damn chipmunk, but that's what he got by not doing that diary entry homework.

"I need a word with my Annabelle and my Fox. All the other players need to inhabit their animals, with every fiber of their being." Miss Violet strode up on stage, the actors playing Annabelle and The Fox—and Miss Violet's long, long lavender scarf—trailing after her. The woman was, as his father would say, a trip and a half.

Gavin pulled out his cell and surreptitiously—surreptitiously, because chipmunks didn't have phones—checked his messages. Erin asked if he wanted to meet up at the BBQ for dinner. **Always up for BBQ. See ya at 7:30,** he texted back. As he slid his cell back in his pocket, he noticed KiKi walking down the aisle, heading toward the corner of the stage where the other teens were gathered. She hesitated for a moment, then climbed the steps and walked directly to Robert. She must have asked if they could talk alone, because the two of them moved off away from the others, something the girl with the long brown hair, Riley, her name was, did not look too pleased about.

The conversation didn't last long, and neither Robert nor

KiKi smiled when it was over, but at least she'd done it. Now it was out of her hands.

Gavin did his best chipmunk as part of the chorus of animals watching The Fox being rescued from the trap by Annabelle Hatherley, Annie's great-great-great-great-great-grandmother. Then he gave his duet with a horse his all, getting an approving nod from Miss Violet. Next up—the BBQ and Erin.

Lillian didn't even have to imagine Owen was with her when she walked into the BBQ. Doing hard things over and over made them easier. Piper spotted her, smiled, and waved her over to an empty table. Becoming a regular had made it easier too. Now when Piper took Lillian's order, they always got a little chat in.

She pulled out her phone to check messages. Just one from her mom. She kept pushing Lillian to quit Boots Camp and meet up with Owen while there was some of her summer vacation left. Lillian wasn't sure what her mother's advice would be if she knew the truth. Maybe then she'd think Lillian was doing the right thing, trying to get Owen back in her own way.

Lillian was close to the end of her thirty days of no contact. She'd really thought Owen would have gotten in touch with her after that care package she had sent him. She knew he'd been at the hostel. Had there been a mix-up there? Could someone have forgotten to give the package to him, or could they have given it to the wrong person? Stop, she told herself. That way lay madness.

The door swinging open caught her attention, and she saw Gavin come in. She smiled, and started to wave, then dropped her hand. She hadn't realized Erin was here. Gavin ambled over to Erin, and leaned in for a kiss.

Lillian looked away. Maybe she'd just peek at Owen's Instagram. No contact. She wouldn't do any likes or anything. She just wanted to see his face.

* * *

"I thought your rehearsal got out at seven thirty." Those were the first words out of Erin's mouth. He didn't even get a hello.

"Sometimes it runs a little late." Hadn't tonight, but sometimes it did.

"Well, Flappy made it over here by seven thirty-five, and he's in the play." She jerked her chin toward the table where Flappy and his family sat.

"Look, I stopped by the Mercantile. I needed toothpaste. I don't think you want my teeth to rot out of my head."

"It's five after eight. Was it that hard to choose between Crest and Colgate?"

"I ran into one of the Booters. I needed to talk him through some things." Erin rolled her eyes, and Gavin felt a burst of annoyance. "It's my job, okay?" A.J. was still obsessing over losing muscle mass if he spent too long on the trail.

"It couldn't wait until you saw him tomorrow?"

Gavin shrugged. Nothing he was gonna say was gonna satisfy her. They needed a subject change. "What'd you get up to today?"

"Went to the Lily Bay beach, did some grilling, swam in the lake. I'm always surprised how cold it is, even in the middle of summer. I'm looking forward to the pools at Pirate's Cove. They have one of those ones where you can float down a river in an inner tube."

"There's great rafting right here on the Penobscot, a whole train of rapids. Nature's better than anything you can find at a resort."

Erin looked at him for a long moment. "I love going out on the Penobscot, but in nature the water's not heated and you can't splash down next to a bar with piña coladas."

"O-kay, princess."

She let out a long sigh. "You could have just said you didn't want to go."

"I want to go."

"Uh-uh. I know exactly what you're doing and why you're doing it. You show up late and make little sarcastic digs at me, so I'll get mad and say you can't go with me to Vermont. All because you're too much of a weenie just to say 'no, thanks.' "

Christ. That sounded like something Rebecca would have said.

Erin stood up. "Your plan worked. Don't come with me. Don't even talk to me again." And she walked off, just like she had that day at the picnic. What kind of way was that to deal with a problem?

Lillian put the phone facedown on the table, then covered it with a paper napkin, as if that would magically make what she'd seen disappear. She'd been so stupid, so delusional, so willing to believe there could be a perfect happily-ever-after for her, even after Owen couldn't even be bothered to acknowledge the package she'd sent. And now she knew why.

That wild, adventurous woman Owen had said he wanted that night at the inn? He'd already had her. There were dozens of pictures of her on his Instagram, including some from the top of Katahdin, back when Lillian and Owen were a couple, or at least when she still believed they were. He must have added the pictures from that part of the hike after she started the thirty days. She wanted to leave, but she was afraid if she tried to stand up, her knees would give, and she'd collapse. All you have to do is breathe, she told herself. Just sit here and breathe, and, in a little while, you'll be able to go.

But with each breath, a new rat came at her. Stupid. Delusional. Doormat. Boring. Worthless. Stupid. Stupid. Stupid. She couldn't find her imaginary wand. And it didn't matter. Because there was no magic. No happily-ever-afters. She lived in the real world, where rats never turned into horses.

"Twinkle, hey. Lillian, look at me." It took a moment for the words to register, for them to turn from random sounds into words she could understand. She raised her eyes and saw Gavin standing there. "What's going on?"

She couldn't find a way to tell him. Instead, she lifted off the napkin and flipped over the phone.

"Ah, hell. I'm sorry."

Piper came over with a glass of water. "Anything I can do, Lillian?" Lillian shook her head. Piper gave her shoulder a squeeze, then left her and Gavin alone.

Alone. Wait. Erin. "You shouldn't be over here. Go back to Erin."

"She had to leave. I can stay, no problem. Want to try drinking some of that water?" Gavin nudged it toward Lillian.

"I'm so stupid. What have I been doing all these weeks?"

"You've been working hard, getting strong."

"It's all been for nothing."

"Nah, don't look at it like that. It was for you."

For her. Stupid, doormat, delusional, boring, worthless her.

CHAPTER 14

"You don't have to take me wherever it is you're taking me. I'm fine."

Lillian sure as hell didn't look fine, her face pale, dark smudges under her eyes. "I'm the one who wants to go. I just needed someone to ride shotgun." She didn't answer, just leaned her head against the window and closed her eyes. Gavin hoped she'd fall asleep. She didn't look like she'd slept since he'd taken her back to the boardinghouse last night.

Taking her on this little trip was probably ridiculous. It couldn't possibly do much to make her feel better. But it was all he could think of, and he had to do something. Just looking at her made an ache start up in his chest.

If he were in Lillian's shoes, he'd want his angry driving music going full blast. Instead, he found a coffee shop chillax mix, and played it low. He didn't know if she slept, but she didn't lift her head for the whole three-and-a-half-hour drive. After he found a parking spot with a clear view of the sign at the entrance, he lightly patted her arm. Here goes nothing. "We're here, Twinkle." She didn't respond. She had fallen asleep. Good.

She gave a little groan and tried to burrow into the side of the car. "Time to wake up."

Slowly, Lillian straightened up. "Where are we?" she mumbled.

"Someplace you told me you'd always wanted to go."

Her brow furrowed as she looked around, then she got it. "You brought me to Story Land."

"That I did."

"That is so—That's so sweet of you. It's probably the last place I should be, though. I need to grow up, stop believing life can be like a pretty story, complete with Prince Charming." She laughed, a high, strained sound, not her usual throaty chuckle.

"Maybe it can be like that just for a few hours. We can check out all the places in that book you read all those times."

"I can't believe you remembered that. I can't believe you brought me here."

"What do you think? Should we get out of the car?"

"I've always wanted to come here. So, yes, we should get out of the car."

"I'm not so up on my fairy tales, so you might need to be my guide," Gavin said as they walked toward the blue and orange house that served as the ticket booth. Its windows and door and chimney were all askew. "Like this place. What's up with it?" He figured asking her questions might help keep her mind off the way her life had been blown all to hell. That was the point of the trip, to give her a little relief.

"There was a crooked man, and he bought a crooked cat, which caught a crooked mouse, and they all lived together in a little crooked house," Lillian recited softly. He'd hoped seeing the place would at least make her smile, but she sounded . . . wistful, maybe.

It'd been crazy to think an amusement park could make things better, even for a few hours. That was his style, not hers. Feel bad? Take a hit from the bong, 'cause there was nothing

like an old-school bong. Power up World of Warcraft. Go to a
bar. Meet someone new. Whatever. Just anything to keep whatever crap he was feeling locked down. He didn't have to have a
technique to get rid of what Lillian called ratty thoughts. He
never gave them a chance to come at him. "So, what first?"

"We have to take a picture with Humpty Dumpty. In the
book, the whole family sat on the wall with him."

It wasn't hard to find the egg-boy. The big fiberglass sculp-
ture was pretty much the first thing you came to. Next to
him was a little box with a button. "You want to press it, or
should I?"

Lillian pressed it, and Humpty's blue eyes rolled back and
forth as he welcomed them to the park. "Can you take our picture?" he asked the dad of a family passing by. The guy said
yes, because they were in Story Land. You couldn't be a jerk in
Story Land. Gavin handed over his phone, and he and Lillian
got up on the wall, one on each side of Humpty. He promised
himself he'd get the picture printed out and give it to her before
they both left town. Was she even going to stay until the Boots
Camp ended? He decided not to ask right then.

"I want to take a drink from a water fountain that looks like
a sunflower, if they still have them."

"I think they still have everything." The place didn't look
like much had changed since it had opened in the fifties, but it
had a campy charm. It looked like something somebody who'd
been spending time with one of those old-school bongs had
dreamed up. He wondered what it looked like through Lillian's
eyes. She still had that little girl in her, the one who had read the
story set right here so many times. "Hey, even I know this one.
The three bears' house. I don't know about you, but I'm goin'
in." He led the way through the door and up the narrow stairs.

"This place leaves a lot to your imagination, in a good way."
Lillian pushed down on the mattress of the medium-size Mama
Bear bed. "A lot of places would have put Goldilocks in here

somewhere, or the bears, but since they didn't, kids can put themselves right into the story." She tested the Papa Bear bed and the Baby Bear bed, and smiled. "They really are too hard, too soft, and just right."

Gavin suddenly started thinking about Twinkle and kids. She had to want some of her own. Wonder if that made her breakup extra bad. She'd been with that Owen guy for something like three years. She had to have been imagining a future with him, and Gavin was sure that future included a family. Was she thinking maybe she'd missed her chance? It seemed like women thought about all that a lot more than guys did, which made sense. Men could have babies as long as their guys kept swimming. Gavin was twenty-seven, and hadn't given any kind of real thought to having kids. He still felt like a kid himself half the time, and he was good with that. Kids had fun.

They stepped back into the sunlight, and Gavin spotted a big cradle, complete with a kind of creepy smiling baby, rocking back and forth in a tree. He pointed it out to Lillian. "What was that nursery rhyme about? When the bough breaks, the cradle will fall. . . . I'm remembering that right, right?"

"Supposedly, it was about the son of King James II, or actually, a baby who was sneaked into the birthing room, to ensure there was a Roman Catholic heir. The wind—when the wind blows—was the Protestant forces coming in."

"Seriously?"

"That's what some historians say. And 'Mary, Mary Quite Contrary'? That one might be about Bloody Mary. The garden could refer to the graves of Protestant martyrs. The silver bells might have meant thumbscrews, and the cockleshells . . . let's just say, you don't want to know what those were."

Listen to her. His Twinkle had the smarts. And at least he'd given her something to think about other than getting cheated on and dumped. "And we still teach these rhymes to children why?"

"Any rhyme helps kids hear the sounds and syllables words are made up of. It helps with reading. And I guess nostalgia could be a part of it. Parents learned them from their parents."

"My parents used to recite Ozzy Osbourne lyrics to me. 'Satan smiling, eyes of fire,' that kind of thing." Her eyebrows shot up, and he laughed. "Nah. I'm just messing with you. My mom was really into Winnie the Pooh, and my dad would jump in with an excellent Tigger voice. We did all go to an Ozzy concert once, but not until I was, like, twelve."

"Oh, well, twelve. Sure."

"We're here because you used to have to read some book over and over until you were exhausted just so you could fall asleep. Speaking of childhoods."

"My mom used to leave me alone when I was kind of little. She wouldn't go until she thought I was asleep. I guess she thought I wouldn't even realize I'd been alone."

"But you did." What was he doing? He was supposed to be making her feel better, and he was getting her to dredge up all this painful childhood crap instead. Well, he'd redirect. "I'm concerned about those pigs." He walked closer to a pen.

"You don't think they have enough space?"

"All three of them are over by the straw house, even though they have easy access to the stick and brick ones." He cupped his hands around his mouth and yelled, "Get to cover! The big bad is on his way." The pigs—real, not fiberglass—didn't even look at him.

They continued walking, passing some goats—real—and a troll—fiberglass. "I'm still looking for your sunflower, but you could get a drink from inside a lion's mouth over there."

"I'll wait." She grabbed his arm. "Look over there! That cow was in the book. You can actually milk it." She was getting into it, even had a little of her twinkle there for a second.

"Well, let's go." He led the way over to the fiberglass Holstein, much more realistic than that creepy ass baby in the tree. They had to wait for a couple little girls to finish up, but then they got a turn to pull at the teats, making the cow moo, as water squirted out. "Don't move. I have to have a picture of this." He pulled out his phone and got a shot of Lillian leaning her head against the cow's side, the perfect pretty milkmaid.

"All that milking made me thirsty. I'm hittin' the Slushie Shed." Gavin read the sign on the nearby building. "You can mix six, count 'em, six flavors, and that's what I'm doing." He got a cup for Lillian, because who wouldn't want to create a slushie masterpiece? She only chose one flavor—white cherry—while he worked at layering the flavors in the best combination. When he was done, he took a long pull on his straw and immediately gave himself brain freeze. He didn't think he'd ever had a pain-free slushie. Lillian took a sip and crinkled her nose. "Brain freeze?" He didn't think she'd sucked down enough.

"White cherry is supposed to be green tea and white tea and jasmine. I wasn't expecting that, but this . . ." She grimaced.

"Hey, I had a buddy who was in the hospital for almost a month. All he kept talking about was how much he wanted a white cherry slushie—not cherry, white cherry. Cherry was like drinking liquid garbage. White cherry, ambrosia." Lillian snorted. "Trouble is you can find cherry plenty of places, but white cherry is elusive. I finally found it at a movie theater a few towns over. Made his day."

"That's so sweet that you did that for him."

Gavin shrugged. "It wasn't like it was a hardship. In my Porsche. Sunroof open. Good tunes. Life is good."

"It's not something everybody would do. Same with taking me here. Extremely sweet."

"Once I heard I could actually meet the Old Woman Who Lived in the Shoe, I was coming, with you or without you."

"I mean it. Thank you."

The expression on her face was so earnest that he had to look away. "You're welcome. You want to head over to the castle? We can ride over in that pumpkin coach." He watched it go by, the horse's hooves floating a good six inches above the ground. "You up for it?"

"Maybe later."

He figured Twinkle for a fairy-tale castle kind of girl, but then remembered what she'd said about Prince Charming, how she shouldn't believe in him. Maybe the whole Cinderella deal was making her think of the son of a motherless goat and how un-prince-like he'd turned out to be.

Lillian consulted the brochure she'd picked up at the ticket booth. "The Farm Follies is starting up in a few minutes. It's 'an award-winning Vegetable Extravaganza.'"

"Just lead the way."

She tossed her slushie in the trash, checked the map, then looked up at him. "I just realized something."

"That there's something very wrong with the phrase 'Vegetable Extravaganza'?"

"Erin probably had today off, and the two of you must not have that much time to spend together. She works mostly nights at Banana's, doesn't she?" He nodded, not liking the turn this conversation was taking. "And you're at Boots during the day, Monday through Friday. You shouldn't be spending a whole day here with me."

He took a pull on his slushie, stalling—and giving himself brain freeze again. "We broke up. No, that's not exactly true. We weren't really together, so—" He was so full of crap. "Scratch that. Our deal was casual, and neither of us was thinking it would last once we went our separate ways at the end of the summer. But that doesn't mean she didn't break up with me. She did. And it was because I did that thing I always do. There was something she wanted me to go to with her, and I didn't want to, but instead of just saying that, I acted like a jerk until she dumped me."

"Can I ask where it was you didn't want to go?" Lillian stepped back to get out of the way of a couple kids racing toward the cow.

"She's up for an internship at a gaming company, one that's really making a name for itself. They invited her up for a meet-and-greet reception, and she wanted me to come with, and have a weekend together in Vermont. It just felt like too much of a couple thing, meeting prospective bosses."

"Do you think she was getting more serious, maybe wanting the two of you to stay together after the summer?"

"Pretty sure not. So, I didn't have any reason to flip out."

A couple more kids ran past them. Lillian sat down on a nearby bench next to a truly horrific fiberglass clown—white, white face and a really big, really red mouth. It could give Pennywise a run for his money. "Glad you took the seat next to that guy." He squeezed onto the bench on her other side. Lillian just looked at Gavin, waiting. "I guess I have a thing about freedom. I like to keep my options open."

"And I didn't want any options. I was happy with what I had. Clearly, Owen wasn't."

"This is not at all to excuse what he did, because there is no excuse for how he hurt you, but sometimes being out on the trail, it starts to feel—It feels like it's the only real life there is."

"There were pictures of him and . . . and the woman at the top of Katahdin. He climbed Katahdin on his first day out, and by the time the two of them got through the Wilderness, they were together. That wasn't even two weeks. And we were together for nearly three years."

Gavin could practically feel the hurt coming off her. "I hate like hell he did that to you." He wanted to offer more comfort, but he couldn't figure out how. "Want to go see some singing squash?"

She smiled, a shaky, and probably mostly fake smile. "Absolutely."

They found seats in the little theater just as a scarecrow came out onstage and started lip-synching a song about how he did more than keep the crows from crowin', including saying "hi" to the frogs. Who knew?

When the seed packets started to sing about needing rain and water, Gavin glanced over at Lillian. She looked like she was enjoying the reaction of the little kids, and as long as she was good, he was good. His mind began to wander as a cow got into the act, saying something about her moo juice. He needed to apologize to Erin. He should have just told her he didn't want to go to Vermont. Maybe she'd still have wanted to end things, but at least he wouldn't have had anything to feel crappy about, the way he did now.

He could almost hear Rebecca calling him passive-aggressive. He'd told her—and himself—that she was crazy, that she was taking things personally that weren't personal at all. Like that time he'd shown up late for dinner with her and her friend. But he'd pulled that same kind of thing with Erin. He'd known she was waiting at the BBQ. He could have just gone there as soon as rehearsal let out, instead of going to the Mercantile.

Gavin still didn't think it was that big of a thing. But a pile of little things could turn into a big thing, and that's what had happened with Rebecca and Erin both. Why was he thinking about this? This was supposed to be a fun day. He was supposed to be enjoying the Vegetable Extravaganza.

About ten minutes later, all the veggies, the scarecrow, and the cow were finishing up the finale. "What'd you think?" Lillian asked once they were back outside.

"A little draggy. I think they should bring in Miss Violet to give the show some pizazz."

"I love her and her pizazz. She lives big."

"I told you how I broke up with someone right before I

came here, right?" He'd shoved the thoughts about Erin and Rebecca down, but they'd come popping back up.

"Yes. That day in the laundromat." Lillian and Gavin paused next to a big fiberglass sunflower with a smiling face, who said her name was Susie, then started to sing.

"Well, even though that scarecrow was dang entertaining, and don't get me started on the carrot, my mind wandered, and I started thinking about her, Rebecca. Looking back at it, she was right. I did push her away, not by doin' anything big, just by driving her crazy with a bunch of little things. But what I don't get is why. Rebecca was great. Not at the end, because she was always pissy about something. Something stupid I'd done," he added. "Before that, though, things were good, so good we'd moved in together."

"You were living together?"

"Yeah. A couple months ago we got a place together."

Lillian looked at him. "That's kind of the opposite of keeping your options open."

He hadn't even thought of that. Moving in with Rebecca had been a lot more serious than going to some work thing with Erin, but, then, he and Rebecca hadn't just been having some summer fun. They'd been . . . serious. "I thought I wanted to do it."

A memory hit him. Looking for houses with Niri. Breaking up after fighting about some house. He had thought he wanted to live with her. They had been about to get married, for chrissakes.

"Sometimes what we think we want isn't what we actually want." Lillian sighed.

This was getting way, way too serious. "This sunflower is getting on my nerves." The thing had started singing the same song again. He spotted a ride a little ways away, a barn that rose up into the air and spun around. That's what they needed. Fun. He'd brought her here so she'd have a little fun. "Come on. Let's go try out the crazy barn."

"I thought you'd never ask."

He grabbed her hand, and, a few minutes later, they were swinging up into the sky, and whirling around, and she was laughing. Yeah, this is what today was for.

"Thank you. Thank you for making me get out. I'd still be in bed with the covers over my head if it weren't for you." And, yet, today, with Gavin, she'd actually been able to forget about Owen for several minutes at a time. Gavin had even made her laugh.

"You gonna be okay? We could go find someplace that's open. I don't think the Dairy Barn over in Guilford closes until eleven."

"If I eat one more piece of junk food, I'll . . . I don't know, but something bad."

"Weren't you listening to the cow in the Farm Follies? Dairy is nutritious."

"I'm fine. I'll be fine." She leaned over and gave Gavin a fast hug. "Thank you."

"You already said that a few times."

"Well, it didn't feel like enough." She got out of the car and gave him a wave before climbing up the steps to the veranda of the boardinghouse. Simon sat in one of the rockers, cradling a guitar. Lillian decided to join him. She wasn't quite ready to be alone. She was pretty sure once she was, the rats would come for her. "You play guitar too? I guess that's a silly question, since there you are, holding one."

He wiped his forehead with a bandana. In the dim light, she hadn't realized he was sweating, and his hand shook as he returned the bandana to his pocket. "I used to play constantly, but I haven't even held a guitar for, well, decades." He lightly ran his fingers, his trembling fingers, over the strings.

"Another panic attack?" Lillian asked.

"Yeah. The visualization technique you taught me helps though. You should have seen me fifteen minutes ago. Dude. I was quivering like a bowl of Jell-O during an earthquake."

"You had an attack when you were playing the piano, now with the guitar. Is there a connection, a trigger?"

"I hadn't played the piano for decades, either. Decades and decades. I just—I stopped for a while. I thought it was only going to be for a while. I didn't mean it to be permanent, but the more time that went by, the harder it seemed to start up again. Then it felt impossible. The few times I tried—well, you've seen for yourself."

Simon gave his hands a vicious shake, then continued. "I was always good at math, so I got an accounting degree, and I've done well. I told myself it didn't matter if I couldn't play. But I turn sixty in a few weeks, and time is passing faster and faster, just the way old people always say it does. I started feeling like I didn't want to get to the end without making music again, even with no one listening. I came here hoping to see The Fox. I had a . . . friend who saw it years ago, decades and decades ago. It changed his life. Made him more successful than he ever imagined he could be. If The Fox could do that, I figured it could help me get back to my music."

"But all it took was Miss Violet."

Simon laughed. "She pretty much dragged me over to the piano that day. If I hadn't at least tried to play, I'm not sure what she would have done."

"She's a force of nature."

"Dude." Simon gave the guitar a light strum, which barely made a sound. Lillian realized the guitar was electric, and not plugged in. "If I'd met her forty years ago, who knows what my life would have been like."

" 'For of all sad words of tongue or pen, the saddest are these: It might have been.' "

Simon nodded, playing almost soundless chords. Lillian stared up at the stars, thinking about the other nights she'd sat here looking up at them, imagining Owen, out there on the trail, looking at them too. It had made her feel close to him.

And that whole time, he'd been with some other woman. A wild, adventurous woman. Someone completely different from Lillian. She felt a salty ball of unshed tears form in her throat. Even now, knowing what he'd done, she missed him so much. How was she going to go back home without him? He'd ripped a huge, ragged hole in her life, and she didn't know how she was going to fill it.

She had the sudden urge to call Gavin, and, when her phone vibrated at that exact moment, she had the wild thought that he'd felt her need for him and called her. Then "Mamma Mia" began to play. Lillian couldn't deal with her mother right now. Lying again, pretending everything was great between her and Owen felt impossible. Telling her mother the truth would mean hearing all the ways Lillian was to blame for his cheating on her, then dumping her. She turned off the phone.

"Everything okay?" Simon asked.

"Just avoiding a conversation with my mom." She'd have to have it eventually, but not tonight. "Do you have any kids?"

"No. No wife, no kids. When I lost my music mojo, I felt like I had nothing left, nothing anyone would want."

"Dude!" For him to think there was only one thing, one talent that gave him worth as a person, was almost unbearably sad.

"Exactly."

Was her attitude so different from Simon's though? Without Owen, or without someone, she felt worthless. Maybe the idea had started with her mother, who definitely felt that way about men, but Lillian had taken it in bone-deep.

"Maybe I'll find out that there's truth to that saying, 'life begins at sixty.' " Simon gave a little shrug.

She was almost half his age. If she was lucky, she had lots of years ahead. And it was up to her what she did with them. Some things were out of her control though. She'd worked so hard, but she wasn't going to get Owen back.

CHAPTER 15

Gavin pulled up in front of his cabin, turned off the engine, then immediately revved it up again. He didn't feel like being alone, and Banana's place would be open for a couple more hours. He drove over, and almost turned around when he saw Erin's cute little Bug—thanks, mom and dad!—parked out back. He reminded himself that he owed her an apology, and it wasn't going to get any easier if he put it off.

He didn't see her when he walked inside. Probably picking up an order in the kitchen. "I'm preparing an invoice," Banana announced as soon as Gavin sat down at the bar. It took Gavin a few seconds to remember that Banana had told him that Erin broke things when she got mad.

"I'll pay it. I was a jerk."

"You're telling the wrong person."

"I'm going to tell Erin too." As if Gavin had summoned her, Erin came striding out of the kitchen, balancing three loaded plates. She shot him a look that he was surprised didn't incinerate him on that spot. "I'm going to have to apologize to Rebecca and Niri too. Probably there are others." He considered that. "Definitely there are others. But I think I'll let the ones from way back when go."

"Sounds like you had a come-to-Jesus moment. Maybe more than one. Where's the mug?"

"Left it in my car, I guess."

"I'll let it slide this time. What'll you have?"

"Whatever's strongest."

Banana filled one of the plain mugs and set it in front of him. "Mule Kick. 19 ABV. I'll take your car keys. I can give you a ride since you're staying till closing."

Gavin handed them over, then took a slug. "Tastes like licorice . . . licorice and molasses."

Banana nodded. "The kick sneaks up on you. Since I'm a bartender, you're pretty much obligated to tell me your sorrows. How'd you screw up so badly you have a list of women to apologize to?"

"Basically, instead of telling each of this multitude of women that I was ready to move on, I acted like a jerk until they were eventually forced to breakup with me. And I got to walk away feeling like it was their problem, not mine."

He caught sight of Erin heading back to the kitchen. "Can I talk to you for a minute?" he asked.

She didn't slow down. "Stick around, and I'll consider it."

There was the sass. He still liked it. He still liked her. He had to find a way to stop being such a . . . son of a motherless goat with women. "Can I blame my parents?" Gavin asked Banana. "Everybody gets to blame their parents for why they're messed up."

"My opinion? You get to a certain age, and you have to take responsibility for your own actions. Not that your parents don't have a big influence. What'd yours do?"

"They were great. I had a great childhood. No bedtime. I could order pizza pretty much whenever. My dad got all the best video games as soon as they came out, and let me play with him. Gave me a bong when I turned thirteen." If Banana had been drinking, he'd have done a spit take. "I got really used to doing whatever I wanted to do, whenever I wanted to do it. I think I get itchy when things feel too locked down. Like with Rebecca, we'd just moved in together a few months before we broke up. And with Niri, we were engaged and lookin' at houses before she gave back the ring. This might be—This *is* an asshole thing to say, but it's the truth: I don't like it when someone starts depending on me. Makes me want to cut and run. Which I guess means makes me drive whomever I'm with nuts enough that she gives me the boot—so I can cut and run."

"You're dishing it up, but I'm not having any."

"What's that supposed to mean?"

"It's supposed to mean that I don't believe you. What about Lillian?"

"What about Lillian?" Gavin didn't see what Twinkle had to do with any of this.

"You told me you were taking her to Story Land."

"Yeah. And?"

"And did you have any interest in going to Story Land?"

"It's for little kids."

"Is that a no?"

"It's a no, but you should have seen Twinkle when she found out that guy had been cheating on her. She was destroyed. I had to do something."

Banana pointed to his nose, then pointed at Gavin.

"And this means—" Gavin repeated the gesture.

"It means, Lillian needed you, and you were there for her. You didn't cut and run."

"That's different. I'm not her boyfriend. I can walk away any time. I'm not even going to see her again once she's done with Boots Camp."

"Were you and Erin planning on keeping things going after the summer?"

"No. I mean, I don't think she was thinking we were. I wasn't. We both knew we were heading in different directions when school started back up."

"So what's the difference between her and Lillian? The finish line's in sight for both of them. No plans to see either of them again."

"Like I said, I'm not Lillian's boyfriend. And we're talking one day. I didn't have any plans, so why not do something to cheer her up?"

"I didn't realize it was just one day. Weren't you spending the summer helping her with some strategy to get her boyfriend back?"

"How do you know—" Gavin raked his hair off his face with his fingers. "Never mind. You always know everything. But again, obviously not her boyfriend, because I was helping her get her boyfriend back." He stood up. "I'm going to go see if Erin will allow me to apologize. Can she take a break?"

"Sure. I'll cover the tables."

Gavin walked into the kitchen. "Banana said you could take a break."

"And you're assuming I want to spend that break listening to you?"

"I'll make it fast. You were right. I didn't want to go with you, and instead of saying that, I pulled enough stupid crap to make you end it, so I didn't have to."

Erin shot a look at Big Matt, the short-order cook, who wasn't even pretending not to listen. "What do you think?"

"I don't think I heard an actual 'I'm sorry.' That's usually part of an apology." Big Matt sprinkled some diced radishes on top of a tower of nachos.

"And I'm sorry," Gavin added quickly. How'd he forgotten that part? "And you're great. And I hope I didn't screw up the entire summer for you."

"Don't give yourself so much credit." Then she actually

smiled at him. "We had some fun. Glad you pulled your head out of your butt. Now, leave. It's my break, and I want to eat."

Fair enough. "Can I get my keys?" he asked when he returned to the bar. "I decided I don't need that 19 ABV, and I only took a swallow."

Banana took the keys from a hook by the taps. "Sometimes apologizing can feel pretty good."

He was right. And that was a good thing, since Gavin still had a few more to give.

"Remember what we talked about," Annie told Lillian.

Lillian didn't have enough air to answer right away. She'd just done forty-five seconds of squat jumps, the third of three sets, with twenty seconds of rest in between. Twenty seconds that felt like two. "Hinge at the hips," she wheezed out. "Thighs parallel to the ground."

"Not that. About making sure your ex has his head on straight before you think about taking him back, because I believe he's over by the picnic tables."

"What?" Lillian jerked around—and there was Owen. Owen. There was Owen. Tears immediately began pricking her eyes, just from looking at him. She blinked them away, walked over to her backpack, grabbed her water bottle, and took a long drink. What was she supposed to do?

Obviously, what she was supposed to do was go over and talk to him. She took three long, slow breaths, then walked—just walked, no hurry here—over to him. Let him talk first, she coached herself. Don't fall all over yourself asking how he is.

"Your mother told me you stayed in town." Lillian hadn't even wondered how he knew where she was. Her brain was spinning. "You're doing a hiking boot camp, is that right?" He sounded baffled, and why wouldn't he be? This was so not the regular Lillian, the Lillian he was expecting.

"Uh-huh. We were just doing some interval training. Good for speed and stamina on the trail. It's so beautiful here. I thought I'd do a few overnight hikes before I headed home, but I need to get in shape first." She wasn't going to tell him that she'd been trying to turn herself into the woman he'd said he wanted. She'd thought about quitting Boots when she'd found out Owen was already with someone new, but she realized that she actually liked it. It was impossibly hard so much of the time, but because it was impossibly hard, it gave her a sense of accomplishment unlike anything she'd felt before. She didn't want to give it up.

"So, why are you here?" Did he want her back? If he did, he had to say so. He owed her that much. He couldn't just expect her to throw herself into his arms and tell him how much she'd missed him. She was sure he'd love to hear how she'd pretended he was with her so many nights when she was eating in a restaurant alone, but he didn't deserve to know that, at least not yet. But he looked so good, sections of his blond hair bleached almost white by the sun.

"I wanted to see you, Lillian. I've missed you, sweetheart."

Wasn't he going to apologize? Not for the cheating. He didn't know she'd found out about that. But for that night at the restaurant when he called her a doormat and walked out on her?

"I should get back to training." She glanced over her shoulder. The group had moved on to lateral lunges, using their backpacks to do single-arm rows. She needed to get away from Owen, at least for a little while, so she could think. Because it was getting hard to be rational with him standing right in front of her, so close she could smell his sweat, sweat and soap. He hadn't come straight from the trail. He'd obviously stopped to shower and shave. For her. "So, I . . ." She took another look at her group.

"I came all this way, and you're not even going to talk to me?"

"Tonight. Meet me at the BBQ on Main Street at six."

"I was hoping we could head back to Vermont this afternoon. I just got to Bromley Mountain, and I'm going to need to pick up some time. Making this trip messed up my schedule."

"If you want to see me, I'll be at the BBQ at six. I understand if you can't." She didn't wait for him to answer. She walked to her pack, picked it up, and started doing the lunges. She couldn't believe she'd sent him away. Would he leave?

He hadn't bothered to send a text for more than a month. If he couldn't be bothered to wait a few hours to see her, well, that was something she needed to know.

He was there. It was five minutes to six, and he was there. He'd gotten there early. Lillian still didn't know exactly what she wanted to say to him. The way he'd arrived, so unexpectedly, had left her thoughts all in a jumble and her nerves jangling. She decided she didn't need to know what she was going to say until she heard what he was going to say.

"Hello." She sat down across from him.

"I've been recalculating my schedule. I think I can still make it to Harpers Ferry before we need to get back for school, but we need to leave first thing in the morning."

"You expect things to go back to exactly the way they were? You're not going to say anything about what happened? You broke up with me, Owen, and you're acting like I've been waiting here—passively—for you to come back and get me." Wow. The words had come spilling out, and they felt right and true. She could do this.

Owen blinked. Long eyelashes. Lillian loved those long eyelashes of his. "Of course, I'm sorry. I just . . . I'd had a hard run of days on the trail. The Wilderness is one of the roughest stretches. I was exhausted. We shouldn't have even tried to go out to dinner."

"I believe I suggested just getting room service, but that's part of what made you explode in the restaurant, my deferring to you, being a doormat."

"I shouldn't have said it like that. But being more assertive is something you might want to work on. Remember how hard it was for you to be firm enough with that parent who said you pulled her daughter's hair? Obviously, the kid was fibbing, but by the time that mother was done with you, you'd started wondering if maybe you'd retied her ponytail too tight, even though you knew you'd never touched her hair."

That was true. But just because she should be more assertive, that didn't mean he could yell at her the way he had. He'd apologized for that though, she reminded herself. She realized she was staring at him, and forced herself to look away, even though it was so, so good to see his face.

Piper came over and handed Lillian a menu. She didn't give one to Owen. She put a glass of water in front of Lillian. Owen didn't get one. Clearly, someone had recognized Owen from the scene in the inn's restaurant, and word had flown around town. Lillian used the menu to hide a smile, then handed it to Owen. "I already know what I want." And she did. Chicken wings, with mac and cheese and baked beans. Owen hated wings. He always said he wasn't paying good money for skin and bones. But Owen didn't have to eat them.

"I think I've gotten more assertive these last weeks." Lillian took a sip of her water.

"That's so great. And I really appreciate your taking that hiking class. It's great that you want to know more about something I love."

Of course, he assumed it was all about him. And it had been all about him, until, gradually, it wasn't. "It's been so hard, but I realized I can do things I never imagined I could. I can dig down and keep going, even when my lungs are burning and my legs are jelly."

"Maybe you could hike a little way with me when we get to

Bromley, a couple miles, to get a sense of the trail. Then you can drive on ahead, like we planned."

She still hadn't said she was going, but it was what she'd wanted, before she had found out about that woman, who he clearly had decided not to tell her about. She'd checked his socials before she headed to the BBQ, and all the pictures of the woman had vanished. "You know what's on the way, almost on the way, to Mount Bromley? Story Land! We should stop."

"What's Story Land?"

She knew she'd told him about the book where the characters went to Story Land. She knew she'd told him she'd had to use it to help her fall asleep. Gavin had remembered, and when she'd mentioned it to him, they'd practically just met. "It's an amusement park. When I was little—"

"I told you, Lillian, I need to make up time. I'm barely going to make Harpers Ferry as it is, now that I had to come back here. I had to rent a car too, so I've blown my budget."

Him, him, him. All about him. Well, this time, she was going to make sure that their relationship was more balanced. She wasn't going to be just a minor character in the story of Owen's life. She had her own story. "I've been thinking about my Boots Camp. I only have about a week left. I want to finish up. You should go on without me, and I'll meet up with you when it's done."

"Why? We both know you were doing it because of what I said, about how I wanted a free, adventurous woman."

"Wild," Lillian corrected him. His words had seared her like a brand, and he couldn't even remember them correctly.

"I was wrong though. That's not what I want. I want you, just as you are."

Just as she was, meaning a passive doormat. "Did your wild, adventurous woman dump you?" More words that felt right and true. It was like she was learning how she really felt by listening to the words that rose up inside her and came out of her mouth. It didn't seem like any words were rising up in Owen. He was looking at her like she'd reached over and slapped him. "Were you going to pretend you didn't cheat on me?"

"It didn't mean anything. It was a trail hookup. They happen a lot. I—"

"I think I'm done." She stood up. "No, I'm sure I'm done. I don't want to get back together, Owen. I think you actually liked the passive, doormat me, and I'm not that woman anymore. I'm an Amazon butterfly."

And it was her turn to leave him behind at the table.

CHAPTER 16

"He called my mother to let her know I broke up with him," Lillian told Honey as she carefully unpacked a shipment of spun-glass foxes. "He didn't mention the part where he broke up with me first, or the part where he cheated on me."

Honey looked up from the laptop, where she'd been running a monthly report on the shop's sales. "She must have been outraged when you told her what was what."

"She reminded me how long I'd been single before I met Owen. She didn't say he was my last hope of getting married, but that was the subtext."

"That's ridiculous! You're a catch, Lillian, and, any time you say, I can line up dates with—"

"Still not ready. I was with Owen so long. I need time to figure out what I'm like when I'm not trying to be who I thought Owen wanted me to be." Lillian ran her finger over one of the little foxes. "This one has a chip on its tail."

"Set it aside. We'll send it back," Honey said. "Would you take a peek up front? I don't want KiKi to have to help too many people on her own."

Lillian pulled back the curtain. "We have three browsers, and she's just finishing ringing someone up." She returned to unpacking. "How's she doing? She doesn't talk to me as much as—"

"She's having a mental health crisis." Evie climbed out of a large box that had held a shipment of needlepoint pillows. Lillian had been meaning to break it down.

"Evie! I had no idea you were back here!" Honey exclaimed.

"That's because I'm P.I., Practically Invisible. It's an essential skill for a detective." Evie adjusted a barrette that had come loose.

"We've talked about eavesdropping, missy." Honey shut the laptop. "When people are having a conversation, you have to make your presence known."

"But if I'm in sight, and am being so quiet that people forget I'm there, then it's okay, right?"

Lillian could see Honey trying not to smile. "I suppose. That wasn't the case this time though, was it?"

"No. Now do you want to hear about Kristina?" Evie pulled out her notebook. "I don't think she even went to bed last night. This morning, she was wearing the same clothes as yesterday, and her toothbrush wasn't wet. Kristina always brushes her teeth as soon as she wakes up. She's been working on a map of every place The Fox has been seen. Miss Violet gave her tons of old copies of that newsletter she writes, and all Kristina does is read them, looking for any mention of fox sightings. She hardly talks to me. She only goes to play practice because Honey makes her. And she hardly eats. I brought her one of the junk-drawer cookies from Shoo Fly's two days ago, and she hasn't even taken a bite. Before that, the longest she'd left one of those cookies unbitten was forty-seven seconds."

Underneath the P.I. rattling off her observations was a scared little girl. Lillian was concerned about KiKi too. Ever since KiKi had insulted that boy she liked, she'd sunk into herself, interacting with customers when she had to, but not engaging with Lillian or her family. "I know you're worried about her, Evie."

"If The Fox is magical, she should know how much Kristina needs to see her, and she should just come over here."

"I agree." Honey gave Evie a hug. "It's lunchtime. Why don't you take KiKi over to Amore for pizza?" She took her purse off its hook and handed Evie a twenty. "Lillian and I will watch the front."

"Kristina might love pepperoni pizza more than the cookies. I'll have to check my log." Evie slipped through the curtain, but was back in less than a minute, eyes wide.

"KiKi said no?" Honey asked.

"You have to come," Evie whispered. Lillian and Honey hurried after Evie. Where was KiKi? She wasn't at the register. Was she helping one of the browsers? As Lillian scanned the shop, she realized every person there was standing motionless, all facing the same direction. What was happening?

Then she saw what they had all seen. KiKi stood on the sidewalk in front of the big front window. Less than three feet away stood The Fox. Lillian could see its black tail tip and white sock. The vixen and the girl stared at each other, as if they were having a silent conversation, then The Fox turned and trotted away.

KiKi let out a whoop! Then she started to dance, head jerking, arms flapping, butt wiggling, knees bopping in and out. She was joy in motion.

Lillian hoped the creature brought KiKi more luck than it had her. Although, maybe she'd received luck, but hadn't recognized it. Hadn't she started her transformation after she saw The Fox? Hadn't she found the strength to let Owen go?

She smiled as KiKi whooped again. *Bring her what she needs little fox, just like you did for me.*

* * *

The young one had needed her mother. The scent of that need had been so strong that The Fox felt compelled to go to her, the same way, many years ago, she had gone to one of her kits tangled in a human fence.

But now, the young one's scent had completely changed, and she was leaping and bucking, like no animal, or even human, The Fox had encountered in all her long years. Her desperate need was gone. The Fox could return to her woods.

"Could I possibly have a dish towel?"

Gavin knew that voice. He looked around Flappy Jacks, where he was waiting for a to-go coffee to get him through that night's rehearsal. Yep. There he was. Ford. "Sure. Here." One of the waitresses leaned over the counter, grabbed a towel, and handed it to him.

Ford headed over to a nearby booth, where what looked like a mom and middle-aged daughter were sitting. The daughter had her arm in a sling. "Your neck is getting raw." He touched his neck in the spot where the sling was irritating hers. "Use this." He folded the towel and handed it to her. Most people wouldn't have noticed the rubbed spot on her neck—Gavin hadn't—and forget about doing something about it.

"Thank you," the daughter said, but Ford was already walking away. Probably afraid he'd start spilling bad luck.

"Here." Scotty, a friend of Erin's, thrust the coffee into Gavin's hand. Erin had forgiven Gavin, but clearly this guy wasn't a fan. Fair enough. He paid, then hurried after Ford. He caught up to him on the sidewalk.

"Hey, Ford, hi." The man turned. He looked wrecked, the lines around his mouth deeper, his skin with a grayish tint. "What are you doing in town?"

"Same as always." He stuck out his hand for a shake. "Looking for The Fox."

"Stephanie convinced you to give it another shot, huh?"

"She doesn't know. We aren't . . . We don't talk. If I see it, I'll tell her. But why get her hopes up for nothing, probably nothing. This is the third weekend I've come looking. I'm feeling like Don Quixote. But if there's a chance to be with Stephanie . . ."

"Next time, let me know, and I'll hit the trails with you. Not as an official fox walk, just to be another set of eyes."

"I think I'm better off solo, but thank you."

"If you change your mind, I'm in town until the end of August."

Ford nodded, then crossed the street. That was one stand-up guy.

Gavin pulled the lid off his coffee and drank it as he walked to POPA, the Palace of Performing Arts. The theater's name was more of Miss V's pizazz. He got a kick out of the woman, and he had to admit, she had chops. The play was really coming together. He'd been doubtful of the chorus of forest animals, but with the costumes she designed, it was going to rock.

"Hey, girls." KiKi and her little sis were sitting on the bench outside the barber shop next to the theater, working on ice cream cones. KiKi smiled at him, and he thought it was the first time he'd seen her smile since it all went south with Robert. The boy hadn't had much to do with her, even with the apology. He wasn't actively rude, but he kept his distance. KiKi made that easy, because she'd mostly been keeping her distance from everyone, sitting by herself until it was her turn to be onstage.

"How's the investigation into the mysterious Mr. Reiser, Evie?" He got a kick out of this kid too. She had almost a full notebook of observations she'd made about Simon. She'd pumped Gavin for every detail he could think of, asking him dozens of questions to fill in what she called her fieldwork, basically spying on Simon whenever she spotted him in town. She came to rehearsals whenever she could convince KiKi to bring her so she could keep gathering her "intel."

Evie fiddled with one of the dozen little hairclips she wore. "It's almost finished. I just need to confirm my conclusion."

"Excellent. Good to see that smile on your face, KiKi. I've missed it."

"It's because she saw The Fox, and now she thinks that boy, Robert, will like her. Or at least not hate her anymore." Evie licked the ice cream drips running down the side of her cone.

"Nobody hates your sister." He turned back to KiKi. "Where'd you see The Fox? I need a new location for my walks."

"Right on the sidewalk in front of Vixen's." Evie licked another drip.

She could have put in another appearance in town and changed Ford's life. Maybe it would still happen. Gavin downed the last of his coffee, then tossed his cup in the can by the bench. "See ya in there." Once inside, he spotted Simon sitting on the edge of the stage with a guitar. "Gibson Goldtop, nice. Is that a '57?"

"Good eye. Miss Violet and I thought maybe we'd get in a guitar solo in one of the scenes that takes place in the eighties, the part with the guy who saw The Fox and became a rock legend."

"You going to take it on?"

He nodded. "It's my era."

"Cool beans. What's goin' on over there?" Gavin angled his chin toward the group of kids in their usual corner of the stage. Something was up with them. There were lots of laughs and snickers and chatter, with a couple phones being passed around.

"Some YouTube video has got them spinning. Not my era."

KiKi and Evie came through the double doors over on the opposite side of the theater, and the group of kids went silent for a moment, then started back up even louder. KiKi hesitated partway down the aisle, all deer in the headlights. Gavin realized she was getting a lot of looks from the under-twenty crowd, and some of the laughter had turned mean. Something was goin' on. He climbed up on the stage, walked over to the kids, and grabbed the phone out of the nearest one's hand.

"That's mine," Riley protested, giving her long hair a flip.

"You'll get it back in a sec." Gavin slid the bar back so the video she'd been watching would start over, and saw KiKi and The Fox looking at each other, an expression of wonder on KiKi's face. The Fox trotted off, and KiKi launched into an epic touchdown dance. He thought she looked adorable as hell. Clearly, not everyone agreed.

Riley snatched her phone back. "That girl needs to go home and change everything about herself." She'd said it loudly, and, yeah, KiKi had heard. She was rushing back toward the doors.

Gavin jumped off the stage, planning to go after her. Before he could, Robert yelled, "Awesome dance, KiKi!" And there wasn't any kind of snark in his tone.

"I can't believe you saw The Fox," a girl called. "I've lived here my whole life, and I've never seen The Fox. Do you feel luckier?"

"So much luckier." KiKi started back down the aisle, heading toward the group. Well, damn. It had seemed like her encounter with The Fox was going to tank her, but look at this.

Evie had been following her sister, but now she stopped in front of Simon. This should be entertaining. So far, she'd been doing her investigating from a distance, but it looked like Simon was about to get grilled. Instead of firing questions, Evie began to sing that "Down in the Deep Dark" song.

And Simon started to shake. He managed to put down the Gibson, then half jumped, half fell off the edge of the stage. He stumbled when he tried to take a step, and collapsed onto the floor. Evie gasped. "I didn't mean to make you do that."

Gavin dropped down next to Simon. "Picture your axe. Picture cutting off the heads of all those bad thoughts coming at you."

"What's this?" Miss Violet exclaimed as she swept onto the stage from the wings. "Simon!" She scrambled to the ground so fast, Gavin thought he was going to have a second person in a heap on the floor. She knelt on Simon's other side and took his hand.

"I'm all right." Simon regained his feet, not letting go of Miss Violet's hand. "Just a little panic attack. I'm fine."

"I'm sorry. I didn't mean to make you fall." Evie's face was pale. "I just wanted to verify that the song, the 'Down in the Deep Dark' song, caused a reaction. It's part of P.I., Painstaking Inquiry. All facts must be confirmed. I know who you are now. I'm sure of it. But I won't tell if you don't want me to."

Simon used his free hand to wipe his face with a bandana. "Go ahead."

"Mr. Reiser is Ryker, part of a duo from back in the eighties. Shane and Ryker."

Gavin stared at him. "That's you?" Simon nodded. "You had that song, the one about the darling dragon. My dad used to play it for me all the time when I was a kid."

"My one-hit wonder. Right up there with the purple people eater." Simon put the bandana back in his pocket. "We couldn't come up with anything that went anywhere after that one. Then Shane came here and saw The Fox. He wrote a song without me, and you all know the rest. He's still coming out with hits."

"Like 'Down in the Deep Dark.'" Evie clutched her notebook with both hands. "I discovered that several of your attacks happened when it was playing, like the one you had when I was listening to it on Kristina's phone at the store."

"Who's Kristina?" Robert asked.

"I am." KiKi brushed her bangs off her forehead. "I was trying out the nickname KiKi, but I think I like Kristina more."

"Me too." Robert smiled at her.

"I researched the song. Research is a big part of an investigation. A lot of people don't know that," Evie continued.

"She also researched the history of French toast, since that's what you always order at Flappy's," KiKi—no, Kristina—added.

Gavin was still trying to wrap his brain around the idea that Simon was the darling dragon guy. The Gibson lying on the stage caught his eye, and he laughed. "That day when Lillian told you to choose the most powerful object you could think of for your visualization, I thought you picked an axe." He made a chopping motion. "But you were thinking of an axe." He did his best air guitar.

"Dude. You got it."

"Am I correct that you are not, in fact, a hiker?" Miss Violet asked.

"That was my cover story. I didn't want anyone to know a washed-up has-been was in town looking for enough luck to let him play again."

"And play you shall! Your solo will stop the show, I guarantee it."

"Thank you for the chance to perform." Simon kissed Miss Violet's hand, and her cheeks went pink. "Is that okay? Now that you know I'm not a damnable hiker?"

"It's wonderful." The word came out in a musical trill.

Gavin grinned. Happy endings were bustin' out all over the place.

CHAPTER 17

Lillian joined the standing ovation, clapping so hard her hands tingled as she watched Gavin, KiKi—no, Kristina—and Simon take their bows. She was so glad she'd decided to stay in Fox Crossing until she had to be back in Sylva for school. The shop was busy, and Honey had been able to give her lots of hours. But in just a few days, she'd be home. She knew she'd made the right decision breaking up with Owen, but she was a little afraid of how empty her old life would feel without him. She'd be fine though. This summer had proven how strong she could be, not just physically, but mentally and emotionally.

"Brava!" she called as Miss Violet walked out on stage. Simon disappeared into the wings and returned with an enormous bouquet. When he handed it to her, she kissed him. "Brava!" Lillian called again, loving the sight of the two of them as a couple, even though the sight of any happy couple started an ache in her chest. She was sure she'd get over it in time. A lot of time.

Pretty much everyone in the theater headed directly to Wit's Beginning. Lillian walked over with Honey, Charlie, and Evie. Banana had closed the place to host a private cast party, although private wasn't all that private because the whole town would be there, and Banana wouldn't turn away any hikers or tourists who came by.

All her fellow Booters had left town, either to go home or to hit the trail. Lillian was going to go on an overnight hike with Gavin the next day. He said she couldn't do all that training and not put it to use on the Appalachian Trail, and she agreed, although she wasn't sure about the overnight part. Because of the *bam*. She still got the *bam* when she looked at him, and now that he wasn't with Erin and she wasn't with Owen, there were new possibilities, possibilities she didn't intend to explore. She'd seen her mother go from breakup to new guy way too fast so many times, and didn't want to make that mistake. She was also sure that, even though he'd been so wonderful to her, Gavin could break her heart. If she let herself get closer, she knew she'd want more. She'd want everything, and that was something Gavin couldn't give; that was clear from all the conversations they'd had.

"Here they are! Our stars!" Banana called as the actors started coming in. He'd pushed some of the tables back to make a dance floor, and Lillian nudged Honey as she saw Kristina and Robert go straight to it.

"She's a vixen. She gets that from me." Honey wrapped her arm around Charlie's waist and gave him a squeeze. "Come on, take me out there."

"When there's a slow song," Charlie promised.

Lillian hadn't seen Gavin arrive. He must have gone straight to the bar, because here he came with a tray of mugs. "Moxie for you," he told Evie, as he handed out the drinks. "Look at KiKi, Kristina, I mean. She's owning it. I like her style."

"She gets it from Honey." Evie took a sip of her soda.

Lillian shook her head as she watched Kristina doing a version of the happy dance she'd burst into after she saw The Fox. Robert joined in, then, here and there on the dance floor, others started giving her moves a try. Miss Violet was mixing them with something that looked like experimental ballet. Simon only did the head jerk, while shuffling his feet back and forth. A woman in a straw fedora approached Simon and Miss V, and the three left the floor for a table.

"You know who that is, don't you?" Banana asked, taking the empty tray from Gavin.

"How come you know and I don't?" Honey demanded.

"How come you know and *I* don't?" Evie demanded.

"It's rare that either of my ladies is out-scooped," Charlie said.

"That, my friends, is Elaine Greenberg, Broadway producer. I met her during intermission when I was getting some air."

"Miss Violet must be thrilled that a big producer saw her show." Lillian put her hand on Gavin's arm, then quickly removed it, because even that little touch gave her the *bam*. "I don't know why she's not over here praising your duet."

"I owe it to the horse—both halves. They gave me so much to work with." Gavin winked.

Evie stared at the little group as she adjusted one of her barrettes. "I'm going over there. I'm going to find out what's what, because I am a P.I."

"What's the P.I. stand for this time?" Lillian asked.

"Private Investigator, of course." Evie grinned.

"Don't eavesdrop," Honey told her.

"I will make sure that I stand in plain sight where any human would realize I could overhear their conversation." With that, Evie headed for the table.

"I say she'll be back within five minutes," Banana said.

Gavin shook his head. "Not that girl. I give her three." He looked over at Lillian. "Want to dance while we wait, Twinkle?"

The music had turned slow. That meant touching. That meant a lot of *bam*. She wasn't going to do that to herself. "No, because I'm giving Evie two minutes."

She was back in a minute and a half. "She recognized Mr. Reiser. She loved that song about the dragon. And she reaaallly loves the story of The Fox and the whole show. She wants to bring it to Broadway! Mr. Reiser couldn't stop saying 'dude.'"

"The Fox came through for Miss Violet big-time." Gavin swung his empty mug by one finger.

"Big-time," Lillian agreed, watching Miss Violet rest her head on Simon's shoulder. "Simon, too, and he didn't even see her."

"Our Fox has had a busy summer, what with Kristina, Miss Violet, Lillian, and you seeing her," Banana told Gavin.

"I wish Ford had seen her too." Lillian would never forget Stephanie's face when Ford told her he couldn't marry her.

"Me too." Gavin gave Banana a friendly punch in the arm. "When I first got here, you said my life was about to change because I saw Miss Fox, but that Broadway producer isn't over here offering to make me a star."

"Just you wait," Banana said. "Sometimes the luck takes a while to arrive, but it's coming."

APPALACHIAN TRAIL
CAUTION
THERE ARE NO PLACES TO OBTAIN SUPPLIES
OR GET HELP UNTIL
ABOL BRIDGE 100 MILES NORTH.
DO NOT ATTEMPT THIS SECTION UNLESS YOU
HAVE A MINIMUM OF 10 DAYS SUPPLIES AND
ARE FULLY EQUIPPED.
THIS IS THE LONGEST WILDERNESS SECTION
OF THE ENTIRE A.T. AND ITS DIFFICULTY
SHOULD NOT BE UNDERESTIMATED.
GOOD HIKING!
M.A.T.C.

"Reading that just gave me goose bumps, literal goose bumps."

Gavin ran his fingers down Lillian's forearm, and, yeah, it was covered in little bumps. Which didn't stop him from noticing how soft her skin was. "You're ready. You trained hard. And it's not quite as wild as it used to be." He didn't mention that it was also possible to get food drops out there. He didn't want to say anything that would remind her of that Owen guy.

"And we're only going to Wilson Valley Lean-to and back."

"Maybe next summer we could meet up and hike the whole hundred." It wasn't like him to make a plan for a year away, but time on the trail was always good, and Nick and Annie had talked to him about a marketing job with Boots after he got out of school. Sounded great to him, so he should be around next summer. He was going to do some part-time stuff on the Fox Fest they had going in the winter.

"I can't even think a month ahead. I'm in day-by-day mode."

They fell silent, needing to keep their attention on the roots and rocks. Put your foot in the wrong place, and you'd be going down. But still. Tall trees. Fresh air. Twinkle. Life was good. As they walked, they entered a stretch of the trail where pine trees grew close together on both sides. He knew the road was nearby. People joked that the Wilderness was a hundred miles long, but only a mile wide. The trees blocked the sounds and sights of civilization, though, and, at least for now, they had the trail to themselves. It felt kinda like the woods belonged only to the two of them.

"It's like we're the last people on earth."

Just what he had been thinking. More and more often, he felt in synch with her like that. She seemed to like the quiet, the way he did. Doing a short little section hike felt good. So many times when he was out on the trail for a longer stretch he'd fall into the mindset of needing to get the most miles possible, even hiking with a headlamp sometimes to make it a little farther. He had a buddy who'd decided to run the whole section. He'd made it his goal to get from end to end in under forty hours. Gavin could be plenty crazy, ask, well, pretty much anybody, but he wasn't that crazy. Although he always said he'd try anything once, so maybe he shouldn't rule it out.

"The mushrooms on that tree look like a staircase for fairies," she said, breaking the silence after more than an hour.

He took a look at the shrooms. They had wavy edges that made them look a little frilly, and they wound around the tree in a way that did look like steps. "You're right. Very cool." They were in synch, but she had this way of looking at things that took him by surprise, gave him a new perspective. "You tired? Want a break?"

"Just for a second." She paused and took a pull on her water bottle. So did he. They hadn't been out long, but the heat and humidity were taking it out of him. She started down the trail again. He'd let her take the lead. She'd been training for weeks. She should have the chance to put it into practice. "We're coming to a pond up ahead."

"Not a big one. And look who's built us a bridge." He studied the beaver dam, looking for rotten spots.

"I don't want to hurt it. The beavers might be having tea, and suddenly this big boot would come crashing through their roof."

Gavin laughed. Beavers having tea. Loved that. "They don't live in the dam. They just make it to create a pond. "They live over there, in that den." He pointed to what looked like a jumbled pile of branches in the middle of the pond they'd made.

"Well, that's okay, then." She walked across, taking it slow, placing each foot carefully, then turned and waved to him when she reached the other side. She was wearing that sky-blue T-shirt of hers, the one she'd had on the day she appeared in the Boots Barn with her toenails painted to match. Hard to believe he'd only known her a few months. "I sounded like such a kindergarten teacher back then, didn't I? With the beavers and their tea. Owen didn't like it when I was silly like that." She gave her head a sharp shake. "But that no longer matters, and it shouldn't have ever mattered. My mom raised me to always let a man be right."

"Your mom sounds like a piece of work."

"She is." They started back down the trail. It was wide enough for them to walk side by side in this stretch. "But not just in a bad way. We had a lot of fun sometimes. When I was little, I loved watching her get ready to go out. I'd play dress-up at the same time, like I was getting ready too. She'd put makeup on me. I loved it when she used a brush to put the blush on, so soft and tickly. I think a lot of times getting ready was the best part of the night for her. She'd get so excited. Giddy, even, full of anticipation. But so many times, when she'd come home she'd just seem deflated. She'd crawl into bed with me, hold me tight, tight." Lillian let out a shaky breath. "Long time ago. And she's still looking." She glanced over at him. "Maybe I should send her to Boots Camp."

"Maybe so."

"You thought I was crazy when I came in to sign up."

"Nah. Well, actually, maybe. Crazy to try to turn yourself into something that Owen guy wanted you to be, especially when he'd just treated you like—" Gavin decided saying Owen had treated her like crap wasn't the best way to put it. "When he'd treated you so badly."

"I just—Owen was the only man I felt comfortable with. He understood how anxious I got, and he'd help me."

"Help you how?"

"Every time I'd start overthinking things, even little things, like what to wear, I'd ask him, and he'd tell me if something looked good or not. He didn't make me feel stupid for not being able to make decisions for myself."

Twinkle saw that as helpful. Sounded controlling to Gavin. Owen should have told her she looked beautiful in everything, which was true.

"But why am I talking about him? I want to soak in"—she threw her arms wide—"everything!"

They fell silent again, soaking in the everything. He liked that they didn't have to fill every moment with talk. "Coming up to our first ford." The current in Little Wilson Stream was fast. It'd be a challenge to cross with their heavy packs.

Lillian rolled up her pant legs. "Buddy system?"

"Buddy system." He got his own pant legs rolled up, then they linked arms and faced upstream. "Ready."

"Ready!"

They started across, sidestepping it. Gavin almost went down when his foot landed on an unsteady rock, but her arm steadied him. They took a break on the bank to dump the water, well some of the water, out of their trail runners, and to wring out their socks.

"I'm so excited about this section, where we get to hike by the falls for miles."

"You've done your homework."

"I've read pretty much every hiker blog I could find, watched all the YouTube videos. I liked to imagine what Owen was seeing. I'd look at his tracker and try to picture everything in as much detail as I could. It made me feel closer to him."

That was so damn sweet. Gavin wondered for the millionth time how Owen could walk away from Lillian and all that love.

"And that whole time he was out here, he was with some other woman. I wasn't picturing that." She started to walk.

"Why would you? Who wants to be that person, suspicious all the time?"

"You're right. Maybe you'd get hurt a little less, but the world would seem darker, and, if the world was darker, maybe that wouldn't look quite so beautiful." She gestured toward the falls, the water rushing down a canyon of the slate that had saved the town of Fox Crossing.

"Last time I was out here . . ." He didn't finish. He'd started thinking about Niri, but he didn't want to talk about her, not now, when it was almost his last day with Lillian.

"Last time you were out here, what?"

"Being out here made me think about an old girlfriend. Fiancée." Didn't feel right not to tell Twinkle the real deal.

"Fiancée? Really? How long ago?"

"I was twenty-four. And at twenty-four, I was not even fully human. I definitely shouldn't have been thinking about marriage. In my gut, I knew it, too, because I pulled my favorite stunt."

"Pushing her away?"

"By being a complete asshole." Son of a motherless goat was not a good enough description. "I end up hurting everyone so much worse than if I'd just be up-front and say 'I thought I was ready for this, but I'm not.' I couldn't even tell Erin I didn't want to go to her meet-and-greet. That's pretty pathetic."

Lillian didn't deny it. She didn't say anything for what felt like forever, but what was probably only a few seconds. "You can't change until you realize you were doing something wrong. Look at me. If Owen hadn't broken up with me, and hadn't done it the way he did, I'd probably still be thinking it was perfectly fine to be a pathetic doormat."

"Impressive the way you turned it around."

"Not really. I wouldn't have signed up for Boots Camp if I hadn't thought it would get Owen back. You completely called me on that."

"But by the time you got him back, you'd changed. You knew you didn't want to be that person anymore. I've gotta do that. I've gotta figure out how to change."

"Well, you apologized to Erin, and to your old girlfriend, you said. That's a start."

"I called Niri, that's my ex-fiancée, and apologized to her too. She was decent about it. She said we would have been divorced in less than a year, because she wasn't any more ready to be married than I was."

Gavin heard voices. Had to happen. It was August. He was surprised they'd made it this far without seeing any other hikers. Well, so much for being the last two people on earth.

The Wilson Valley Lean-to already had nine people in it when he and Lillian arrived, but they found a spot where they could eat, just the two of them, after he'd borrowed a little time on another hiker's camp stove to heat up their food. "Freeze-dried beef stew. Yumm-o," Lillian said in the growly monster voice she used at her story times with the kindergarteners. Silly Lillian was one of his favorite Lillians. But pushing-herself-to-her-limits Lillian was right up there. Can't-flirt Lillian. Wand-waving, rat-banishing Lillian. Hard-question-asking Lillian. He was happy spending time with all of them.

Ah, crap.

He loved her.

Why hadn't he seen that coming?

It wouldn't work. He wasn't thinking marriage until maybe thirty-five. He needed a few more years of having fun. Having fun without being an asshole, but having fun. Lillian wasn't the kind of woman for that kind of fun.

"What's wrong?" Lillian asked. "I don't think the food's that bad."

But he was having fun with her now. He'd had fun with her lots of times. And, Banana was right; he'd wanted to help Lillian when her life got wrecked. He'd been there for her. Any other woman, and he'd have been lookin' for the door. Actually, any other woman, and he'd have been showing up late, making sarcastic digs, spending all his time playing video games, anything to make her tell him to find the door.

"I was thinking . . . I just started thinking . . . I'm just gonna say it. I didn't realize it was happening, but somehow . . . I don't want to let you out of my life. If I can't be with you, it's like there'd be a big Lillian-size hole in me."

She scooted back, not much, but enough that he noticed. "It sounds like what you're saying is . . ."

He'd gone too far to stop now. "I'm saying I love you. I'm saying I want us to find a way to be together." He cupped her cheek with his hand. "I could do online classes for my last semester, get a place—"

"I can't." She put her hand over his and slid it off her face. "I can't be with anyone right now. I'm still figuring out who I am without Owen making all the decisions for me."

"I want that for you too. I won't get in the way of that."

The expression in her bluebell-blue eyes told him there was no chance, before she said the words. "You're wonderful. You've been so wonderful to me this whole summer. I can't even begin to thank you enough. But it's impossible. Gavin, it's just absolutely impossible."

The Fox let out a cry from all the way down in her belly. These humans, these humans. Even they, with their limited senses, should be able to feel the glowing cord between them, as beautiful as the moon and stars. But the female did not. She could not. If she did, it would not be possible for her to try to rip it free of him. It would be like a rabbit running to The Fox and baring its throat to her teeth.

Lillian would be glad when school started. She usually liked setting up her room, especially doing the bulletin boards. This year they were going to be Matisse-inspired, not that the kids would know, but they'd like the crazy shapes and beautiful colors. But even as she worked on them, there was part of her that was always thinking, thinking of Gavin. Well, why wouldn't she? It had only been three days since he told her he loved her. Telling him that anything between them, anything romantic, was impossible, might have been the hardest thing she'd ever done.

The kids would distract her. At least a little. She reminded herself that she'd only known Gavin a few months. It was just that he'd gotten under her skin, and into her heart, without her quite realizing it. She'd known she got that *bam* of attraction, but that was just superficial. The thing about Gavin was that she could be herself with him. Her actual self. The self she hadn't let anyone see. Well, she showed the kids her silly side, but she let Gavin see it all, even the ratty thoughts.

She used to think that Owen was the only man she could feel comfortable with. But she really hadn't been comfortable with him at all. She'd constructed a version of Lillian that was exactly who he wanted, and, since she had, their relationship was smooth. The crazy thing was, she hadn't even realized she was doing it. She'd thought she and Owen were the perfect couple. They never fought. He was always sweet to her, well, until that horrible night. Why wouldn't he be sweet, with her spending every moment she was with him trying to anticipate his every want and need?

Lillian threw away the scraps of leftover paper, turned out the lights, and locked her classroom door. Time to go home. She'd stayed as late as she could. It was easier at school than in her apartment, even though she'd bagged up everything of Owen's as soon as she got home and had taken it out to the dumpster.

She stopped at the Panera drive-through for a soup and salad combo. She didn't feel like cooking. She needed to put that on her list. Cook! She'd cooked all the time for Owen, amazing meals. She deserved those meals even now that she was alone. No, especially now that she was alone. She'd already ordered season tickets for the opera in Asheville. Barb and her husband were skipping this year. They had a new baby. But Lillian wasn't going to let having to go by herself stop her.

Tomorrow night it's chicken tortilla casserole, she promised herself as she pulled into her parking spot. Forget tomorrow night. She grabbed her to-go bag as she got out of the car. Tomorrow morning it's cinnamon baked French toast. The perfect Saturday morning breakfast. She hadn't had it in forever, because Owen didn't like French toast. She might make it every day until she was sick of it. Why not? It was her one and only life.

Lillian made a stop at her mailbox. Bill, bill, junk, junk, letter. An actual letter. Her heart seized up, just looking at the envelope. It was addressed to Twinkle. She didn't let herself open it until she was sitting at her kitchen table. She closed her eyes for a long moment, then opened them, and began to read:

> Dear Lillian,
> Started writing this as soon as you left town. Here's what I've been thinking. When I haven't been thinking about you. Which I do most of the time. I really haven't ever been on my own. Like this summer. I broke up with Rebecca, and, less than a week later, I'm flirting with Erin, trying to get her to go out with me.
> Even when I'm with someone, I'm usually doing something to shut off my thoughts. Playing WoW. That's World of Warcraft. Which is the best video game ever. But for a while, I'm not logging on. Time for me to see what all those thoughts I shut off actually are. Maybe if I get good at that, I won't act like such an enormous asshole so much of the time. Sorry, kindergarten teacher.

The thing about you? I let you see all the crappy parts of me. I've never talked to a woman the way I talked to you. Never talked about the way I screw up. Never talked about the downside of having parents like mine. Well, I talked to Banana, but everybody talks to Banana. Probably I could talk to you because at first you were so hung up on that other guy. Since there wasn't a chance of anything starting up between us, I guess I figured why not just say whatever.

I miss talking to you, Twinkle. I miss your face. If you tell me to get lost, I will. But I hope you'll let me keep writing, so you'll know I was serious about what I said. I love you.

Gavin

Lillian slowly refolded the letter, her hands trembling. She wondered how long he'd stay interested. She wondered how many letters she would get. Because when she wasn't right there in front of him, his feelings would fade. He had admitted it himself. He was always on to the next thing, the next woman.

He said she was different, though. That he could let her see all of him. The way she'd let him see all of her.

She wouldn't tell him to stop writing. She wasn't going to get crazy and invite him to visit or anything. But she wouldn't tell him to stop.

EPILOGUE

The Boots Barn had been transformed into a winter fairyland, with little twinkly lights and pine boughs everywhere. Lillian barely took it in. Her eyes went straight to him, straight to Gavin, even though the huge space was crammed with people. He immediately turned and looked at her, as if he'd sensed her gaze. She let him walk over to her. The *bam* was still there.

"You came."

"I've heard wonderful things about the Fox Crossing Fox Fest. Snow tubing, ice sculpting, sleigh rides."

"My marketing strategies at work."

"Don't forget the ornament workshop with the vixen of Vixen's," Honey said as she joined them. She wrapped Lillian in a tight hug.

"It is so, so good to see you." Lillian straightened the fox ears Honey wore.

"Maybe it's even better to see someone else." Honey gave her a wink. "I'll leave you two to it. But find me later. I want to hear everything about this." She gestured from Lillian to Gavin.

"So, you came for the snow tubing?"

"And because you wrote me every day for three and a half months. It was kind of a crazy thing to do."

"Crazy like a fox."

Crazy wonderful. Because with every one of those letters, he'd let her further in, brought her closer to him. After she'd received ten, she'd started writing him back. She'd thought limiting their relationship to letters would somehow protect her. That when he moved on, which she'd been sure, almost sure, he would, it wouldn't hurt so much.

But here he was.

"I think there was one day when I wrote twice."

"Lillian, welcome back!" Banana came over, holding two paper cups. He handed one to her and one to Gavin. "I took a break from beer and have been experimenting with white mulled wine. It may be a little early, but, as they say, it's after five somewhere. And it's a party."

She'd made sure to arrive in time for the celebration kicking off the town Fox Fest. Gavin had been working for months generating buzz about the winter festival. She took a sip of the wine. "I'll never go back to red. How've you been, Banana?"

"Not too well. I've been having trouble sitting. Maybe it's my knees acting up. But I'm having trouble standing too. Knees again. They sort of lock up on me. I told all this to my doctor. He said, 'Hmm, trouble sitting, trouble standing. I guess the only option is to hang yourself.'"

"I should have seen that one coming. You've been reading *Philogelos* again?" Gavin asked.

"Those jokes have been around for more than two thousand years for a reason."

"When you figure out what it is, let me know."

Banana gave his haw-haw-haw as he walked off. Lillian and Gavin looked at each other. "My heart is pounding." Her mother would say she shouldn't admit that. But Gavin still made her feel like she could say anything to him.

"Mine too."

"I've missed you," she confessed. Sometimes the letters had made her feel like he was right there in the room with her. And sometimes they'd made her miss him so much that her whole body ached.

"Missed you too." He shoved his fingers through his hair. "But spending time on my own, probably something I needed to do,"

"Me too. I've been figuring out what I really like and don't like. Sometimes I can hardly tell. I've spent a lot of time trying to be who someone else thinks I should be. My mother, definitely. And Owen."

"I've been acquiring some new skills. I tried out some of the recipes you sent me."

"You unlocked the Baked French Toast achievement?"

He laughed. "I did."

"And I unlocked the Bounce achievement."

His eyes widened. "Seriously? You started playing?"

"I wanted to try it, since you love it so much." At first she'd been a little afraid she was falling back into her old relationship habits—not that she was in a relationship with Gavin—deciding what to do based on what she thought Gavin would want. But she had genuinely been curious.

"And I'm going to go see *La Bohème* at the Met. I wanted to try it, cause you love it so much."

"Lillian. I'm so glad you came." Now, it was Annie interrupting them. That was the thing about Fox Crossing. You stayed there a while, and you knew absolutely everyone.

"I think I hear Nick calling you." Gavin cupped one ear. "Yeah. He's definitely callin' you."

Annie ignored him. "Have you been taking care of yourself?"

"I am. Even joined a gym. I couldn't live without picking stuff up and putting it down." That's how Annie had always described weight lifting.

"Now, Nick is saying that he smells smoke," Gavin said.

"Fine. We'll talk later." With a shake of the head, she left them.

"So, anyway, I ended up with an extra ticket. When I say I ended up with it—"

One of the barn doors opened so hard it hit the wall with a bang. Ford staggered in, a child cradled in his arms. "Call 911."

"On it!" Nick called from across the room.

Annie was at Ford's side in moments. "Lay him down. Everybody stay back." She positioned the little boy on his side with one of his arms cradled under his head.

"I was out walking." Ford struggled out of his snowshoes. "I saw a sled, but no kid. Then I thought I heard something. A cry. I followed the sound. There was this hole by one of the pines. Deep. I don't know how it got there."

"Tree well," Annie said.

Lillian shot Gavin a questioning glance. "Hole around the base of a tree. Low branches keep the snow from compacting around the trunk."

"You're okay, Elton. Just hang in there. Nick, call his parents too."

"Already did. They're heading to the Greenville hospital."

Annie kept talking to the boy, keeping him calm, until the EMTs arrived and quickly got him on a stretcher and wheeled him out to the ambulance.

"He's going to be okay," Annie announced. "Just shaken up. Nothing broken."

Ford paced in a tight circle. "He was down there headfirst. I was afraid to pull him straight out. I kind of figured out where his head would be and started digging."

"That was exactly the right thing to do." Annie put her hand on Ford's shoulder, stilling him. "If you hadn't found him, he could have suffocated."

"Dude!"

Lillian hadn't realized Simon was at the party. He stood close to Miss Violet, arm around her waist.

"Ford, I think your luck has changed," Gavin called.

"When I saved that one"—Annie jerked her chin toward Nick—"he told me the Talmud says if you save one life, you've saved the whole world."

"You hear that, Ford?" Lillian exclaimed. "You just saved the world. Your luck has changed. It has!" Please believe it, she thought. Please believe it down to your bones.

"Anybody have a phone?" Ford asked. "Mine's wet."

Gavin had his out in a second and tossed it to him. "I have to call Stephanie and ask her to marry me. Think we could have the wedding here? With all the lights and boughs, it's already decorated."

"Of course," Annie said.

"Tomorrow?"

"Of course," she said again.

Ford smiled. Wow. Pure joy. "You're all invited."

"You want to be my date to the wedding?" Gavin asked Lillian.

She felt like she was standing at the edge of a high dive. When she was little, she could never make herself jump. She'd always have to turn around and do the climb of shame back down the ladder. This time, she leaped. "Yes."

His grin was as bright as Ford's. "And, I was saying I ended up with an extra ticket to *La Bohème*. Because I bought it. Valentine's night. You want to go?"

"Yes, yes, yes."

The human male had looked directly into The Fox's eyes, but somehow had not seen her, and for a moment it seemed that he would not be able to hear the child, even though the cries were loud enough to reach every creature from here to her mountaintop. The child did not belong to The Fox, was not one of her kin, but she still felt the cord between them, felt the pull as the child's terror grew. At last the male seemed to feel it too, and he went to the child before it was too late.

The Fox did not think she would ever come to understand the humans, even if she dwelled beside them for hundreds more years. So often they seemed unable to sense the cords of connection binding them to one another and to the world. The Fox had seen one of them try to hold tight to a cord, even though it was splotched with rot, and then try to rip in half a cord that shone like moonlight. Somehow, that human had saved herself. The moonlight cord was so strong now, The Fox didn't believe it could ever be broken.

It was time for The Fox to leave the humans behind, at least for now. She needed to be deep in her woods. She needed to be high on her hilltop. She needed to be in a place where things were as they had always been, where mothers nursed their kits, males searched for mates, predators hunted prey, and all felt the connections that bound them.

Keep reading for a special excerpt!
FOX CROSSING
by Melinda Metz

In the mountain village of Fox Crossing, Maine, everyone knows the story of The Fox. According to local legend, one of the town's founders crossed paths with a curious-looking fox with a distinctive white ear and paw. The unusual fox sighting not only inspired the town's name, it sparked a fantastical piece of folklore that's been passed down for generations. Some people say that whoever sees The Fox will be rewarded with good fortune, love, and happiness. Others say it's just a silly folk tale . . .

Annie Hatherley doesn't believe The Fox legend—even though it was her great-great-great-grandmother who spotted the critter centuries ago. But now it's part of Annie's legacy, along with her family business, Hatherley's Outfitters. For years, Annie's been selling gear to hikers on the Appalachian Trail. But she's never seen The Fox—until now. Out of nowhere, this little white-eared vixen leads her to Nick Ferrone, a woefully unprepared hiker who needs her help. The Shoo Fly Bakery owner also spots the sly creature—who takes him to a homeless dog that needs his love. Annie can't deny that something magical is happening—because she's starting to fall for a certain foxy hiker named Nick . . .

Look for **FOX CROSSING**, *on sale now.*

CHAPTER 1

One look was all it took. He's not gonna make it, Annie
Hatherley thought. She watched the lanky man cross the street
toward the store, the sun bringing out glints of auburn in his
curly brown hair. He wasn't the worst noob hiker she'd ever
seen. That would be the guy last year wearing jeans, flip-flops,
and an aloha shirt, cotton of course, his pack filled with three
more of the gaudy shirts, a carton of Clif Bars, and a large bottle of water. And nothing else.

This guy wasn't that guy, but his backpack probably weighed
close to seventy pounds. Nope, he wasn't gonna make it.

Forget the pack and the boots, his calves showed her that he
hadn't been doing the kind of training he needed to take on the
100-Mile Wilderness. They weren't scrawny. They were, in
fact, nicely muscled, with just the right amount of hair, at least
in Annie's opinion. She had a friend who liked her men to look
half-bear. Took all kinds to make a world.

But this guy's calves, nice as they were, were the calves of a
casual day-hiker. A serious hiker's calves usually expanded a

half inch in circumference, thighs about two inches. Sadly, Annie couldn't see the man's thighs. His prAna Stretch Zion shorts hit him a couple inches above the knee. He'd made a smart choice there, the shorts stretchy and cool, with a wicking finish. And only two pockets. A lot of noobs thought they needed way more pockets than they actually did. But, despite the sensible shorts, he wasn't gonna make it. He—He was coming through the door. "Okay if I bring this in?" he asked, holding up the paper cup he carried.

"Sure." Annie watched him take in the store, her store, since her mother had gotten herself elected first selectman, basically CEO of the town, about four and a half years earlier. He took his time, looking at everything.

"These hardwood floors are amazing."

"They're juniper maple." The hardwood floors were the first change Annie had made when she took over. Her mother hadn't bothered much with aesthetics. Hatherley's Outfitters was the only game in town, the only place to buy gear in Fox Crossing, and Fox Crossing was the last town before the 100-Mile Wilderness, the wildest, and in Annie's opinion, most beautiful stretch of the Appalachian Trail. But just because the store had no competition didn't mean it shouldn't be inviting. Fox Crossing had changed over the years since her great-great-great-great-great-grandmother opened the store. An antiques store was a few doors down from Hatherley's, the Wit's Beginning Brewery was included in one of the Brew Ha-Ha Bus tours out of Bangor, and Foxy Loxy Books had just been selected as one of Maine's best used-book stores.

"Perfect with the slate." The man appreciatively ran his fingers over the smooth slate counter Annie stood behind. For a crazy second, Annie flashed on those fingers running over her skin with that same—Inappropriate thought! He was a customer. Also, a complete stranger.

"Slate from Fox Crossing is in high demand," she said, as

crisply as a new schoolteacher being observed by the principal. "There are several political graves in Arlington Cemetery made by the black slate from the local quarry. Although I preferred gray for—"

"Political graves?" he repeated, raising one eyebrow. Annie had been trying to learn to raise one eyebrow since she was about seven. Still couldn't do it.

"Don't be pedantic." Had she actually just used the word *pedantic*? People who used the word *pedantic* were pedantic. "You know I meant graves of people in politics, including Jackie and John F. Kennedy's," she continued, unable to shake the lecturing tone. At least it was keeping her brain from creating more inappropriate thoughts.

"Guilty. License to be pedantic comes with the glasses." He pushed his slightly geeky, definitely stylish tortoiseshell specs higher on his nose. "The girl—woman—who sold them to me said they gave me a 'modern intellectual look.'"

He laughed and Annie joined in. Even though he was a noob who shouldn't be within a hundred miles of the 100-Mile Wilderness, she was starting to like this guy, dammit. And not just for his perfect-amount-of-hair-and-muscles calves. And not just for his warm chestnut eyes, which she couldn't help noticing when she was looking at his glasses. He was kind of funny, and kind of smart, and had good taste in flooring and countertops.

You have to find, at the very least, a new friend-with-benefits, Annie told herself. It had been a little more than a year since Seth had decided to head west to hike the PCT, and she hadn't even started feeling lonely. Truth? Seth had been starting to get on her nerves, and she was more than kinda glad he was gone. But her zero-to-sixty attraction to this guy showed her she was getting itchy.

"So, what can I help you with?" she asked, all professional-like.

"Wait. First you have to tell me your name. I don't allow myself to be mocked by strangers."

"Annie Hatherley."

"Of Hatherley's Outfitters." She nodded. "Nick Ferrone." He held out his hand, and she shook it. His grip was also just right. Not you're-a-delicate-lady-and-I-must-not-squash-your-fingers soft, but not I-must-show-dominance-to-all hard. Also, it sent a little tingle from her fingers to low in her stomach. Dammit.

When he let go, Annie caught sight of the tattoo on his fore-arm, and she could feel a wide grin, the kind that gave her chip-munk cheeks, stretching across her face. The tat was of what was clearly supposed to be a fox since it had the words I'M FOXY underneath. Nick noticed the direction of her gaze and flushed. "I—"

"You had an encounter with Noah and Logan, otherwise known as Nogan," Annie finished for him. "I'm quite familiar with their hand-drawn temporary tattoos, as well as their strong-arm sales techniques. What else did you buy?"

He took a swallow of what Annie knew was Nogan's drink of the day—blackberry lemonade sweetened with local honey. She'd had one herself at lunch.

"Just a piece of the Canine Candy," he admitted.

He had a dog? Bad idea. She opened her mouth to give Nick a list of all the reasons he should absolutely not bring a dog on his hike, starting with how it would greatly lower his odds of completing the hike, and those odds were pathetic to start out with. She forced herself to take a beat. Find a way to say it nicely, she told herself. Be professional. Last hiking season she'd gotten a bunch of negative social-media reviews about her attitude. One had even called her surly. Surly! Not that it mattered. You wanted to buy gear in Fox Crossing, you bought from her.

"You're planning to hike the Wilderness?" she asked. Even though she already knew the answer.

"Yep." Those chestnut-brown eyes of his gleamed with enthusiasm.

Nick was clueless about what he was in for. Annie felt prickles of irritation run down the back of her neck. The irritation prickles were stronger than the attraction tingles. A license should be needed to hike the Wilderness, and a test—written and practical—to get one. Don't go there, she told herself. "Then I'm assuming you want to go up Katahdin when you get to the end." She managed to keep her tone pleasant. No surly to be heard.

"I couldn't say I'd hiked the whole thing if I didn't."

Couldn't *say* he'd hiked it. Was he doing it for bragging rights? Who was he trying to impress? What was he trying to prove? None of your business, she told herself. You're here to sell him stuff.

"Just so you know, dogs aren't allowed in Baxter State Park, which is where the mountain is." Yeah, that was a good approach. Nothing personal about his hiking skills. "You'll need to board your beastie before that last stretch. There are kennels in Millinocket, but that's twenty-five miles east. It's not easy. You'll only have logging tr—"

"No dog. Just me."

"Oh. Good." She let out a breath. "Then why the Canine Candy?"

"The boys convinced me it tasted just as good to humans and that there was nothing in it that would hurt me, so . . ." Nick shrugged. "Wasn't too bad."

"Wait. You actually ate a piece!"

"Well, yeah. They were watching. It tasted like an extremely healthy, very dry, mostly flavorless cookie, if you want to know."

He's nice, too, Annie realized. Dammit. He wasn't just smartish and funnyish, with excellent taste, plus the calves, and the eyes. He'd humored two nine-year-old boys by buying a dog treat when he didn't have a dog. And he'd eaten it! That was exceptionally nice.

But he's also exceptionally ill prepared, she reminded herself. He wasn't gonna make it out there. The only question was, How badly was he gonna get hurt?

Not at all, if Annie could help it. She'd try to be nice herself, but if that didn't work, well, she could deal with another "she's so surly" review. Surly sometimes saved lives. "So how long have you been training?" Annie asked nicely.

"Almost three months. Every weekend, and I usually got in a few weeknights. And I carry my pack whenever I can, like now."

"Not enough." It felt like the two words hit the ground with a thud.

"What?"

"That's just not enough time to get in shape. I can tell by looking at you you're not up for the Wilderness." Was that surly? No, Annie decided. She hadn't raised her voice. She hadn't called Nick an idiot. She'd just given him the truth, plainly spoken, and he needed to hear it.

"Just by looking at me?" His eyes weren't warm anymore.

"Yep. I've been working here since I was a kid. I can tell when a hiker's not ready, and you, my friend, are not ready."

Nick snorted. " 'My friend,' " he muttered.

The prickles of irritation were back, but they were more like ice-pick stabs now. He was already shutting down. He didn't want to hear her. Well, too bad. "Look, you could die out there. Do you get that? This slate"—Annie slapped the counter—"it's what a lot of the rock out there is made out of. And it gets slippery as shit." She managed not to say *my friend* again, but it was truth time, and she was giving him all of it. "Which makes falling and bashing your head in a definite possibility. Also, there's snow melt. We've got snow melt this time of year, and it can turn streams into white-water deathtraps. And there are swamps—"

"I read about all of this." Nick planted his hands on the counter and leaned toward her.

Annie mimicked his position, leaning in, getting right in his face, glaring at him. "Oh, you read about it. My bad. So, you know it all. Happy trails then."

"Have I interrupted something interesting?"

Annie's grandmother had come in. Of course. Why not make this situation a little worse by having her as a witness?

"Just giving a customer the rundown on what to expect out on the trail." Annie pushed herself away from her side of the counter.

Nick took a step back from his and planted a smile on his face. He turned to Annie's grandmother. "Hi. I'm Nick. The customer."

"I'm Ruth Allis. But you can call me Honey." She fluffed up her blond curls and straightened the pair of cloth fox ears attached to her hairband.

"I'm honored." The fake, being-polite smile—because, of course, he had to be polite, too—became genuine.

"Don't be too honored," Annie snapped. "Everyone calls her Honey, including me, and I'm her granddaughter. You'd think I'd call her Grandma or Grammy or Nana or the like, but, no, I'm forbidden from using any appellation that makes her sound over twenty-one." Annie knew she was taking out her frustration on the wrong person, but kept on going. "That's actually what she puts on forms, even medical ones, twenty-one-plus."

"All anybody needs to know." Honey shot Annie a reproving glance. It didn't work. Annie was way too riled to be reproved.

Nick laughed. "I agree completely. I'm going to start using that myself. Twenty-one-plus."

Honey gave Nick's arm a pat. She was such a flirt. "I hope Annie's told you how beautiful the Wilderness is."

"She was just about to tell me about the swamps," Nick answered, keeping all his attention on Honey.

"There *are* sections of trail that were blazed straight through bogs," Honey began.

Annie had to interrupt her. "Just so you know, you're not going to find much resembling an actual *trail* out there. Don't be expecting a nice dirt path."

"You'll get muddy, but you'll also see pitcher plants." Honey went on as if Annie hadn't spoken. "You're not going to get a look at those too many other places."

"I read about them!" Nick exclaimed. "Definitely going to make sure I see some of those bug eaters in the wild."

He was trail-struck. Nothing Annie was going to say would make a difference. Suddenly, she felt tired. This happened way too many times. "Was there something particular you were looking for today?" She wanted him out of there.

"I was thinking about a bug net."

"This time of year? Absolutely necessary," Annie answered. "I have several types."

"Around now, the blackflies and mosquitoes can get so thick you can't see your hand in front of your face," Honey added, finally giving Annie some backup. "The man who owns the bakery? He was found standing on a bog log shouting, 'Shoo, fly,' over and over, tears streaming down his face. And he was a marine. He got his trail name that day and has been called Shoo Fly ever since."

"Bug net it is," Nick said.

He's probably hoping for a cool trail name, like Thoreau or Seeker, Annie thought. He's one of the ones who imagines he's going to be *transformed by the journey*. She didn't bother telling him to get over it.

"Looking at your pack, I'd say you should have Annie do a shakedown for you," Honey told Nick.

"Shakedown?"

He couldn't have done that much reading about the trail if he didn't know what a shakedown was. "To let you know what's unnecessary, noob," Annie explained.

His eyes narrowed as he looked at her, and she could hear tension in his voice when he spoke. "Everything I brought is important. You're the one who said I wasn't prepared, but I have everything I'm going to need in this baby." He patted his pack.

"Take it off and open it up," Annie ordered. She wanted him out, but that didn't mean she was willing to send him into the Wilderness carrying enough weight to blow out his knees, or end up with a rolled ankle, or a stress fracture. If he managed to avoid one of the dozens of possible injuries, he could still end up so fatigued that he'd take a fall.

When Nick hesitated, Annie insisted, "Do it."

"Fine. But you'll see I have everything I need and nothing more." Nick yanked off his pack, put it on the floor, and unzipped it.

Annie crouched down and started checking out his supplies. She gave a snort of laughter when she got to a worn copy of *Walden*. Had she called it or had she called it? "Everything is necessary, huh?" She tossed it to the side.

"It's one book," Nick protested. "And it is necessary. I know a big part of the trail is mental preparation, and—"

Annie didn't bother to listen. She pulled a solar phone charger from his pack. "Don't need this. Cell service sucks out there." Annie kept on going through his stuff. She pulled out a box of Band-Aids. "Don't need this. If the injury is small enough for a Band-Aid, you don't need a Band-Aid." She pulled out a deodorant stick. "You're gonna have to stink." She pulled out three pairs of boxer briefs. "Nope."

"Come on!" Nick yelped. He probably wouldn't call it a yelp, but it definitely was.

"Bring those and you'll have to bring Boudreaux's Butt Paste for the chafing," Annie explained.

"Fine." She noticed a flush was creeping up his neck. She wasn't sure if it was caused by anger or embarrassment or both. And she didn't care. About ten minutes and fifty protests later, she had Nick's pack at a manageable weight. It took her another five to convince him to trade in the boots for trail runners.

"Is that it?" Nick asked. She noticed a little muscle in his jaw twitching. Good. Why should she be the only one who was pissed off?

"That's it." She shoved herself to her feet.

"Except that we wish you a wonderful hike," Honey said. "It's the experience of a lifetime."

"Thank you." Nick smiled at her. "Hey, we match." He held out his arm so she could see his fox tattoo.

"We're twins!" Honey smoothed down the front of her T-shirt to show off her I'M FOXY fox.

Annie took a long breath, trying to calm down. "I assume you have an extraction plan."

"I did. But the solar charger you nixed was part of the plan. I tried to tell you that."

"And I told you, you can't rely on cell service," Annie shot back. "You need a tracker."

"Yeah? And how much profit are you going to make off one of those?"

He thought this was about money? She was attempting to keep him alive, and he thought she was trying to make a profit. Not that she didn't want the store to be successful, which it was, but that didn't mean it was all she cared about. "I'll rent you one. Hell, I'll loan you one. For free. You can give it back tomorrow afternoon when you come back to town with your tail between your legs."

"Annie!" Honey exclaimed.

Nick jumped in. "I don't—"

"Shut up and take it." Annie jerked open a display case and took out one of the satellite messengers, then thrust it into Nick's hand. He stared at it, as if things were going too fast for him. "Call the number and they'll get your profile set up. If you get in real trouble, send an SOS. It will go out to a rescue coordination center. You can also send your support person a link to an app. They'll be able to watch your progress in almost real time."

Nick's forehead furrowed as he continued to look at the small device. Annie read his expression. "And you don't have a support person, do you?"

"If I needed help, I planned to call for help." He held the tracker out to her. When she folded her arms, refusing to take it, Nick set it on the counter. "I'll take the solar charger and my phone."

Annie pressed her fingers against the bridge of her nose. "Were you not listening? You might not get service and you might not always get sun for the solar. Which means"—she said the next words slowly, and deliberately—"you. Might. Not. Get. Help."

He was close to walking out. She could see that. She pressed her lips together to stop herself from saying something that would push him out the door. He needed the tracker.

"Go ahead and take it, Fox Twin," Honey told Nick. "It might come in handy." She picked up the tracker and gave it to him. He slid it into his pocket.

"I want to pay for it," he told Annie.

"Fine. How many days?"

"Ten."

"It's fifteen bucks for three days."

"Fine."

She could tell he wanted out of her place as much as she wanted him gone. She quickly rang up the bug net, the trail runners, and the rental, ran his card, and gave it back to him. "Do you need me to go over how to send the SOS?"

"I'll google it." He hefted his pack back on his shoulders. "I'll see you when I return the tracker. In ten days."

"I'll be here," Annie said to his back. He was already heading to the door. She and her grandmother watched as he crossed the street, turned the corner, and disappeared from sight.

"You can call me Grandma if you really want to," Honey said.

"I like calling you Honey."

"I know you do." Honey smiled. "That man had everything, and then some. You could have been sweeter to him. Then when he returned the tracker, he'd probably have asked you out for drinks. Or you could have asked him. Then who knows?"

Annie shook her head. "He's way too impulsive for me. He's one of those guys who thinks he's going to change his life by hitting the trail. Walking around with his copy of *Walden*. Which, fine. But you can't just *go*. You need to prep. You need to plan."

"Looked like he'd done some of both to me."

"Some. Not nearly enough. And did you see how he almost walked out of here without the tracker? Just because his pride got dinged a little? He should have thanked me for pointing out he needed the thing." Annie took her phone out of her pocket. "I have the app that will let me see how he's doing. I'm going to keep an eye on him. He clearly isn't capable of taking care of himself out there."

CHAPTER 2

She acted like I wasn't capable of taking care of myself out there, Nick thought as he spooned the last bite of cobbler into his mouth. He knew it was fantastic—the perfect combo of buttery crunch and sweet, tangy blueberries. But he might as well have been eating that Canine Candy. He'd made a dinner reservation at the Quarryman Inn as a treat before ten days of eating dehydrated meals, dehydrated fruit, jerky, protein bars, and instant oatmeal. Believe it or not, Annie Hatherley, he *had* researched, and he knew what he should be eating on the trail.

He'd also decided to splurge on a comfortable bed for his last night in civilization and promised himself he'd enjoy both again when he returned, scraggly bearded and stinking, since Annie Hatherley had taken away his deodorant. Probably, make that definitely, he should go upstairs and get into that comfy bed early, get a good night's sleep, but he was too wound up. He decided on a walk. He thought about getting his pack from the room, but one more night of carrying it wasn't going to make a difference on the trail. And he'd been training plenty, despite what Annie Hatherley thought she could tell by looking at him.

Annie Hatherley. Annie Hatherley. Enough with the thinking about Annie Hatherley, he told himself as he headed out of the Inn in his new, comfortable trail runners. He got that he might not make it all the way through the Wilderness. He knew people had to give up for all kinds of reasons. He wasn't an idiot, even though Annie Hatherley clearly thought he was.

He was still doing it. He had to forget about all her negative bullshit. Haters gonna hate. Crap. Annie Hatherley had reduced him to thinking in Taylor Swift lyrics. "Shake it off," he muttered.

You're in a new place. You're at the start of an adventure. Look around. Take it in, he thought. He slowed his pace, smiling as he noticed Honey in a lit store window across the street, putting a sundress with a frolicking-fox pattern on a mannequin. The sign, all flourishes and curlicues, read VIXEN'S. That explained the fox T-shirt and the cloth ears. He wondered how much business it did. Was there a market for all fox stuff? At a glance, it looked like that's all the shop sold. Maybe people just went in to talk to Honey. She was a charmer. Unlike her granddaughter.

Nick gave a growl of annoyance. In another minute, he was going to have to take out the pocketknife he'd bought for the trip—an Opinel No 7—and excise the part of his brain that held the memory of those few minutes in the outfitter's. At least Annie Hatherley had let him keep the knife. She'd actually said it was one of the best backpacking blades.

Crap. He was doing it again. He shoved his hands through his hair. Maybe it was because before Annie Hatherley had turned into a shrew, he'd thought he felt some mutual attraction between them, a *click*. He knew he'd felt it on his side. That hadn't happened in a long time. Actually, not since Lisa. It's like being happily married had switched off that part of his brain. Not that he hadn't noticed attractive women, but he hadn't noticed them in the same way. He'd have a flash of speculating what they looked like naked or what it would be like to have sex with them, your basic guy stuff. But not with any . . . intent.

But he wasn't married anymore. And he hadn't been happily married for a long time. He'd *thought* he was happily married, but how could he be if his wife was thinking divorce? How could he have been happily married if his wife—ex-wife—got married the day their divorce went through? Not even one day later. The same day.

Today, in those first few moments with Annie Hatherley, it's like an old part of himself had woken up. He usually didn't like short hair on women, but her short, dark brown hair let him focus on her face, on her clear blue eyes, her perfect creamy skin, her lips, her neck, that little dip between her collarbones.

It wasn't just the physical though. He'd liked how she busted his chops, so playful, about being pedantic. Then she did almost a Jekyll and Hyde. It was like she couldn't wait to get him out of her store and out of her sight.

Enough. He needed a drink. Something to settle him down. Get him ready for that good night's sleep. He'd seen a bar with a crazy sign on his way into town. He walked up a block, then turned left. Yep, there it was. The Wit's Beginning Brewery, with a presumably dead donkey, all four legs in the air, on the sign. He'd try one of the local microbrews, then head back to the Inn. And tomorrow the adventure started!

He could have, and probably should have, asked one of his friends to be a support person, but he wanted the Wilderness to be his thing. He didn't want to be checking in every day, didn't want even that much connection to the outside world. It felt like it would . . . like it would somehow diffuse the actual experience, suck some of the meaning out of it.

As soon as Nick stepped inside, the bartender called, "Welcome, friend." He was tall, wiry, and bald, with skin the color of a pine cone. The greeting felt so genuine that Nick headed to the bar instead of settling in at one of the tables. Most were empty, although a group of about ten was settled in at a table in the back, probably town regulars. It was early in the season for hiking the Wilderness. In a few weeks, Nick bet the place would be much more crowded.

"First time here?"

"First time in Mai—"

"Banana, is it or is it not endless-nacho night? Because we are perilously close to the end over here," someone called before Nick could finish answering.

"Big Matt, you got that?" Banana—Banana?—yelled.

"Got it," a guy called back from what Nick assumed was the kitchen.

"Let's start again. As I'm sure you heard, we have endless nachos tonight, if you're interested. Big Matt sprinkles chopped radishes on top. Sounds crazy, but . . ." Banana let out a groan that sounded almost orgasmic.

"Wish I could. But I just finished a big meal."

"What'll you have? The first drink's on me."

Nick had picked the right place. A little *pleasant* conversation would help him unwind as much as a drink. "In that case, what do you suggest?"

"My specialty. The Spirited Banana. It's a wheat beer, but in the German vein, not Belgian."

"Bring it on. But I'm gonna tell you up front that I'd have an easier time telling Coke from Pepsi, than German from Belgian beer."

"Honesty is appreciated." Banana grabbed a plain brown ceramic mug and held it under one of the taps. "Belgian is more citrusy. Esters and phenols give German wheat beer banana and clove flavors." He set the mug in front of Nick.

Nick took a long swallow, trying to pick up on all the ingredients. He got the banana and clove, but also a little apple, and, weirdly, a little bubble gum. "Smooth." He took another swallow. "I wasn't sure I'd like banana in my beer, but it works. Is that why they were calling you Banana? Because of your special brew?"

"Nope." Banana grinned at him.

"Are you going to tell me why they do?"

"Nope." Banana's grin widened.

"How about a different question. What's the story with the donkey?" Nick nodded toward the display of deep blue mugs with the legs-in-the-air donkey on the front.

"It's in honor of my first donkey. I called him Bucky." Banana pressed one fist against his heart and closed his eyes for a long moment, before he opened them and continued, "He was a feisty son of a gun. But smart. I taught him all kinds of tricks. Taught him how to count to ten. Taught him to add. Even taught him to do a kind of a hula shake. Then I decided to try something harder. I decided to train him not to eat."

"Train him not to eat," Nick repeated, his shoulders relaxing with the story and the alcohol.

"Yeah. I cut his food back a little at a time, and he was really getting the hang of it, then he died. Right when he almost had it down."

Nick laughed. It might have been the stupidest joke he'd ever heard. Which is exactly why it was so funny.

Banana laughed even harder than Nick, a low, loud *haw-haw-haw*. "That's from *Philogelos*, the world's first joke book. Or at least first surviving. It was written in Greece, fourth or fifth century CE."

Now Nick understood the name of the bar. "Hence Wit's Beginning." The bartender pointed to his nose, then pointed to Nick. "So, what's the deal with the mugs. Is it a membership thing?"

"Yep, but not the usual kind. There's no membership fee. All you've got to do is walk the two thousand, and I hand one over."

The two thousand. As in miles. The whole Appalachian Trail. "Do you have one?" This was where Nick needed to be. Banana could be Nick's Yoda. He'd send Nick on his way with everything he needed to know, the stuff you couldn't read in books or blogs.

"It's my place, so I could have as many as I want. But I'm not taking one until I finish the damn thing, and I still have a hundred miles to go."

"The Wilderness?"

Banana nodded. "Made sixteen attempts, had sixteen failures."

Nick let out a low whistle. "You never wanted to just throw in the towel?"

"Of course, I did. Sixteen times, for sure. Probably a lot more. But I'm not a quitter. I only have a hundred miles left, and I'm getting them done. This time, though, I'm waiting until I see The Fox."

"What's that?" Nick asked eagerly. "Some kind of flower that blooms at the best time to start? Or when the sunrise is a certain color? Or—"

"Why don't I just tell you?"

"That might work better."

"This is a story that takes some telling."

"Why am I not surprised?" This guy was a story himself— trail hiker, teller of ancient jokes, a beer maker, a business owner. All that, and Nick felt as if he'd barely scratched the surface.

A skinny guy carrying a plate with a mountain of nachos on top headed for the back table as Banana began. "A long time ago, before you were born, hell, before I was born, before my sweet grandmama was born, back in 1803, a fox was caught in a trap around here. Now, I don't know why, because back then there weren't a lot of animal-rights types, but a woman named Annabelle rescued that fox. She'd just lost her husband, and her baby, and was desperate to keep her little boy, not more than two, healthy and safe. The whole settlement was about to go under, and the scraggly group of settlers with it. Maybe that's why she freed that fox and took her home. Maybe she was so heartbroken that she figured any company was better than none. Or maybe death had taken so much from her that she refused to let the Reaper take another, not if she could help it."

Nick bet Banana had told this story a dozen times at least, but he looked as if he was seriously considering the reasons why this woman had saved the fox. "Some say the only reason it lived was because she nursed it. And I'm not talking with a bottle."

"You're shitting me!" Nick took a long pull on his beer.

Banana held up both hands. "All I'm telling you is what people told me. And some have said the milk, the same milk Annabelle still used to feed her little boy, saved The Fox. Some say it did more than that." He turned, took a mug, one of the plain brown ones, and poured himself a drink from one of the taps.

"I don't get you. What more could it have done?" Nick had the feeling he was walking into another bad joke. But he had to ask.

"It's just rumors and supposition. Not much worth passing on."

He's messing with me, Nick thought. He tried not to sound too eager when he said, "I like a good supposition."

"What do you think, Big Matt?" Banana asked as the skinny guy headed past on his way back to the kitchen. "Should I tell our friend the secret about The Fox?"

The man rolled his eyes. "As if I could stop you," he answered without pausing.

"I do like to tell a story," Banana admitted. "I said the settlement was close to dying out. Then a gentleman, Celyn, who had immigrated from Wales, was out riding. A fox ran right between his horse's feet—a skinny, skittish gelding named Mud. Mud dumped Celyn on the ground and took off into the woods. Celyn took off after the animal, who was not nearly as smart as my donkey, Bucky. Before he reached Mud, Celyn caught sight of something sparkling along the side of a cliff. Now, Celyn had worked at a slate mine back in the old country, and he knew what he was seeing. Mica. And where there was mica, there was usually slate."

Nick jumped in. "And that was the start of the Fox Crossing Mine Company." Banana again touched his nose and pointed at him. "I saw some slate from there today. Beautiful."

"And profitable. Turned the luck of the settlement around. Annabelle's especially. She owned the land, and she teamed up with Celyn on the mine."

"This is the part where you tell me the fox was the fox that Annabelle saved, right?" Nick loved the story, even though he knew it had to be heavy on rumors and general malarkey.

Banana gave an exaggerated shrug. "She had the same markings—one white sock, one almost-white ear, black-tipped tail, same as the one Annabelle saved. Same as the one I'm waiting to see."

"Wait. You mean same as in same?" Banana nodded. "You should take this show on the road. You're a master bullshit artist. You've almost got me believing that there's a more-than-two-hundred-year-old fox running around. And that you had an exceptionally smart donkey named Bucky." Nick was glad he'd come in. He hadn't had an Annie Hatherley thought since Banana started spinning his stories. Except that one thought he'd just had, but that one didn't count, because it was about how he wasn't thinking about her.

"Well, some people think she's a descendant of the first

one," Banana admitted. "I disagree. And you can see Bucky's gravestone out back." Banana crossed himself.

"And you're seriously not going to make another try at the Wilderness until you see this fox—or its great-great-great-et-cetera-granddaughter?"

"That's right. When I see The Fox and get me some of that luck, I'm heading straight to the trail. My backpack's packed. Big Matt is ready to take over." Banana's eyes flicked up and down Nick's frame. "Maybe you should wait for a sighting. It'd give you a little more time to condition."

"You, too?" All the good feeling Nick had going circled the drain. "You think you can tell just by looking at me that I'm not ready? Don't bother with the lecture. I heard it all and then some from Annie Hatherley."

Banana let out another of his deep *haw-haw-haws*. "Our Annie, she's a pistol. She also has a good heart."

"In a jar on her bedside table," Nick muttered.

Banana laughed again. "It's why she's so hard on hikers. She doesn't want anyone to get hurt. I wasn't trying to say you're not ready, by the way. But anyone on the trail can use some extra luck." Banana pulled several baggies out of the pockets of his jeans. "I got chicken. I got ham. I got berries. I got a hard-boiled egg. I go out to likely spots in the woods every night and morning, scatter fox treats around me. The Fox is going to come to me. This is the year. This is the year I get my damn blue mug. Speaking of mugs, you need a refill." He got Nick a refill. "I like to talk, as you've probably already concluded. But now it's time for you to tell your story."

"My story."

"Everyone who hikes the Wilderness has a story."

"Ah." Nick took a swallow of the beer. "My thirtieth birthday is in a few days. Thought it would be a good way to mark the decade. A couple buddies and I used to talk about doing a thru-hike when we were in college. It ended up just being talk, but lately I started thinking about it again. . . ." He shrugged. "And here I am. Not a thru-hike, 'cause I don't have time, but a real challenge."

"Try again."

"What?"

"Try again."

"That's it. I'll have my birthday while I'm on the trail. Seems like a good way to close out my twenties and kick off my thirties doing the kind of thing I hope I'll be doing the next ten years."

"Sounds good. But, no." Banana nudged Nick's mug closer. "Try again when you finish that."

Another guy, short, stocky, starting to go gray, poked his head through the door. "Right back," Banana told Nick. Banana took a ceramic bottle from under the counter, filled it from one of the taps, and brought it to the guy. The guy handed him some cash.

"Shoo Fly, want to join—" a woman from the back table called. Before she could finish the sentence, the man had disappeared.

"You tried, Bev." Banana patted the woman on the shoulder before he headed back to Nick.

Shoo Fly. The name was familiar. For a few seconds, it wouldn't come to him, then the memory clicked into place. "The marine who cried because he got swarmed by blackflies, right?"

Banana nodded. "I'd still be crying if I was him. Those flies are little mofos. You got a bug net, right? This early in June, you gotta have a bug net."

"Yep." Nick finished his beer. "I should go. I want to get an early start in the morning."

"Before you go, let me ask you one more time. Why are you hiking the Wilderness?"

"Sorry. My reason hasn't changed. Unless my wife about to have a baby is a thing."

The good humor disappeared from Banana's face. "Your wife is about to have a baby and you're heading into the Wilderness? I'm going to have to ask you to leave my place. I misjudged you."

"Not my wife. My wife that was."

"And bingo."

"Bingo what?"

"Bingo was his name-o," Banana shot back. "Bingo, I think we've unearthed your reason for taking on the Wilderness."

Nick tilted his head from side to side. His neck felt stiff. Must have slept on it wrong. "I wouldn't say—"

Banana slapped the bar with both hands before Nick could finish. "Another drink on me if you want to share your sad story." Nick hesitated, giving a few more neck tilts. Banana refilled Nick's mug.

Fifteen minutes later, the mug was empty. "Oh, and did I mention that she got married the day the divorce got finalized?"

"You did not. And may I say, harsh."

"That same day." Nick stared into his empty mug. Banana refilled it. "Same day."

Connect with Us

Visit us online at
KensingtonBooks.com
to read more from your favorite authors, see books
by series, view reading group guides, and more.

for sneak peeks, chances to win books and prize packs,
and to share your thoughts with other readers.

facebook.com/kensingtonpublishing
twitter.com/kensingtonbooks

Tell us what you think!

To share your thoughts, submit a review,
or sign up for our eNewsletters, please visit:
KensingtonBooks.com/TellUs.